DEATH IN THE SPIRES

KJ CHARLES

This paperback edition published in 2026.

Paperback ISBN: 978-1-83700-380-8

Cover design: Lisa Horton
Cover images: Trevillion, Shutterstock

Published by Storm Publishing.
For further information, visit:

www.stormpublishing.co

For Charlie, who always believed in this.

Golden lads and girls all must,
As chimney-sweepers, come to dust.

—*William Shakespeare,* Cymbeline

NOTE

The Oxford University academic year is divided into three eight-week terms. It begins in autumn with Michaelmas term, then Hilary term (spring), then Trinity term (summer). Each week is numbered, so First Week, Second Week and so on.

PROLOGUE

Nobody knows. (But…)
Nobody will find out. (They can't. They won't.)
Nobody can ever find out. (If they do, if they know, if they tell…)
Nobody will tell. It's all in the past, buried, six feet under and rotting away. Nobody knows.
But what if someone looks?

CHAPTER 1

November 1905

Jeremy Kite is a murderer.

Jem stared at the words. They sat stark and accusatory, too brutal for the typewritten letters that made them, or the thin cheap paper that bore them. The ink was a little faded, as though the typewriter's ribbon was almost worn out. There was no date, no address, no signature, nothing but three lines of text.

Jeremy Kite is a murderer.
He killed Toby Feynsham.
Ask him why.

Jem turned the paper over, as if there might be more on the back. It rattled slightly, betraying the tremor of his hands. He turned it back again to the poisonous words, and looked up at Mr Leighton, who sat across the mahogany acreage of desk, regarding him with disfavour.

'I'm not.' Jem put the letter carefully on the desk, facing Mr Leighton. He lined up the top parallel to the wood's edge, adjusting it with microscopic movements to be quite, quite straight. 'A murderer, I mean. I didn't kill Toby Feynsham.'

'I did not ask you if you did,' Mr Leighton observed.

You handed me the letter rather than throwing it away. What was that meant to mean?

'No, sir,' Jem said aloud. 'But I'm answering the question anyway.'

Mr Leighton tapped his fingers to his lips. He wore a wide moustache, its ends twirled and pointed with wax that had stained the hairs a little yellow over the years. Most of the clerks in the Registrar-General's Bureau at Somerset House wore similar facial adornments. Jem had followed that fashion for a couple of years, but he'd shaved clean as something to do in one of the endless weeks last summer and hadn't been able to stomach growing it back. He found himself rubbing his naked top lip with a finger now.

Mr Leighton exhaled. 'You must see, Kite, that this is a most peculiar communication.'

'Yes, sir.'

'It is hardly the kind of death notice with which we deal.'

'No, sir.' Jem could keep this up all day, the bland answers, the blank stare. He'd had practice. And if Mr Leighton wanted to know something, then he could damned well ask, rather than waiting for Jem to offer it.

Jem had no doubt he would ask. They always did.

His superior frowned. 'Why would anybody write this? Why would you be linked to the Feynsham case?'

'I was at Oxford with him, sir.'

Mr Leighton's brows drew together. 'I don't think I was aware you were an Oxford man?'

'I didn't take a degree.' Jem made himself meet the man's eyes. Tempting though it was to simply rise, turn and walk away, he must not. He'd lose this post and then he'd have to summon up the energy to find another. He could sit through this. 'I was one of Toby's closest friends. If you know the case, you'll have heard—'

'You?' There was audible incredulity in Mr Leighton's voice. '*You* were one of—what was it they were called—the Seven Wonders?'

'I took a First in Mods, sir. First-year exams,' he added, because Mr Leighton was not an Oxford man. 'With a scholarship. I coxed for the college in Eights Week of ninety-four.'

'But—'

'I was one of Toby's friends, and some people called us the Seven Wonders. We were a group of friends, that's all, and then Toby died. Was killed. Murdered. And I…fell ill.' Sitting in the Examination Rooms, watching the tremor of his hand, watching the ink dry, unused, on the nib of his pen, and his future dry up with it. He had not written a single thing except his name on the paper that day. 'I don't like to think of it.'

'Naturally, naturally. I had no idea. I remember reading about the case, of course: it was fascinating. And dreadful,' Mr Leighton added hastily. 'Needless to say. But as an intellectual challenge, you understand? Mrs Leighton followed the story closely too. She always thought it was the black.'

Jem shut his eyes, feeling the old, futile fury rise. 'It isn't a story, sir. It was our lives. And the man you mention was about the only one of us to have an alibi. As to this…' He picked up the letter between thumb and forefinger. 'I received a lot of them when it happened, from people who "followed the story closely" because it was "fascinating".' He saw his superior flush and knew he shouldn't have said it, but he couldn't hold back the contempt. 'We all got them, even Ella. Her brother—her twin—had died, and she opened a dozen letters a day calling her unspeakable names and accusing her of his murder. So you will forgive me if I do not treat anonymous spite as a serious matter, sir. I'm used to it.'

'Yes. Well.' Mr Leighton cleared his throat. 'I shall have to advise Mr Radley, naturally, and seek his guidance. The breath of scandal, attaching to the Bureau—We have a responsibility to uphold. You may take the rest of the day off.'

'I should rather work.'

Mr Leighton's moustache humped. 'You will kindly go home. Mr Radley and I shall discuss the matter and advise you of our opinion tomorrow.'

'Yes, sir,' Jem said, since there was nothing else to say, and took his leave.

He walked home. The afternoon spread endlessly in front of him, and he had nothing to do with it. His foot hurt a little, but the new built-up shoe made walking quite tolerable as long as he did not hurry, and he had no reason to do that. London roared around him, motor cars jostling horse-drawn buses for space, pavements crowded with stalls and placards and kiosks and goods on display. The air was speckled with water—not enough to count as rain and justify an umbrella, but quite sufficient to coat Jem with moisture after a few paces and make the paving slabs underfoot slippery. It was three o'clock, and the gas lamps were already being lit.

Grim, grey November weather. It had been blazing bright, the summer Toby died.

You were one of the Seven Wonders? The shock in Mr Leighton's voice wouldn't leave him. Of course he'd been astonished. There was nothing at all wonderful about Jeremy Kite now.

Here he was, halting through drizzle, a drab man in a drab world. Club-footed and short of stature, always a little shabby, never quite paying attention. He arrived at work on time, left on time, limped his way through a succession of empty days with unremarkable competence, never good or bad enough to be noticed. He could scarcely remember how it had felt to be golden.

He'd known once.

When he got back to his room, he started looking for the photograph. He had not looked at it in years; it was probably still in the chest where he'd hidden it. He had never put it up, but he'd never thrown it away either.

It was there, with other things he didn't look at: books, letters, papers, pictures. The whole-cast photograph, although he didn't pause over that. He wanted the special photograph, which Toby had insisted they take. The one showing just the seven of them.

Assuming he still had it. He'd burned his gown and mortarboard in a fit of rage, and some papers and photographs with them before his father had stopped him, and the thought came to him now that he might have burned this one. If he had, it was because he'd wanted it all gone, but even so, his hands were shaking a little as he worked his way through the books and papers and blurred sepia faces frozen in time.

And there it was.

Jem hauled himself onto his armchair and looked at the framed print. Seven of them, all in their costumes and make-up, Old Quad unfocused in the background. It was a good clear photograph of them. The light had been excellent. It always was, back then.

They all looked serious, neutral-faced, as one had to, since a smile wouldn't survive the long exposure. All except Nicky. Nicky had cocked a hip and arched a brow, and looked into the camera with a taunting expression that was so himself Jem had to shut his eyes for a moment to block it out. He stood with Hugo, both of them in Roman tunics, and Aaron in his glinting wreath and toga, all three of them displaying bare, muscular arms. The two women had chairs: Prue in her boy's garb, eyes wide with glee that shone down the years; Ella, vivid hair greyed out by the photograph. Toby lolled at Ella's feet, forever bright, forever youthful, and Jem curled on the stone by him, the crutch that had been his prop lying in front. Toby had insisted they were all photographed in costume, but Jem still regretted the crutch.

He looked at the photograph, smelling greasepaint and lilies, champagne and sun-warmed stone and the faint scent of meadow vapours.

It had been their second year, Trinity term, an idyllic summer. The play was *Cymbeline*, one of Shakespeare's later, odder ones; they'd staged it in St Anselm's Old Quad. It was the perfect space, with its low medieval buildings in greying stone, the gnarled tree in the corner, clematis flowering all around. He remembered Prue sitting in a window—Nicky's tutor's room, requisitioned for the occasion—her face alive with pleasure at the sheer joy of success. *Being the centre of attention suits her*, Nicky had remarked, unkind and accurate as ever.

The play had crowned a year of triumphs, and it had been marvellous, mostly. There had been rows, tensions, but it had been a roaring success in the end. Sold out, critically praised, exhilarating. Until the last night.

The last night, the last Saturday of the term and the academic year, should have been the climax of the best year of his life. It should have been glorious. It almost had been.

They'd been so young and so innocent in the picture he held, but as Jem looked at it now, he felt a surge of anticipatory dread ten years too late, a sense of a terrible inevitability. It hadn't happened in *Cymbeline*, where tragedy was averted by an attack of conscience and the intervention of the gods, but it had come to them in the end.

He headed to the office the next day with fear curdling in his stomach, as familiar and hateful as the sensation of a brace on his foot.

He knew what was going to happen, today or tomorrow or soon, because it always did. Nobody could resist gossip when it involved murder and notoriety and unsolved crimes. *Do you know that fellow Kite in my department? Well...* Someone would tell one person, in strictest confidence, and that person would tell one person, and Jem would find himself halting into the office through a gauntlet of accusing eyes. Opening his desk drawer to discover unsigned letters. Trapped against a wall while people explained their theories of who put a blade into Toby's heart, who took the light from his eyes and the vitality from his body and left him cold, greying meat on the floor of his own room, as though this were a puzzle in a magazine, solution on the back page.

He couldn't do it again. Not the eyes, the surreptitious watching, the words just out of earshot, the reminders over and over again that Toby was dead and the rest of them were merely waiting to die.

Unless they weren't, of course. How should he know? He hadn't spoken to any of his friends in a decade, since Toby's murder had ripped them apart.

He didn't want to go to work, but he didn't have a choice about that. He'd exhausted his savings and his days off in dealing with his parents' funerals, just four months apart, and the rent had to be paid. So he set off on the trudge to Somerset House, telling himself the whole way that he was panicking. Of course nobody cared about a ten-year-old murder. Of course nobody would be interested in him. He was no longer twenty-one, no longer flayed raw with grief and fear and guilt. He could manage this.

He told himself that all the way along the Strand, walked through the doors of Somerset House into the lobby where thirty or more clerks were gathered in morning gossip, and hit the buzz of conversation like a stone into water, sending silence rippling outward. It looked as choreographed as any performance, heads turning, mouths closing, until the whole room was silent, and watching him.

Jem stalked through the silent lobby, his dot-and-carry-one tread echoing off the high ceiling. He hung up his coat and hat, approached his place on the long bench among the clerks, and read *Murderer* scrawled in black ink across the blotter. The ink had spread faster than it could dry, leaving the letters thick and blurry. That word always spread quickly.

He carefully detached the sheet from the blotter and took it through to Mr Leighton's office. He was hanging up his coat when Jem walked in, and swung round, affronted at the breach of etiquette. 'Mr Kite—'

Jem dropped the blotting-paper on his desk. 'I see you told everyone.'

Betraying colour swept across Mr Leighton's face. 'I'm sure I don't know what you mean.'

'It says *Murderer*. I had that from a lot of people after Toby died. Letters, whispers, people saying it to my face. I had to leave Oxford, and then I had to leave my home town because people were saying things to my parents in the streets, and now it's followed me here. And it's always the same. It's one person who hears about it and says, *Did you know*, with no harm intended, and within half a dozen repetitions it reaches the ears of someone who does *this*.' He stabbed a finger at the scrawled word. 'Could you not have spared me that? Could you not have kept your mouth shut?'

'You forget yourself, Kite!'

'That is what I have been trying to do,' Jem said. 'For ten years I have been trying to forget, but one spiteful letter by a lunatic, and you decide to ignore my years of service in the joy of spreading gossip about the *intellectual challenge* of my best friend's murder! How did I deserve such treatment at your hands, Mr Leighton?'

Mr Leighton was scarlet. 'I might as well ask how you deserved the accusation in the first place.'

'Have a care, Mr Leighton.' Jem heard the shake in his voice. 'There is such a thing as slander.'

'It is not slanderous to wonder why someone felt it necessary to advise me of your history.' Mr Leighton drew himself up. 'And whatever justification you feel you have, sir, I am your superior in this office, and I will not have you question my conduct.'

'Whereas this, I suppose, is an entirely acceptable questioning of mine.' Jem's hands were shaking with anger and tension. 'Will you pursue whoever is behind this piece of malice?'

'I hardly think that would be possible. And if you put yourself in a position where you are vulnerable to accusation—'

'I did not put myself in this position!'

'It is your responsibility to uphold the good name of the Bureau, as is clearly stated in your contract of employment. Did you advise the Bureau of your situation when you applied for the post?'

'What situation?' Jem said furiously. 'I have never been charged with any crime in my life, let alone convicted.'

'The shadow of guilt…' Mr Leighton began, and Jem stopped listening. He'd been in this damned job three years; all he'd wanted was to be left alone to do it. Now notoriety had been forced on him again, and it didn't really matter whether his superior sympathised or was the sort who believed there was no smoke without fire, because everyone in the building would have their own opinion, and most of them would tell him what it was.

You can put your head down, wait it out. Nine days' wonder, said the dreary voice in his head, the one that drove him back and forth between his desk and his little cheerless room, and, quite suddenly, Jem knew he couldn't.

Mr Leighton was still talking about the Bureau's need to be Caesar's wife, free from even the shadow of suspicion. Jem broke in the second he paused for breath. 'I quite agree the situation is untenable. I believe the notice period is a week.'

Mr Leighton looked startled but recovered quickly. 'I think we may waive that under the circumstances. You may leave at once and be paid the week.'

'I was halfway through a task, sir, which I should like to conclude, as it would be difficult for another to take up. Perhaps I might finish that first.'

'Very well. Today, please.'

'Yes, sir,' Jem said, and got out of there.

He limped back to his desk, feeling an unfamiliar crackle of energy, driven by an anger that was equally unfamiliar because it was focused.

He was sick of this. Sick of the letters, the spite, the corrosive *not knowing*, the arid wasteland of memory and misery. Sick of all of it, and, in particular, sick of the bastards hunting him down. Why would they even bother? He wasn't a public figure. He wasn't Hugo Morley-Adams, up-and-coming Liberal politician, engaged to the daughter of a duke.

Had Hugo received letters? Had the others?

He looked down at the surface of his desk, the blotter and the pointless papers pushed to its side, then he got up again and headed for the indexes of public records. By the time he reached them, he had an intention, hardening into a mission. He did not spend the day finishing off the task in hand; he had better things to do.

By three that afternoon, he had achieved all he could. He collected his week's pay, went out onto the Strand, and headed for the British Library. On the way he bought a notebook.

Hugo proved easy to look up. The Liberal seat, backed by his father's money, the meteoric rise, the magnificent marriage planned to the Duke of Breighford's daughter: it was easy to see why he was causing a political stir. None of the articles Jem read made any reference to the events at St Anselm's. Perhaps Hugo had managed to put the sordid business behind him, or perhaps having an extremely rich father helped discourage malicious speculation, at least in public.

Ella's activities were equally easily found. She'd sat the Examination of Women with her brother still unburied, and gained first-class honours, though of course, as a woman, she had not been awarded a degree. Now she worked in the University of London's chemistry department. Her name was on a number of papers whose titles left Jem baffled. He could find no indication of her home address.

Aaron was a doctor, partner in a practice off Harley Street. Prue had married, and that was astonishing in itself because the date was the third of August 1895. Two and a half months after Toby's murder. It seemed impossible; he'd sat staring at the record in the green leather index book, barely crediting what he read, but there it was. Prudence Matilda Lenster, spinster of the parish of Aldbury in Hertfordshire, marrying Mr John Alan Warren.

He remembered her weeping, that dreadful day: the heaving, sobbing howls of a woman destroyed. And she'd married ten weeks later.

She seemed to be the only one who'd married, as far as he could find. Not that he'd expected Nicky to. Nicky, like Hugo and Aaron, had sat his Finals in the middle of the chaos, and won the top First in the university as Toby's body cooled, and he was now senior lecturer in Anglo-Saxon at St Anselm's.

He hadn't even left the college. Prue had fled a couple of days after Toby's death, Jem after that first dreadful examination paper, and the others had gone after Finals, he supposed, but Nicky had stayed on. Jem found himself wondering where he lived. In college? In Front Quad, where he and Toby had roomed in their first year? Old Quad, looking out into the courtyard where *Cymbeline* had come to its calamitous end? Summoner Quad, where Toby's blood might still stain the floorboards?

Nicky would see St Anselm's and Toby around him every day of his life. Jem had spent ten years trying to forget them both.

CHAPTER 2

Michaelmas Term, 1892

'Hey. You, with the limp. Grammar boy.'

The voice was upper-class, commanding, with a sneer in it, and Jem turned swiftly and incautiously. The ill-fitted mortarboard he wore, caught by the air, flew off his head. He lunged for it, just a short step, but he stumbled anyway, and the hot rush of humiliation made his clumsiness even worse. His fingers scraped the edge of the brim, couldn't grasp it, and he saw the black square tumble towards the paving slabs.

A hand swiped it up before it hit the ground.

'I say.' His rescuer straightened, holding the mortarboard. He was of medium height and build, which made him substantially larger than Jem, and strikingly good-looking, with a square-jawed, open face and an extraordinary head of wavy red-gold hair. The early-autumn sunlight caught at its strands, turning the mass to a blaze. 'Is this yours?'

Jem mumbled thanks and reached for the mortarboard. The redhead smiled, wide and happy. 'Good afternoon. My name's Feynsham. Are you one of us?'

'Hardly,' interjected the fellow who'd startled Jem in the first place. 'It's the scholarship boy. Some creeping toady from a grammar school, at Anselm's. I call it a disgrace.'

'Quite right,' came a third voice, a tall, lean blond, standing a little behind Feynsham. He was no older than the rest of them judging by his face, but his drawl suggested a decadent, world-weary forty-year-old. 'It's an outrage. Here you are, Lewis, ready to drink champagne and smash up other people's property, and instead you find yourself forced into company with an intelligent and hard-working scholar. At Oxford, of all places! They'll be asking you to read books next.'

The offensive man, Lewis, reddened. 'I say, Rook—'

'Oh, don't worry,' the blond man said over him. 'There are still plenty of ill-mannered braying clodpoles who are only here to vomit in the wellspring of education. You'll fit right in.'

That left Lewis speechless with indignation. The blond waved a languidly dismissive hand at his splutters, and turned to Feynsham, who was grinning broadly. 'And with the formalities concluded, do introduce me to your new friend.'

'I'd love to if I'd got so far as his name,' Feynsham said cheerfully. 'Starting again, I'm Toby Feynsham.'

Jem stuck his mortarboard awkwardly under his arm, and shook the proffered hand. 'Uh, Kite. Jeremy Kite. Pleased to meet you.'

'And this is Nicholas Rook, don't mind him. He's determined to make a reputation as the rudest man in Oxford.'

'No determination required. It's effortless.' Rook held out his hand in turn, giving Jem an assessing look. His eyes were brown, strikingly so against his fair hair and pale skin. 'I take it you are indeed the gentleman from the Midlands, of whom we have heard so much?'

Jem had hoped that nobody would know of his origins. The scholarship award had made him famous in his small factory town as the first there ever to go to the great university at Oxford, but he had not expected to make the slightest ripple here, nor wanted to. His coldest fear, lying awake in the summer nights while he'd waited for autumn to come, had been to be singled out as the grammar school boy, the lone plebeian among gentlemen of breeding; the odd one. He'd spent so long being different; all he'd wanted was to be unnoticed, and he'd failed at that on his first day.

It had been inevitable. He didn't look right here, in the magnificent sixteenth-century quadrangle with its gables and gargoyles and wrought-iron gates, and the perfect lawn with its great oak. Feynsham and Rook and even Lewis seemed perfectly at home among the ancient glory, as comfortable in their flowing black gowns as any academic. Jem's gown looked new, ill-fitting, wrong. *He* looked wrong.

He swallowed, knowing his accent would betray him even if he tried to lie. 'Yes. That's me.'

'Excellent,' said Feynsham with enthusiasm. 'I was hoping we'd meet you, and here we are.'

Rook rolled his eyes. 'A welcoming committee. Do you know anyone here, at all? No? Well, you haven't missed much. Place is full of Etonians, God help us.'

'Oh, Nicky.' Feynsham took Jem's arm, a confident, casual gesture, as though they'd been friends for ever, and started walking towards an archway. Jem, taken entirely off guard, hopped to keep up. 'I have high hopes of at least a few bright sparks. We decided, you see, that we'd collect the interesting people.'

'Collect?' Jem repeated.

'Exactly. Rather than mingle with all the men one went to school with—'

'As though one hadn't seen enough of them for a lifetime,' Rook put in.

'—we thought we'd look out the fellows with something different to them. Something new. I say, Kite, is your foot all right? You're limping.'

'Of course it isn't all right, you thundering lout, that's a built-up shoe,' Rook said. 'Are we going to the buttery?'

The buttery was a public house of sorts inside the college, where undergraduates could buy drink. Jem had wondered, in the fearful nights, if he'd ever be able to summon up the nerve to enter such a place by himself, and if one day he might have friends who would greet him there. The prospect of entering for the first time in company felt like a small miracle, such an unexpected relief that he could only assume this was some sort of cruel joke and brace himself to become the punchline.

Feynsham drew him on, making no concession to Jem's limp, and Jem let himself be drawn, since he had no idea what else to do. Rook strolled at his other side, towering over him, long legs meaning that he seemed to idle where Jem hurried. He and Feynsham both knew where they were going, as though the geography of the college was second nature to them. Born to be here.

Feynsham steered Jem through a door, Rook claimed an oak table for them in the buttery, and just like that Jem found himself ensconced at the heart of St Anselm's College, with a brimming tankard of beer in front of him and Feynsham—'call me Toby, won't you, and this is Nicky'—talking to him as though they'd been friends for ever.

'My sister's at Anselm Hall. The women's place, you know, it's up Park Road past the Museum. Studying chemistry, would you credit it. She has all the brains of the two of us.'

'And all the beauty,' Nicky said. 'And most of the brawn.'

'Ella is the only person who doesn't put up with Nicky's nonsense. Well, and me, of course, and I trust you won't. His bark's worse than his bite.'

'No, it isn't. I simply haven't bitten you hard enough.'

'I'm reading history, for my sins,' Toby went on. 'Nicky's reading English. What are you here for?'

'Mathematics.'

'Ah.' Nicky gave him a measuring look. 'A cyphering man. And—Oh, wait a moment.' He leaned back as he spoke, putting out a long arm that blocked the passage of another undergraduate to the bar.

'Excuse me?' that gentleman said, looking down with some affront, and then, 'I say, aren't you Rook of Winchester?'

'I am, and you're Morley-Adams,' Nicky said. 'My colleagues Kite and Feynsham. Meet Hugo Morley-Adams, Harrow's best fencer.'

'If by that you mean the only one to beat you—'

'That is precisely what I mean. Care to join us, unless you have another engagement?'

'Delighted,' Morley-Adams said. 'Anyone need a top-up?'

'Morley-Adams?' Jem asked in a whisper as he went to the bar. 'Like the shipbuilding man?'

'So like he could be his son, and indeed is,' Nicky said. 'Morley-Adams is, to use the vulgar parlance, swimming in lard thanks to Papa's industry. But he's excellent with the foils and remarkably tolerable for a Harrovian.'

Jem couldn't help glancing at Toby. It wasn't that Nicky had been making a request, or a suggestion, or anything other than a statement, but still he had a sense of something presented for consideration, and he found himself thinking, *One for Toby's collection?*

Morley-Adams returned with a drink and settled at the table. He was as confident and charming as the others, effortlessly courteous if perhaps a little less open; he treated Jem with a politeness that had a little distance in it, at first. Hardly surprising. Jem's father worked in a factory, while Morley-Adams's father owned them, and dockyards too.

Jem's instinct was to be entirely mute in this confident gathering of Winchester and Harrow and breeding and money, and he had to force himself to be audible when asked direct questions. But he stayed doggedly in his seat as the first glasses were replaced by the second, and then the subject changed to books. It turned out they were all addicted to the works of Conan Doyle, though only Nicky preferred *The White Company* to the tales of Sherlock Holmes. He also thought that 'Lord Arthur Savile's Crime' in Wilde's story collection was better than 'The Canterville Ghost', which was simply wrong. Jem took issue, at first shyly and then with increasing heat, and the argument leaped into full flame when Nicky said he couldn't respect an opinion on William Morris's *News from Nowhere* that wasn't grounded in some medieval text or other, and then had the gall to admit he hadn't even read *New Grub Street.*

Jem planted his finger on the table and talked about books that were written by the people, about the people. Morley-Adams—Hugo—said he'd rather read this George Gissing fellow than whatever incomprehensible tripe Nicky was talking about. Nicky called Jem a radical agitator. Toby laughed at them all and bought more beer.

Well into the third pint, they were rowing joyously about *Salome*, Oscar Wilde's banned play, when a loud low groan erupted from the back of the room.

Jem knew what that noise meant: public schoolboys made it where others might boo. He looked up, as they all did, and saw that a black man had come in, alone.

He wore a scholar's gown but looked slightly older than the rest of them, into his twenties, well-built, with dark skin, a broad nose, and magnificent cheekbones. His face was closed and expressionless.

There was another groan, even louder, in which several more voices joined.

'For God's sake,' Hugo said. 'Quiet over there! Shame on you.'

There were more groans, and more cries of protest at them. The man at the centre of this sudden storm stood still, poised, looking entirely calm except for the tension around his mouth. Jem had noticed him when they had all stood taking the matriculation photograph, heard people whispering that he was the first black man Anselm's had ever admitted. He had hoped at the time that this other novelty might take attention away from himself, and now felt a stab of guilt, as though his wish had caused this.

'Could we not, uh—' he began.

'Yes indeed. I say,' Toby said loudly. 'We've a spare seat here, if you'd care to join us.'

There was, in fact, no other chair at the table, but Nicky was already pulling one over with a long arm, as if he'd anticipated Toby's words. Hugo and Jem shifted up. The newcomer hesitated for a second, then walked over.

'Thank you.' His voice was deep, with a cultured English accent that took Jem by surprise. That was stupid: of course he would be Eton or Harrow or wherever. They all were.

Toby held out his hand. 'I'm Toby Feynsham, and these are Nicky Rook, Hugo Morley-Adams, Jeremy Kite. History, English, history, maths.'

'Aaron Oyede. Medicine.'

'What a pity it's not dentistry,' Nicky said. 'I was just considering punching someone in the mouth.'

'I can help if you split your knuckles on his teeth,' the newcomer said very seriously, and then he smiled. He smiled, Toby and Nicky crowed with laughter, Hugo asked what he would have to drink, and before long they were piling into Hall together at the sound of the dinner bell. Toby, Nicky, Hugo, Aaron, and Jem.

Jem had dreaded the idea of formal Hall, the gowns and grandeur, the tradition and pomp, the terrifyingly alien people. He had pictured himself sitting alone in silence, or perhaps, one glorious day, venturing intelligent remarks about mathematical theorems.

He had never dreamed he'd enter his first Hall with interlinked arms as part of a raucous group several beers to the good.

The magnificent interior sobered him up as nothing else could have. Long oaken trestle tables under a majestic vaulted ceiling; dark wood panelling hung with dark oil portraits of unknown greats; flagstones underfoot and voices echoing around him; and then silence as the Master pronounced Latin grace in a sonorous voice. Jem listened with rapt attention, and then promptly forgot to be overawed by the servants and surroundings because he was too busy talking.

When they left Hall, Toby announced that they were going back to his room in Front Quad, steered them there, and uncorked several bottles of wine in a fashion so expert that Jem was seized with a strong desire to learn the skill. He wanted everything about Toby's rooms for himself. It was a large set, the sitting room offering a table big enough for dinners, decorated with Indian rugs and gilt-framed pictures, photographs of school and of Toby with a striking young woman, several decanters, and more *things* than Jem had ever seen. His mother had owned four china ornaments that took pride of place on the mantelpiece and were too precious ever to be played with. Toby had porcelain bowls, a brass elephant, some sort of hookah-pipe, a Russian samovar, and any number of decorative objects, just lying casually around.

'The Old Curiosity Shop itself. What's this?' Aaron asked, picking up a knife in a gilt-encrusted scabbard off the table.

'Watch out,' Nicky said. 'That thing is unreasonably sharp. Don't test—'

'Ow!'

'—it on your finger.'

'It's a stiletto, from Sicily,' Toby said. 'Our father travelled rather a lot before he married. I use it as a paperknife.'

'That's rather a dangerous way to open envelopes,' Aaron said, sucking the puncture he'd given himself.

'Yes, but if it turns out to be a bill, I'm ready for it.'

When they finally called it a night, Jem weaved his way back to his bare little room in Old Quad, buoyed by the evening's events, at least until he was alone in his bed and the gleeful optimism began to fade.

He lay there, unable to sleep, room spinning and stomach heaving, increasingly convinced that he had made an abject fool of himself and that none of his new acquaintances would want to speak to him on the morrow. Why had he thought he could argue about socialist literature with an English student and a millionaire's son? What must they have thought of him, shouting the odds in his glaringly wrong accent? Had he ruined everything with some stupid remark; had they all been laughing at him; would any of them even talk to him again?

He woke the next morning with a shocking head, to the sound of banging at the door.

He sat up and swung his feet out of bed. It was chilly. He reached for slippers—his bare foot was not a sight he liked anyone to see—and his warm new flannel dressing gown, limped across the uneven floor, and opened the door.

Toby was there, looking what Jem would soon learn to call *disgustingly healthy* or *loutishly energetic*, as Nicky did. At the time, he thought only that he looked wonderful. Glowing.

'Good morning, Jeremy! Gosh, this is rather a cell, have you not unpacked your things yet?'

Jem didn't have *things*. He hadn't known he was meant to trick out his room with personal possessions, though that ignorance had just spared him soul-searching about how little he had to bring. 'I, uh, didn't come with much,' he managed.

'I'll lend you some pictures. Brought far too many. Now, come on. We're meeting my sister for breakfast, and we don't want to be late. Get dressed while I chase Hugo up, and we'll collect Nicky on the way out.'

'Isn't he next door to you?' Jem asked rather dizzily.

'My dear chap, Nicky Rook in the morning is a very different beast to Nicky at night, and a rather more dangerous one. You may trust me, after seven years at Win Coll. I poke him with a sharp stick from a distance and leave him to surface in his own sweet time. Come on, hop to it, meet you in the quad in fifteen minutes.'

Jem made it down with two minutes to spare, and then had a ten-minute wait, shivering in the crisp air of a sharp, clear October morning. Old Quad, his home for the year, was the oldest of the four areas that made up St Anselm's, each of them a courtyard surrounded by buildings that housed staff and students. Front Quad was imposingly Elizabethan and held an impeccable never-to-be-walked-on lawn. Old Quad was low, paved, and gloriously medieval: he suspected it would be freezing in winter. Summoner Quad was three storeys of Georgian elegance looking out onto the formal gardens, while the newest part, Bascomb Quad, was off to one side, a Victorian building far less exciting than any of the others, though it overlooked a rather nice stand of trees.

He was sure that Old Quad was the best and most beautiful, but he was undeniably getting a little bored of the view by the time Toby returned with Hugo in tow. They swept him up and strolled through to Front Quad, where Nicky was resentfully hunched in a startlingly huge dark fur coat of the kind Jem imagined Oscar Wilde wearing.

'If we must go, we must,' he said sourly. 'But you are all ridiculously energetic. Except Jeremy. You look much as I feel, Jeremy. I like you.'

'Jem, please,' Jem said. 'Jeremy makes me feel as if I'm in trouble with my grandmother. Which actually…that coat…'

Hugo and Toby exploded with laughter, slapping thighs and doubling over. Nicky gave him a narrow look, but the corners of his eyes creased with amusement. Someone stuck his head out of a window to request with emphasis that those sleeping should be allowed to continue doing so.

'Come on,' Hugo said, grinning. 'Let's get going. Oh, there's Aaron.'

Aaron was striding along the quad on the other side of the grass with a book under his arm, gown flapping. Toby and Hugo both shouted, with sublime disregard for the unhappy would-be sleeper, Aaron raised a hand, and they headed along the parallel gravel pathways to meet at the porters' lodge.

'You really cannot be starting work already, term's barely begun,' Toby announced to Aaron. 'We're off to breakfast with my sister at Seal's, just at the end of the Broad. Coming? She's a chemist, at Anselm Hall. She told me I had to make friends with some sort of scientist, not just airy artistic types like Nicky, and the best I've done is Jem here and he's only mathematics. Come and help me prove that I'm not entirely trivial.'

'That may not be in my power,' Aaron said seriously. He had a knack for deadpan remarks that Jem would have liked to acquire, but for which he probably lacked the gravitas. There was a supportive chorus of jeers from the others and a crack of laughter from Toby, and they set off together, pausing only to stuff Aaron's gown and book into his pigeonhole.

CHAPTER 3

Jem had explored Oxford a little bit when he'd come for interview, but Toby appeared to know the town intimately. Seal's was an impressive three-storey building on the corner of Catte Street, the sort of place that looked worryingly large and grand for Jem's budget. He had won a scholarship that covered his expenses and day-to-day living but drink, new clothes, and dining outside the college were his responsibility, to be paid for from the little allowance his parents could give him. He cast a glance at the bill of fare as they entered, trying not to make it too obvious.

None of the others looked twice. Toby led the way upstairs into a bright, yellow-painted room into which the autumn sunshine streamed, and where two women sat at a large table.

'Ella!' Toby called, and led his party over, brushing the startled waiter aside.

The women turned. One was small, mousy-haired and round-faced, looking extremely young in a rather severe hat. The other was the woman from Toby's photographs. She had a mass of red-gold hair pinned in a casual manner so that it spilled from under her own plain but clearly expensive hat, and Toby's blue eyes.

'You see?' the redhead told her companion. 'I told you we needed the space; he always has a retinue. Good Lord, Toby, you haven't lost time, have you? And you even roused Nicky. We *are* honoured. This is Prudence Lenster.'

Miss Lenster, mathematics, was rooming with Miss Feynsham at Anselm Hall, one of the new women's halls. Her father was sexton in a village called Aldbury: she was short, sharp-minded, and clearly as adrift as Jem in this new milieu, surrounded by people who'd been born to the right families and gone to the right schools, people who were tall and handsome and confident and educated, and seemed absurdly older and more self-possessed than them. She and Jem recognised one another with relief and hit it off at once.

After a good hour and a half of lively conversation, when Jem was just beginning to wonder if they were going to spend all day here drinking tea, Toby threw up a hand to summon the bill, announced the meal was his shout and waved off Jem's effort at protest. He left a couple of guineas and leaped up without waiting for his change, decreeing that it was time for a walk. Neither Nicky nor Ella looked startled at this abrupt decision, and the seven of them were shortly strolling down Holywell Street, which, Jem was told, led towards the water meadow. Toby detached Prue from Jem with effortless grace, saying he absolutely *had* to make her acquaintance properly, and Nicky took Jem's arm instead. That was slightly awkward, since the coat made him bulky as a bear, and he was a good inch over six feet, compared to Jem's five foot three.

They were all tall. Hugo and Aaron were both around Nicky's height; Toby a few inches under. Even Ella Feynsham was not a great deal shorter than her twin. Jem felt like a dwarf among giants, except for Prue, who was arm in arm with Toby and had a distinct, if repressed, skip in her step.

'So, uh, you know Miss Feynsham already?' Jem asked, realising he ought to make conversation.

'Oh, for ever,' Nicky said. 'Tobes and I went to the same prep before Winchester. Can't be rid of him, despite my best efforts.'

Going to the same Oxford college would do that. 'She's very beautiful, isn't she? Miss Feynsham, I mean.'

Nicky glanced down. 'Really? I thought the little Lenster had captured your interest.'

'Nobody's captured my interest,' Jem protested, feeling the blood rise in his cheeks. 'Not that I'd presume—It was an observation. I mean, having met Toby—'

'You thought his sister would look like a hod-carrier? Well, I can understand that.'

'I thought nothing of the kind, and you can't possibly say that. He's awfully handsome.'

Nicky's eyes flicked forward, to Toby's rear view. 'Tolerable, I suppose. From a distance.'

'Are you always this rude to everyone?'

'I find it saves time. Do you object?'

Jem didn't precisely object, as such. He had been brought up to say please and thank you, never to speak out of turn or show disrespect, to know his place and hold it with decency and pride. Nicky's casually appalling manners were, he assumed, part of the aesthetic pose. It was disturbing, and unsettling, and fascinating in a way he couldn't quite define.

'Well, as long as you don't mean it,' he tried.

'My dear Jeremy, of course I mean it. It would hardly be effective if I didn't.'

He's the same age as you, Jem reminded himself. 'Very well, then: as long as you don't mind me speaking in kind.'

'Ah, now we reach understanding.' Nicky had a slow, lazy, rather mannered smile, the sort that conveyed world-weariness, but his eyes crinkled when he meant it. Jem felt his breathing hitch, just a little, and focused on the sinewy, fur-coated arm through his on the way to the water meadow.

That first morning felt like a dream to Jem, then and ever after. The seven of them circled Addison's Walk in pairs or threes, until Jem's foot was afire, a fact he would not have mentioned at gunpoint. The sky was clear and bright, the grass lush and green though the trees were turning to autumn colours, the air full of meadow vapour, an indefinably delicate fresh, wet fragrance, and Jem was overcome with a dizzy exuberance. He was at Oxford University, on first-name terms with the upper classes, discussing politics with women who studied chemistry and mathematics in this glowing ancient town, and his life seemed to be unrolling in front of him with infinite potential.

That feeling didn't go away as their group solidified. He wrote to his parents in Second Week, feeling guilty that he had let so long go by, and found himself laughing aloud at the improbability of it all as he imagined their expressions, reading in the little dark parlour.

I've made a fine set of particular friends already. There is Hugo (Morley-Adams—the shipping magnate's son!), very charming, without the least condescension. Toby, an excellent fellow, turns out to be the grandson and heir of a marquess, and will one day have a great house and a fortune. But he's awfully friendly, no side to him at all, and his twin sister—Mother, hold onto your hat—is studying chemistry! My other friends—

He thought about sophisticated, drawling, fur-coated Nicky, who lounged against doorways and uttered witticisms that bit.

are all very pleasant too. I have met a lady mathematician—we mix a reasonable amount with the ladies of Anselm Hall, as Anselm's takes a progressive view on women's education, and of course Toby is permitted visits from his sister. We even have an African man, educated in England, and a very decent sort. He is, like me, the only one of his kind here, though there are several Indian fellows, largely of the maharajah type so above my touch. Then again, I am friends with a marquess-to-be, so who knows? I feel as though

I've learned more in a fortnight here than I did in all my eighteen years till now.

Also, and you will be astonished by this, I am now a sportsman!

The Boat Club had come for him in the first week. He'd imagined at the time that he'd been considered worthy of notice because he was one of what was already dubbed 'Feynsham's set', though he soon understood that his appeal lay in the fact that he was the smallest man in the college. They'd asked him to try out as cox for the rowing team, and Toby had agreed on his behalf.

Jem hadn't agreed. Jem had sat in the buttery, frozen in terror as a pack of huge hearty second- and third-year men clustered around him, loudly assessing his meagre form. He couldn't swim. He'd never been on a boat in his life, didn't know what a cox was, and had never aspired to do anything with sport except avoid it. He'd been summoning up the courage to convey that he'd vastly prefer to be in the library than on the river when Toby had given a brisk nod and said, 'Marvellous. Of course he will, he'll be splendid. We'll see you on the river, Jem.'

So Jem had tried out, huddled at the stern of the boat, bewildered by his responsibilities, trying not to fall in. The river had been misty that autumn morning, his breath steaming, the world green and grey around him, the only sounds plashing oars and grunting men, and his own voice shouting commands that came out as faint requests at first, and soon increased in volume as the Eton and Harrow and Winchester and Rugby rowers obeyed without question. He'd hurried back to St Anselm's bubbling with the news that they wanted him to return, and Toby had slapped him on the shoulder with a crow of satisfaction.

'Of course they do. I knew it.'

Nicky rolled his eyes. 'Marvellous. He'll be braying like a boatie any moment. Why must you ruin all the good men?'

Jem was the only rower of their group. Toby laughingly disclaimed interest in sport. Aaron, who had magnificent shoulders, had been wooed by the boat crew but refused, preferring to run; he and Hugo had already started sprinting together. Hugo was a natural athlete, all muscle and grace. He and Nicky had joined the university Sword Club at once, and it was a matter of course that they would be representing St Anselm's at fencing.

Jem hadn't quite been able to imagine Nicky the fencer: he didn't seem like an athlete of any kind, with his languid ways that gave Jem doubt he'd have survived a less rarefied atmosphere than Winchester College. That lasted until Hugo and Nicky decided to get some time with the foils at a gymnasium, and Jem was permitted to watch.

He perched on a bench at the edge of the echoing hall. Both men wore tight white breeches and padded jackets, with faces masked in silver mesh, but Jem had no trouble distinguishing them. Hugo had powerful athlete's thighs and calves; Nicky longer legs and a narrower frame. They were both barefoot. Jem watched Nicky's feet with fascination—perfect, long-toed, flexing for balance in an almost animal way—and was almost shocked when the foils were swept up into glittering salute.

It was enthralling. Jem had never seen fencing, didn't understand the rules or why they moved in such an odd, sidling manner, but he was compelled by the whip of the flexible blades, hissing and scraping, the movement of attack and retreat, the play of strong bodies under the anonymising, close-fitting uniforms. Hugo looked like a warrior: powerful, fast, steady of wrist. Nicky was sinew to his muscle, supple and swaying, then moving with vicious speed and decision. They shifted up and down the hall as though testing one another, blades glancing and dancing, and Jem watched in an ecstasy of longing. For the grace and strength, for the physical prowess, for the fact of this noble medieval pastime as a living thing, for Nicky's long, elegant lines and the surety of his movements and his shout of triumph as he landed a hit.

Finally Hugo flung up a hand and stepped back. Both swords flashed upwards in salute, and then the two pulled their masks off, sweaty of face and dishevelled of hair. Nicky looked more vibrant than Jem had yet seen him, eyes bright and gleaming with victory.

'Well played,' Hugo said, and they launched into analysis of Nicky's final move, which had apparently been very clever, ignoring Jem on the bench. He didn't mind. Nicky looked his age for once, the eighteen he was rather than the jaded forty he liked to appear, lean body held tight by the clinging white jacket. Jem watched, lost in the room's echoes and the scent of male sweat.

'Nicky takes too many risks,' Hugo explained afterwards, as they left together. 'It pays dividends in the short term, granted—'

'As now, when I beat you.'

'Not, however, when we met in the Cup.' Nicky tipped his head. 'Those moves are pure reaction, without control.'

'That's what training's for,' Nicky retorted. 'Think in training, act in fighting.'

Jem let the argument wash over him. They argued about everything: sport and politics and books and theatre and wine and the relative merits of subjects and tutors and anything else they could think of over the endless, impossibly short eight-week term. He made friends among his fellow mathematicians and among the rowers; he attended lectures religiously and chapel as a matter of obligation; he spent afternoons in the Bodleian Library, stunned by his good fortune and breathing the book-saturated air, and nights in the buttery, or sprawled on the couch in Toby or Nicky or Hugo's rooms, in front of a blazing fire, learning to drink port, talking about everything and nothing.

When he went home at the end of that first term, his mother said, as she always did for any length of absence, 'My goodness, you've changed! I shouldn't have known you!' This time, Jem thought, she might have meant it. This time, he wasn't sure he knew himself.

CHAPTER 4

He started with Hugo.

In some respects he seemed the least accessible of the Seven Wonders now, excepting, of course, Toby. Hugo had become an important man, a Liberal MP. Parliament was in session, and doubtless he had many demands on his time: society, his father's business, his forthcoming excellent marriage. Nevertheless, he might spare an hour for an old friend. Hugo had always been reasonable.

All the same, Jem didn't write in advance. It wasn't precisely that he thought Hugo's door would be closed to him if he did, but still he decided to go straight there.

Jem arrived at the elegant Georgian townhouse on Stratton Street before nine that morning. A footman, or for all he knew a butler, in a coat rather newer and smarter than Jem's own, opened the door and gave him the most disdainful look he had received in some time. 'Yes?'

'I'd like to see Hugo Morley-Adams.'

'Have you an appointment,' the footman enquired, not bothering to make it a question.

'Tell him it's Jem Kite. Jeremy Kite. From St Anselm's.'

The footman didn't do anything so vulgar as react. He simply shut the door, leaving Jem on the doorstep. Jem waited, and waited longer, until he was forced to decide between hammering on the door and giving up and walking away. He had his hand almost to the knocker when the door opened again.

'Mr Kite,' the footman said. 'Mr Morley-Adams will see you now.'

Jem was shown into a drawing room. It was gracious, airy, well-appointed and about twice the size of the room to which his own life had dwindled. Hugo had electric lights instead of gas, he noted, and the chairs looked new.

He was examining the titles on the bookshelves—all classics, he noticed, not a modern novel in sight—when the door opened and Hugo came in. He was beginning a greeting, but it died on his lips as they looked at one another.

Hugo at thirty-one was in the prime of life. He'd grown a moustache, which was something of a shock, but suited him. His hair was a little less thick and his hairline a little further back, and his frame undeniably a little less muscular after a decade of fine living, but he was bright-eyed and straight-backed as ever, and very well dressed indeed in a superbly cut suit. Jem knew that Hugo, observing him, would see a shabby clerk, bowed of shoulder, elbows shiny and cuffs frayed, boots worn despite efforts at polish, and tried not to care.

'Jem,' Hugo said at last. 'It's been a long time.'

'It has, yes.'

'How are you? Can I offer you a drink? Tea?' Hugo was watching him, not suspicious, but careful. Jem would doubtless have been careful too if one of the others had arrived out of the blue.

'No, thank you. I'd like a little of your time, please.'

'Of my time,' Hugo repeated, then smiled. 'That you may have. Please sit. Are you sure you won't have tea, coffee? Sherry?'

'It's a bit early for me,' Jem said, with some understatement, and then felt his face heat as he realised what the question meant. 'And if you're asking whether I've come to you because I'm some drunken breakdown—'

'Not at all. To be quite honest, I'm a little off balance. I didn't expect to see you.'

'Have you seen any of the others?'

Hugo frowned slightly. 'No. Should I have?'

'I don't know,' Jem said. 'One more question: have you received any interesting letters recently? The kind to which the writer doesn't sign his name?'

'Ah. May I ask—'

'Sent to my place of work,' Jem said. 'Accusing me of killing Toby. I lost my position over it.'

'I'm extremely sorry to hear that. May I help?'

'Yes. You can answer the question. I want to know if that letter was specific to me, or if anybody else had one. I want to know why, after ten years, someone felt it necessary to write that, to see me dismissed from my post. I want to know who wrote it and why, and why now.'

'But there are so many letters.' Hugo's voice was flat. 'Is that really your first in ten years?'

'In the last three, I suppose. There have hardly been any since I moved to London.'

'You are doubtless harder to find than I am. I suppose I have... oh, no more than one or two a month now, unless I make a notable speech, when they increase again. My secretary opens all my post, so I don't see them. My fiancée puts a special mark on the envelopes when she writes, so that he knows to pass those to me unopened.'

Jem hadn't imagined what it might be like, in practical terms, to be in the public eye. It had been bad enough as a private individual. 'I'm sorry,' he said.

'Yes, well.' Hugo made a face. 'It happens in some degree to all prominent men, you understand. I'm informed that if it wasn't this subject, it would be accusations of adultery with the writer's wife, or embezzlement, or some such.'

'But that would be imaginary,' Jem said.

'Yes. Yes, that makes it worse. That people sit at home, take pen and paper, find an envelope, find a stamp—'

'All to write spite to people they don't know. And so many of them do it. *Why?*'

'You'd have to ask a medical man. I don't know, Jem. I cannot imagine.'

They sat together in silence for a moment, then Hugo gave his head a slight shake. 'Anyway, as I say, I don't read them. My secretary has instructions to keep them all—'

'Why?'

'In case,' Hugo said, with a twist to his mouth. 'He puts aside those that need to be reported to the police—the more specific death threats, or anything that suggests the writer is observing me—and keeps the rest in case of a pattern developing. My most faithful correspondent has been writing intermittently for six years.'

'God.'

'That's why I don't look at them. You are welcome to consult Grey, if you'd care to do so.'

Jem nodded. 'Thank you. But those are all to you. What I really wanted to ask was whether anyone else received one recently. Your fiancée, or your father, I uh…' Who would a Liberal Member of Parliament be answerable to? 'Sir Henry Campbell-Bannerman?'

Hugo's brows drew together. 'Why do you ask that?'

'Mine was sent to my place of work. I've been in the same lodgings for three years; I cannot see that I'd be easier to find at work than at home. It was malice, and of more than the usual kind. Someone wanted not just to accuse me but to cause trouble for me.'

'And you came here—'

'Because I wanted to know if it was just me, or if anyone else had the same.'

'And if we did?' Hugo asked.

Jem hadn't thought that far ahead. He wasn't sure he'd thought at all, driven as he had been by anger and unfamiliar energy. 'I don't know. I'd like to know who wrote it.'

'There's probably no chance of finding that. I have enquired into the possibility more than once, especially with the death threats. There is very little to be done, except when the writer includes a return address, which has happened, believe it or not.' He flashed Jem a grin and, for a moment, the years fell away. 'When was your letter received?'

'Wednesday morning.'

'Wednesday morning,' Hugo repeated. 'I see.'

'Is there something?'

Hugo hesitated, then his shoulders dropped. 'I can't see a reason not to tell you. My fiancée, Lady Lucy, received a letter of this sort on Tuesday. She was extremely distressed. It didn't occur to me that even the kind of lunatic who writes these abominations would consider sending my fiancée such a thing. That a complete stranger would endeavour to distress a gently bred lady, or try to break my engagement—'

'Or lose me my job,' Jem said.

Hugo paused. 'Yes. That is a coincidence.'

'Did you see the letter Lady Lucy had?'

'It was the first one I've touched in a while.' Hugo looked down at his hands. 'I had forgotten what they were like. Seeing it in black and white again was more of a shock than I'd expected. Of course Lucy was distraught, and that was uppermost in my mind, but…it was a shock.'

'What did it say?'

'*Hugo Morley-Adams is a murderer*,' Hugo said, voice precise. '*He killed Toby Feynsham. Ask him why.*'

Jem stared at him. Hugo's gaze snapped back from wherever it had been—Tuesday, or ten years ago—to focus on Jem. 'Is that similar?'

'Word for word. Except the name.'

'Damnation,' Hugo said. 'And—you said the others?'

'I don't know. I came here first. I'm going to ask them all.'

Hugo nodded. 'This does seem to me rather odder than the usual run of things. The same letter, written to someone who would be less likely to ignore or throw it away.' He drummed his fingers. 'At the very least it seems a particularly cruelly calculated bit of malice. Will you tell me what you find? I think I'd like to know.'

'If you like, certainly.' Jem clasped his hands together. 'Hugo?'

'Yes?'

'Who killed Toby?'

'How the devil should I know?'

'I don't know,' Jem said. 'It wasn't me.'

'And it wasn't me.'

'And Aaron and Ella gave each other an alibi. So that leaves Nicky or Prue—'

'Unless Aaron and Ella were lying.'

'Or you're lying,' Jem said. 'Or I am.'

'Indeed.' Hugo gave a tight smile.

Jem took a deep breath. 'It was one of us.'

He didn't think he'd ever said it out loud. He'd known it; they all had. They'd known, and kept silent, and damned themselves and their friendship by complicity, but they had never said the words.

The expression on Hugo's face suggested it wasn't a sentiment he'd faced either. 'Don't.'

'You know it's true.'

Hugo glanced round, an involuntary, fearful motion that had no place in this lavish room. 'It may be, but don't. Please.'

'Do you not think about it?'

'No. No, I don't. I didn't kill him or want him dead, but I have a life to live, ambitions to achieve. I won't have my time on Earth overshadowed by a horror of someone else's doing. If there was anything I could do…but there isn't. It's ten years too late for that.'

'Well, someone wants to find out,' Jem said. '"*Ask him why,*", it said. And I'd like to know too.'

'Are you sure this is wise? If someone is writing these letters, and you go around asking questions…'

Jem met his eyes. Hugo flung his hands up, the movement speaking of frustration. 'Let's be honest. I haven't sought out any of the others in ten years for a reason, and I expect you haven't either for the same reason. I don't think you should do this.'

'How can I not?' Jem asked. 'I'm not you. You have a life and a fiancée and ambitions and a career and all those things. Well, I don't. I didn't take my degree, I couldn't return to study. I've done nothing for a decade but drudge. It might not have affected your life, Hugo, but it ruined mine.' The words came out louder than he'd meant, stark and bare. 'It ruined my life,' he repeated more quietly. 'St Anselm's was my chance, and when I lost it, I lost everything. Whoever killed Toby took my future from me as well, and now it's ruining my life all over again. So I'm going to do what the letter says. I'm going to ask why and see what I find, because I have nothing else, and it seems to me that I never will have anything else while this shadow hangs over us.'

Hugo was watching him closely. 'I can't stop you, but I wish that you will be careful.'

'I will. Hugo, where were you that night?'

'You know where I was. After that ghastly evening, I went up to visit a friend in Christ Church who was celebrating a birthday, but decided before I got there that I didn't like the idea of company after all. I thought I might drop in on Summoner's Gift instead, so I walked back to college and went in through the back gate, but I wasn't in the mood. I didn't speak to anyone and left after a few minutes. Returned to my digs in solitary splendour and sat there feeling like a fool. I expect we all did that.'

'Yes.'

Hugo tapped his fingers on the arm of his chair. 'I don't know if people ever speculate to you on who did it.'

'They used to, all the time. My supervisor called it an intellectual exercise.'

'Oh, yes. People at dinner parties treating it like a parlour game, or amateur sleuths who write with their theories. At whom did you find fingers pointing?'

'Aaron. Always Aaron.'

'Yes. I suspect he might have found himself in very hot water if Ella had not sworn she was with him. She swore they were together, and he agreed they were.' He paused, then grimaced. 'A terrible actor, Aaron.'

'Yes,' Jem said. 'Yes, he never could lie for toffee, could he?'

'I *don't* think it was him,' Hugo said, as if Jem were arguing it. 'If Aaron had wanted Toby dead, he'd have done a better job of it. That sounds appalling, but you understand me. He isn't a fool: he would not have set up an alibi that depended on his sweetheart's word and his non-existent histrionic skills, because even with Ella's testimony, it was a tight squeak for him. I don't suspect Aaron. I would point the finger at…others before him.' A slight hesitation there, as if he'd considered saying a name. 'But I also don't believe that alibi.'

'If he was lying, so was Ella.'

'Ella has a cool head,' Hugo said. 'I have always assumed she took one look at that brute of a detective inspector, concluded that he would hang Aaron on the colour of his skin, and acted accordingly. And, presumably, Aaron realised he should go along with it.' He rubbed the back of his neck, an awkward, boyish movement, slightly at odds with his stiff, high collar. 'So where does this leave us?'

'Prue and Nicky.' The words tasted sour. 'Prue adored Toby.'

'She did, and hell hath no fury like a woman scorned, but she was only a slip of a girl. Granted it was a sharp knife, and she was hysterical that evening, but the blow that killed Toby required a great deal of force. Could she have mustered that?'

'I wouldn't have thought so. Whereas Nicky is a tall man who can handle a blade,' Jem said, and thought he tasted bile in his throat.

Hugo gave him a sharp look. 'In your shoes, I should be careful about accusing Nicky. It might look as though you have a score to settle.'

The blood burned in Jem's face. 'I'm not accusing him. We've spoken about all the others.'

'To no purpose. Look, Jem, it wasn't me, and I will take your word it wasn't you. Aaron and Ella gave each other alibis, Prue is too small, and Nicky…I fenced with him. He always fought fair. And he adored Toby. I can't sit here and speculate on which one of us might be a murderer; I don't believe it of any of us.'

'But it was one of us,' Jem said through lips that felt a little stiff. 'I quite agree that none of us could possibly have done such a thing, but we all know that one of us *did*.'

Hugo shook his head. 'I have no answers for you, Jem. Nobody found an answer then, when the trail was fresh, and none of the sleuths, amateur or professional, have found an answer since.'

'Because we kept our secrets,' Jem said. 'Nobody told the inspector about what really happened that evening. None of us mentioned the trick with the door. Ella gave Aaron an alibi in which none of us believed, and nobody said he was lying. We hid everything, and Toby's murderer walked free because of it.'

Hugo's face had hardened as he spoke. 'If you wish to suggest we were all guilty of perverting the course of justice—'

'Weren't we?'

'Toby's murder almost destroyed us all. Do you wish that to happen again?'

'Are you saying you don't want to know who did it?'

Hugo shook his head, eyes half-closed. It looked like a rehearsed movement, something he'd do in the House to convey weary rebuke. 'I should very much like to know who did it. What I don't want is for everything we hid then to come out now, another scandal, ruining the lives we've since built for ourselves, to no purpose. Because the fact is, nobody saw the murderer, all our movements were examined in detail to no effect, there was no physical evidence. All we have is inference, implication, and suspicion. And I am tired of the suspicion, the sound and fury that signifies nothing. Aren't you?'

The clocks were chiming as Jem left Hugo's townhouse. It was only ten o'clock, which seemed extraordinary. He felt adrift in time, unmoored, as he had done since that damned letter had made him think of things he'd held under the water for so long that he'd almost believed they'd drowned.

He needed to think. He hadn't thought when he'd set off to see Hugo—or rather, he hadn't faced the question of what he wanted in its stark truth. Now it was unavoidable.

The air was cold and wet, leaving a shimmer of droplets on him as he walked. He headed up to Berkeley Square and sat on a bench, staring at the winter-sodden shrubs without seeing them.

What he wanted was to know who had killed Toby. Not who had sent one more malicious letter: that didn't matter. There were always letter-writers; they were legion and would never stop. He wanted to know which of them, which of his friends, which of the people he'd most loved and trusted in the world had put a knife in Toby's ribs, jammed the door, and walked away.

That was the great unspoken truth that had festered for a decade. It was one of the six of them, and they knew it for the simple reason that Toby's door had been stuck.

Toby had died on the night of Summoner's Gift, an ancient Anselm's tradition involving a procession around the quads, followed by free beer for all in the formal gardens. They should have been there, along with other Anselm undergraduates and alumni and passers-by who wandered through the open back gate to see what was going on, walk in the torchlit gardens and drink the college-brewed ale. But Toby had asked them to meet elsewhere beforehand, and they had, and the slide into hell had started there.

They had argued, terribly and destructively, with unforgivable things said on multiple sides. They'd walked away from one another a little after eight o'clock. Jem had never seen Toby again.

Jem hadn't known or cared what the others did after the row. He'd just walked, as though pounding Oxford's pavements could somehow blot out the words echoing in his brain, and, when he'd exhausted himself with walking, he had trudged back to his digs, and let loose the choking sobs of humiliation he'd been holding back. He'd huddled on his bed, wondering how he could possibly face the morning, until it *was* morning and he had to. He'd gone into college horribly aware that the others might be present, that he might see them, they might see him. He hadn't wanted to speak to any of them. He'd never wanted to speak to Nicky again.

Late that afternoon he had been in the library, because Finals wouldn't wait, when he had felt a tap on his shoulder and looked round to see a white-faced porter.

Toby had been found dead a couple of hours earlier, lying in his room in Summoner Quad. The curtains were drawn, windows closed, and the door stuck fast. His scout had been unable to get in to clean that morning, but Toby had often been known to put a chair under the doorhandle when he didn't want to be disturbed. He had missed a tutorial, but it was the fourth he'd skipped that term, and his absence had caused annoyance rather than concern. Goodness knew when the murder would have been noticed, in fact, except that Toby had borrowed someone's gown and its owner had become tired of waiting for its return. Hammering on the door had garnered no reply, neighbours had offered that the habitually loud Toby had not been heard from all day, and then someone asked if there was, perhaps, a smell.

A porter came with a spare key and found the door was already unlocked, and still wouldn't open. Eventually he put his shoulder to it, and everything changed.

Toby had been killed with his paperknife, the Italian stiletto. It had been driven deep into his chest, under his ribcage, upwards to the heart. There was surprisingly little blood; he would, the doctors thought, have died almost at once. Time of death was settled on as the previous evening, at some point between quarter past nine—when the upstairs man had knocked in the hope of borrowing a bottle of ink, and been told to go to the devil in a bellow that carried through the door—and two in the morning, going by the body's rigor. The college gates had been locked at ten o'clock.

Some students who lived in the surrounding rooms agreed they had heard raised voices at various points, including one that might have been a woman's, but there were always raised voices in Toby's room and it had been Summoner's Gift, the gardens full of visitors and chatter and ale. Nobody had paid particular attention at the time, or observed anything unusual. Nobody had noticed who'd come and gone.

If it had happened a few years later, the paperknife could have held the answer. The new study of fingerprints might have identified the killer; just this year, two men had hanged thanks to the fingerprints they left at the scene of their crime. But a decade ago fingerprints had been the preserve of scientific discussion, not criminal detection, and a doctor had pulled the knife from Toby's chest without a thought.

The police had needed evidence, and there was none. Summoner Quad had buildings on three sides of the quadrangle, forming a U shape looking down onto the college gardens. Staircase Thirty-One was the furthest away from the rest of the college, with a high wall behind it separating St Anselm's from neighbouring Trinity. Toby's was the end room on the ground floor. They had sometimes used to clamber in through the window from the quad or the garden rather than troubling to enter by the staircase door; one could also take the cellar route that ran from Old Quad under Summoner Quad, and came up, via a serving stair, in Thirty-One.

Someone had come to Toby's room that night, by whatever route. Someone had killed him with his paperknife, made sure the windows were fastened, left the room, and jammed the door. That had given the murderer the rest of the night and all the morning to wash hands, dispose of stained clothing, recover their composure, and come up with a story.

It was the jamming of the door that had given the killer those hours to dispose of evidence and let the trail go cold. It was the jamming of the door that said Toby's murderer was one of them.

Hugo had discovered it early on, quite by accident, in their third year. The doors of Summoner Quad were old and panelled and a little on the rickety side, and when he had slumped against Toby's one evening and turned the handle, the thing had stuck fast. They had all been rather drunk, so Toby had resorted to Nicky's sofa rather than complain to the porters' lodge. The next morning, after much fruitless rattling, they'd found the trick to release the pressure on the old wood, and from then on Toby's door could be jammed and released at will from the outside. They had kept that fact to themselves, Toby not wishing to spend the rest of the year having to let himself out by the window. But they'd all known how the murderer had jammed the door and prevented the discovery of the body for those crucial hours. And none of them had said.

It ought not to be possible that it was one of them, whatever had passed earlier. But as the nightmare had unfolded around them all, huddled together first in shock at the news and then because the detective inspector had asked for their presence for his enquiries, they had known it, and everything between them had begun to wither and die.

CHAPTER 5

Hilary Term, 1894

If Jem's first year at St Anselm's was revelatory, his second was magical.

Examinations, at the end of the first year, had been triumphant. Jem took a First and a college prize; Nicky bested that with the top First in the university in his Anglo-Saxon paper, and came third overall. Hugo also claimed a First, though not one of such distinction. Only Toby missed out, with a Lower Second that probably flattered the amount of work he'd done. He laughed about it, as he could because he was going to inherit a title and a fortune, and congratulated the rest of them wholeheartedly.

With nothing but the occasional collection to worry about in the way of examinations, their second year was dedicated to glory. Jem secured his place as cox of the college boat and tried out for the university. Nicky and Hugo both took Blues in fencing; Hugo also represented Anselm's on the running track along with Aaron, and even the stuffiest of Anselm's men proved ready to cheer for a champion of the wrong colour but the right prowess. Toby made a good run for Secretary of the Oxford Union, losing narrowly to a man of less charm but more political acumen, while Prudence became Treasurer of the Oxford Women's Association. Ella made sufficient impact in the lecture theatre that Toby began to be described by some scientists as 'Ella Feynsham's twin'. The world was before them, a great sunlit path through pleasant meadows with a glittering city at its end ready for them to conquer.

They were punting along the Cherwell one spring day in Seventh Week of Hilary term when Nicky mentioned the play.

'That chap Helmsley, the one with the hair, wants to put on a college production of *Cymbeline* next term.'

'I didn't know we had a dramatic society,' Jem said idly. They had mostly discarded their hats in a heap at the end of the punt, and he was watching the way the dappled light fell through the green tunnel of willows, turning Nicky's hair to an inappropriately angelic halo.

'We don't,' Nicky said. 'Helmsley's desperate to start one. He has artistic ambitions, so it will naturally be Shakespeare. *I* think he should do *Salome* and recruit Ella to do an exotic dance with someone's head on a platter.'

Prue flicked water at him. Ella ignored him.

'Don't OUDS always use professional actresses?' Toby asked. The Oxford University Dramatic Society was a time-honoured and convention-bound institution.

'Indeed they do. Helmsley's secured authorisation from the Master and the Hall to have Anselm's ladies instead. It will make rather a noise, which is why he's doing it, I expect.'

'Oh, I say, that's jolly good. Ella, you ought to do it. In fact, we should do it. All of us.' Toby waved his bottle of champagne in a wide circle to encompass the whole punt. 'It would be marvellous fun. Nicky and I both acted at school. We *should* do it, shouldn't we?'

Prue sat up, eyes bright. Nicky shrugged, in the casual way that meant he was extremely interested. Ella tilted her head in acquiescence. Toby looked around. 'Jem?'

'I'll be on the river a great deal next term, but I don't mind trying out.'

'It might be a lark,' Hugo agreed from his lofty position wielding the pole. 'I'm in. Aaron?'

'I can't act.' Aaron was sitting at the far end, with Ella. He still wore his straw boater, tipped to keep the sun from his eyes.

'Nonsense,' Toby said. 'Everyone can act.'

'I can't.'

'Of course you can. One just says things convincingly.'

'I can't,' Aaron repeated patiently.

'You should learn,' Nicky told him. 'You'll need the skill when you're saying, *Of course I'd like to hear about your bad knee*, and, *Two guineas is a reasonable fee*.'

'Anyway, it's not *Othello*, you won't have hundreds of lines,' Toby added. '*Cymbeline* has plenty of parts for spear-carriers and noble captains and things, doesn't it, Nicky?'

'You've never read it in your life,' Nicky said. 'But it does indeed have many small parts. Highly appropriate for an Oxford college production, really.'

Jem clamped his lips together; Hugo had a coughing fit. Prue said, 'That sounds perfect. I've never read it either, I must admit.'

'Let's do this,' Toby said. 'I really feel like something spectacular. *All* of us, Aaron, I absolutely insist. It will be such fun.'

Helmsley, the aspiring director with the hair, looked somewhat daunted at being presented with the Feynsham set en masse, but that year they were unrefusable. They were golden.

Prue made a very convincing boy in breeches and was cast as the heroine; Ella spoke the wicked stepmother's lines with a cold, false sweetness; and Nicky was naturally the smooth villain Iachimo. The problem lay with Toby and Hugo. They both auditioned for Posthumus, the hero, and Hugo got the part, leaving Toby as Cloten, the clownish villain.

It made sense. Iachimo and Posthumus had a big fight scene, and two fencing Blues would make that spectacular. And Cloten was the wicked stepmother's son, so Toby and Ella's resemblance would be useful. It was a big role, an important one. But it wasn't heroic by any means, and Toby had wanted to be the hero.

He was very gracious about it. Nicky was not. Nicky argued that Toby was a notably better actor than Hugo, who was handsome but wooden. He made the point forcefully and repeatedly, and he would not let it drop. Jem rather thought that if he were Toby, he'd want Nicky to let it drop.

It wasn't that Nicky made his feelings obvious, precisely. He was flamboyant and mannered, of course, but so were many others, adopting poses of decadence and talking about Wilde and Beardsley, the Aesthetic movement and the *Yellow Book*. Only, Jem saw him watching Toby, and it made something inside him crumple.

Nicky watched Toby, and Jem knew it because he watched Nicky.

He couldn't help it. Nicky was so far from what Jem was. His lounging grace, his casual rudeness and the confident way he didn't care, the flex and grip of his bare toes as he fenced. He was as far from Jem's grasp as the moon, and would have been even if he didn't always watch Toby. And in any case, Jem would leave Oxford and pursue a career—he thought, ambitiously, of the civil service, even Whitehall—and doubtless marry, because one *did*, and even if he was one of the Feynsham set, one of the golden ones, there were some things that were unthinkable for the son of a Midlands factory hand.

But he watched Nicky all the same, and Nicky watched Toby, just as hopelessly.

Toby didn't mind. He took Nicky as he was, and none of the others objected to Nicky's postures either. Jem wasn't even sure how much they thought it was a performance, and how much acting a truth. Except, once, a man in the buttery called Nicky a damned queer and Hugo and Aaron turned shoulder to shoulder on him: two large, muscular men moving with open menace, as though Nicky needed defending. So maybe they knew and didn't care. Maybe Nicky was permitted to watch Toby as Aaron watched Ella—with a longing that was entirely permissible if it was understood to be impossible.

One couldn't help one's feelings. But one could certainly avoid making an embarrassing display of them, and, after Summoner Quad's peace was shattered for a good half hour by a discussion between Nicky and Helmsley conducted with the lexicon of dramaturgy and the savagery of a pub fight, Hugo muttered in Toby's ear, and Toby agreed that, really, he was very glad to take the part of Cloten. After all, his decapitation in Act Four would give him plenty of time to relax while the others sweated.

With that resolved, rehearsals proceeded. Jem, whose duties on the river were all-consuming, would have preferred the smallest possible part, preferably a single appearance, but Helmsley had seized on one of Cloten's lines to the servant Pisanio—'Where is she, sir? Come nearer; No further halting'—and decided to interpret 'halting' as a description of Pisanio's movements.

'He's an old soldier. Loyal to Posthumus not just as a servant but as comrade-in-arms, wounded in battle, all that. Hence your limp, you see.'

'Do I have to explain my limp?' Jem asked mildly.

'Well, I'd think so, otherwise everyone will wonder what you're doing hobbling about like that.'

'I think it sounds jolly good,' Toby said. 'Suppose he had a crutch too? For the look of it?'

'I think that's an awfully good idea,' Helmsley agreed, and there they were. Jem would have liked to argue, but they'd had enough of that for any production. And in truth, the idea of taking a decent part had its appeal, even if he wasn't quite sure when he'd sleep between rowing, acting, and the odd spot of mathematics. *You won't get another chance*, he told himself, and decided to get up earlier in the mornings.

The rehearsals went well. Hugo was handsome and charming. Nicky chilled the blood as the villain: louche, malicious, purring. Toby clowned wonderfully as Cloten, but insisted that he should not only be a fool.

'He's frightening,' Toby said at one rehearsal. 'An oaf, but a villain too, every bit as dangerous as Iachimo. I think we should see that in the scene with Pisanio.' Toby cast an assessing eye over Jem. 'Pisanio is a plebeian and a cripple, exactly the sort of person Cloten would bully. Look, Jem, play the scene, would you?'

He took the centre of the room, beckoning imperiously to Jem, who leaned on his crutch to listen. '*Where is thy lady? Or, by Jupiter—I will not ask again. Close villain, I'll have this secret from thy heart, or rip thy heart to find it. Is she with Posthumus?—from whose so many weights of baseness cannot a dram of worth be drawn.*'

'*Alas, my lord, how can she be with him? When was she missed? He is in Rome.*' As rehearsed, Jem turned and began to hobble away.

'*Where is she, sir?*' Toby bellowed, striding towards him. '*Come nearer; no further halting. Satisfy me home what is become of her!*' His voice rose almost hysterically on the last words, and he lashed out, kicking Jem's crutch from under him.

Jem didn't see it coming. His full weight had been on the crutch, because he'd been on his feet for the best part of an hour now, and he fell hard, with a yell of shock and pain as he hit the floor.

'God help us.' Nicky was at his side, pulling him up to a sitting position. Jem wished Aaron were here. His foot was throbbing badly. 'Are you all right? What the bloody hell, Toby?'

'I'm awfully sorry.' Toby dropped to a squat by him, looking shocked. 'I'd no idea you'd go over like that. I didn't mean to kick so hard.'

'I'm sure that will mend his damned foot,' Nicky snapped. 'You utter bollox.'

'I'm fine.' Jem glared at them, both to hold back the tears of pain that prickled behind his eyes, and because he wanted to lean into Nicky's arms and feel them close round him. 'It's fine. I just didn't expect it.'

'Well, that was what I intended.' Toby grimaced. 'I really am sorry, Jem. I thought if Cloten kicked over a cripple, it would be a shock to the audience.'

'It certainly surprised me,' Jem said, and Toby's brilliant smile flashed out.

'Exactly! And if we can work it so you go over, like that—then Cloten's terrifying. Unpredictable. The audience will believe his threats.'

'And see why Pisanio agrees to do as he says, I suppose.' Jem's voice still sounded shaky in his own ears, but he was not, *not*, going to make a fuss. Anyone else would take this in their stride. It *would* look marvellous on stage.

'I must say, it could be a magnificent effect,' Helmsley agreed. 'If you can do the fall safely?'

Jem agreed he could, and learned how, and had his reward in the gasps of horror from the audience every night, their scene eliciting almost as much tension as Iachimo's prowl around the sleeping Imogen.

That, for Jem, was the play's finest moment. Iachimo had himself smuggled into Imogen's bedchamber, creeping up to the helpless woman as she slept. Nicky moved in a soft-footed prowl, circling Prue on the bed, eyes intent. The menace was sexual and palpable; Jem watched in rehearsals, feeling slightly nauseated and at the same time lost in admiration. *Though this a heavenly angel, hell is here.*

It was, Jem thought, the best part in the play, and it was notable that Iachimo, alone of the characters, was never ludicrous. Nicky would not have consented to play Cloten; he did not ever choose to make a fool of himself.

Aaron, who only agreed to take part under intense pressure, proved to be without question the worst actor Jem had ever seen. His deep, resonant voice went hopelessly flat when tasked with reciting other men's words. Toby insisted on his participation, saying it wouldn't be the same without him, and he was given the part of Jupiter, who had twenty-one lines. Ella coached him over and over, the two of them pacing up and down the gardens outside Summoner Quad as Jem sat on Nicky's window ledge and watched.

'It won't matter,' Nicky said. 'He'll look divine, in every sense, in a white toga with a gold wreath. Give him some firecrackers to throw and nobody will listen to a word he says.'

He was right. Ella made up some remarkable firecrackers that went off with coloured smoke, and encouraged the stagehands to wobble their thundersheets with volume, and even Aaron admitted that the experience might be worth the cold night sweats.

They were all good. They were marvellous. Lewis and his cronies sarcastically dubbed them the 'Seven Wonders of St Anselm's' when the college boat coxed by Jem swept all before it at the Eights Week regatta. The nickname was meant to be insulting in its extravagant flattery; Toby shouted with laughter and repeated it everywhere. Why not? They *were* wonders, and the first night was triumphant. Toby brought out champagne afterwards, as students and dons crowded around to offer congratulations. *Awfully good. Rook really is alarming. Wonderful fighting. The Imogen girl was superb. Is that your sister, Feynsham?*

Jem loved it, every second. It was a hot, clear June, the skies endlessly blue; he'd taken his boat to Head of the River, a sporting success that would be written forever in the college's history; his friends were together, and around him everything was perfect.

Until the last night.

The problem was, Iachimo disappeared from the play between the second and the fifth acts. That left Nicky with nothing to do for a long time, and Jem's mother always said that idle hands were the devil's workshop.

He was already sozzled when they started, that last evening. Jem could see it: the sheen in his eyes, the slightly distant expression. He held his drink as well as anyone Jem knew, and he knew a lot of heavy drinkers, but Nicky had nevertheless been quite obviously bending the elbow.

He caught Nicky's arm when he came offstage after the second act. 'Good work, but for heaven's sake lay off the sheep dip, will you?'

'The hell's it to you?' Nicky enquired with cold, careful precision, and a little too loudly.

'Ssh. You're sodden. Go have some water and splash your face.'

Nicky grabbed his chin, forcing it up. 'Oh, my dear provincial Jeremy, always responsible. You'll never shed that tight little Presbyterian shell around your soul, will you? Have some fun, for once.'

His eyes were too bright, his fingers too tight, hot on Jem's skin. 'We can have fun after the performance,' Jem said, placatory. 'Wouldn't that be better?'

Nicky's lips curved nastily. 'Oh, darling. I thought you'd never ask.'

There were people around them. He had to get back on stage. 'Stop it,' Jem said urgently.

'I thought you said fun.' Nicky's voice was slurred. 'Any time, Jeremy. Ready when you are.'

Jem jerked his face away, hating the ugly flash in Nicky's eyes, telling himself, *He's drunk, only drunk.* 'Just sober up a little, will you?'

By the interval, Nicky was nowhere to be found. Jem went to Aaron, as the sensible one. 'Have you seen Nicky?'

'I saw him on stage. He's drunk.'

'He's drunker than that,' Jem said. 'Extremely drunk. I don't think he knew what he was saying to me.'

Aaron screwed his face up, a gesture that in another man would have translated to a lungful of profanity. 'Curse the fellow. No, I haven't seen him. Toby's not around either. Maybe he's talking some sense into Nicky.'

'You think so?'

'Anything's possible,' Aaron said without much conviction.

Toby reappeared just before the play was to restart, looking rather flushed and exuberant—tiddly, Jem diagnosed, but not juiced. He brushed off Jem's efforts to ask about Nicky, hurrying on stage, and, by the time he came off, Jem had to be on the other side of the wings to go on. He told himself the director would handle it. *And anyway, of course Nicky won't make a fool of himself. He never does.*

He did.

Act Five included the swordfight between Posthumus and Iachimo. It was a highlight of the performance, drawing shrieks of applause as Nicky and Hugo battled it out across the stage. It wasn't proper fencing, of course; it was all wild sweeps and dramatic clashes, with Nicky at one point hanging off the tree in the corner off the quad as Hugo slashed at him from below. Pure play-fighting, Hugo called it, with a disapproving shake of the head undermined by his obvious glee. It looked marvellous and had won them cheers every night.

Nicky managed to get on stage, but that was it. Hugo did his best, but there was no way to hold a dramatic fight against a man so drunk he dropped his sword three times. Hugo managed a few half-hearted exchanges in which he was mostly using his blade to keep Nicky's up, put his sword to Nicky's throat with a convincing look of murderous rage, and left the stage, grimacing at Jem, who watched with horror from the wings.

Alone on stage, Nicky was supposed to embark on his soliloquy of remorse and defeat. He wandered around the stage instead, as though he wasn't sure what he was doing there, prodding at papier-mâché rocks with his sword. The prompter hissed at him a couple of times, finally getting through; Nicky said, loudly, 'What?', repeated the first line, 'The heaviness and guilt within my bosom takes off my manhood,' and started to giggle. He laughed for a couple of moments, as the audience stirred in bewildered confusion, then sat abruptly on the stage, hunched over.

'Get him off,' Helmsley snarled. A couple of Roman soldiers hurried on to drag Nicky out of the way. He fought then, kicking out, and it took several agonising minutes and four people to get him off the stage. Helmsley furiously detailed a couple of stagehands to get rid of him, upgraded a blond soldier to speak a few vital lines on his behalf in the final scene, and expressed his firm intention of throttling him once the cast had retreated, after polite but not triumphant applause, to the rooms they were using to dress.

'What the devil was he thinking!' Helmsley bellowed. 'On stage, that drunk—What's *wrong* with the man?'

'It's not his usual practice,' Aaron said. 'He must have been putting it away all day.'

'He was hitting it hard in the interval,' Toby said, rubbing his face. 'I tried to stop him, but he was high as ninety.'

Hugo was in a towering rage, face red. 'Wretched swine. He made us, me in particular, look fools out there. Damn the man.'

'It's the last day of the year,' Jem said, with a sudden sense of emptiness. 'I'm going home tomorrow. I wish—I wish he hadn't done that.'

Jem didn't see Nicky again before he left—there was no answer when he knocked at his door, and no sign of him in Hall. At the start of the next term, Nicky greeted him as usual, without reference to his behaviour or explanation for it, still less an apology. It was never brought up again.

CHAPTER 6

Jem decided to go to Aaron next. It was Aaron or Ella, and after that he'd have to leave London to pursue his nagging need to know.

Ella and Aaron, Aaron and Ella.

He'd known the two were close. They were all close, of course, the seven of them, but some of the individual relationships were special. Toby and Ella. Nicky and Toby. And Aaron and Ella.

Ella and Aaron were so similar. That might have sounded odd to an outsider, but among the seven of them it was obvious. Fierce intelligence, fierce determination to be judged by that intelligence alone. A certain reserve too, which Jem put down to being 'the woman' and 'the black' in a sea of white men, because he felt it himself as 'the commoner' or 'the cripple'. He couldn't react as they did, though. Jem reddened, stared at the floor and felt his inferiority in every biting word, where Ella swept majestically through objection with a cool contempt that made mockery shrivel and die, and Aaron was simply unreactive, unreadable.

He had attended an expensive boarding school from the age of six, which doubtless meant he was used to abuse, and he had all the self-belief of the well-born and well-off. Not that he had any of what people called 'side' to him. He never flaunted his achievements in study or sport, and Jem had sometimes thought he was the only one to see that Aaron disregarded applause not because he was humble, but because he was magnificently sure of himself.

Except that Ella had seen it, of course. Like calling to like.

Aaron and Ella, walking up and down the gardens learning Jupiter's lines, or discussing research papers and scientific innovations in language that left the rest of them yawning. Rarely the jokers, never the leaders.

If it hadn't been impossible, it would have been obvious to everyone. It *had* been obvious to Jem, who knew wanting when he saw it in other eyes because he feared it was all too obvious in his own, but he had still assumed that it was impossible. Aaron was a black man, and Ella was a marquess's granddaughter, one day to be a marquess's sister.

Aaron hadn't seen it as impossible, and nor had Ella, and the two of them had proceeded on their own path until it all came tumbling down.

Jem wasn't sure how best to approach Aaron now. He was nervous in a way he hadn't been with Hugo, and he didn't like that he was nervous.

He'd always thought Aaron to be deeply decent, with an air of calm that, along with his age, made him seem comfortingly reliable in their dizzy, glittering, overheated little world. He'd surely be a superb doctor; one felt better for speaking to him.

But he wasn't a good liar.

Aaron and Ella's alibi was straightforward enough. She said they had left the Mitre Hotel after that last great row, and had walked around together for a while before heading back towards Anselm Hall. That took them past Anselm College's back gates, standing open for the Summoner's Gift festivities, and Ella had decided to go in and wish her brother goodnight. 'Never let the sun go down on a quarrel,' they agreed she had said. Jem couldn't imagine the homely words in her icy voice.

Ella said she had spoken briefly to Toby and left him alive and well, while Aaron waited for her in the gardens: he at least had been noticed there by a few people. They had left through the garden gates at around nine o'clock and taken several turns around the Parks before returning to Anselm Hall a few minutes after ten, for which she had been written up. Aaron had arrived back at his own digs not more than ten minutes later.

That was Ella's story, to which Aaron had lent his voice. They had left at nine; Toby had been heard alive and well at nine fifteen; the college gates had been locked at ten. If they had been together from nine until ten, neither of them had killed Toby.

If.

Jem was absolutely sure Aaron had lied in supporting Ella's story, and equally sure the others had all concluded the same thing. They'd all known, and not said anything at the time because their shattered friendships had still had remnants standing then, like houses broken by an earthquake but not quite ready to fall down.

Had Ella lied in response to the detective inspector's obvious prejudice, or because she was the one who needed an alibi? Had Aaron asked her to lie for him, or let her do it for his own safety, or had he been lying for hers? Who had protected whom? If that alibi was false, where had they both been, and was it together or apart?

Jem wished he could just ask. Just sit down with Aaron and say, *I know as a certainty in my soul that you didn't kill Toby, so tell me the truth.* He couldn't say that, no matter how much he wanted to defy his wormy suspicions for the sake of the golden years.

He needed to be strategic, not sentimental. He'd realised in those long minutes of waiting that he'd made a mistake giving his name to Hugo's footman. If Hugo had anything to hide, he'd had plenty of time to prepare himself. Jem wanted to take the others by surprise, to speak without giving anyone the chance to think first. That was a foul thought, planning to trap his friends into admissions, but they weren't his friends any more, and one of them had murdered Toby.

So he made an appointment to see Dr Oyede on Monday as Jeremy Dunnidge, using his mother's maiden name, and tried not to wince when advised of the consultation fee.

The fire that had driven him out of his boring, safe work ebbed over the empty weekend, leaving him with a distinct sensation of doing something ludicrous, or foolish, or mad. But he'd made the appointment, so he turned up, and when the stern lady at the desk announced, 'Mr Dunnidge? Dr Oyede will see you now,' Jem plucked up his courage and went in.

Aaron was writing at his desk. He didn't look up for a second, and Jem saw that his very close-cropped hair was as dark as ever. Jem's was starting to grey.

Finally he looked up, said, 'Good afternoon, Mr Dunn—' and stopped dead.

'Hello, Aaron. Sorry about the subterfuge.'

Aaron stared at him for a second, mouth slightly open. '*Jem?*'

He made a movement, as though he was about to come round the desk, but didn't. He stood, though, and held out his hand. Jem gripped it, and Aaron's far larger hand engulfed his, warm and strong and familiar, and for a second Jem felt a lump in his throat so hard and painful that it couldn't be borne.

'Great Scott, man.' Aaron surveyed him. 'How are you? What on earth are you doing here: are you unwell? Why…' He paused, then said, a little more slowly, 'Why the false name?'

'I wasn't sure if you'd want to see me. I'm not unwell.'

'It's been a long time.' Aaron's deep voice was a little vague, as though he was thinking. His gaze flicked to Jem's foot. 'Let's sit down.'

Jem moved to the chair on the opposite side of the desk, then hesitated. Aaron took up his own chair and moved it so that they faced each other without furniture between them.

'Very well,' Aaron said. 'I suppose this isn't a social call. Or is it?'

'No. I wish it was.' He wondered whether to plunge into it, and decided to prepare the ground. 'Have you had many letters recently?'

'Letters. That sort?' Jem nodded. Aaron shrugged. 'Three or four a month, perhaps. Fewer than I used to.'

'My God. Even Hugo only gets one or two.'

'You've seen Hugo?'

'Last week. I went to him after a letter was sent to my employers. I lost my position over it.'

'What?' Aaron demanded. 'You were dismissed for a letter?'

'More for objecting to my superior letting the rest of the office know about it. You know how it is, people scrawling *Murderer* on my desk blotter, that sort of thing.'

'Oh, Jem. I'm extremely sorry to hear it.'

'It's all right. I loathed the job anyway. It was tedious paper-pushing. I've done nothing but tedious paper-pushing since—since…'

'I'm sorry,' Aaron said again, his voice deep and irrationally comforting, making Jem realise just how much he needed that comfort.

He pushed the longing aside. 'Did your superior or your colleagues receive one last week? Last Wednesday, or thereabouts? I expect it would say, *Aaron Oyede is a murderer. He killed Toby Feynsham. Ask him why.* Three lines, typewritten. And addressed to the head of your practice, not to you.'

'We're equal partners. I'll ask; Miss Hirsch throws them away for me. Wait here.'

Aaron went out, and returned a few moments later, looking grim. He shut the door behind him. 'Miss Hirsch is of the opinion that there was indeed one in the middle of last week, and that the wording rings a bell.'

'Hugo's was to his fiancée. Someone set out to cause all three of us trouble. Or, for all I know, all six of us. I don't know about the other three yet, but I'm going to ask.'

'You're going to see—'

'Ella next,' Jem said, watching his face. 'Have you seen her?'

'No.'

'I wondered if you'd kept in touch.'

'No. What about the others?'

'Prue is in Hertfordshire. She married.'

'Good.'

'And Nicky is at Anselm's, teaching.' He tried to say it without any particular weight, but Aaron was watching his face, and Jem could feel his cheeks warming. 'I'm going to talk to them all.'

'To what end?' Aaron leaned back a little, frowning. 'To learn if we are all being harassed by the same lunatic?'

'Someone has written to at least three of us to accuse us of killing Toby,' Jem said. 'One of us did.'

Aaron went absolutely blank, the way he did when people said things he didn't choose to hear, the way he had that first night in the buttery. After a moment he blinked, slowly. 'You can't say that.'

'We all know. We all knew back then. After the row—'

'It was an argument. Nothing more.'

'It was more. You know it was. Toby said some awful things. And someone killed him.'

Aaron blew out a long breath. 'If someone had given Toby, or indeed Nicky, a good thrashing, it would have been understandable. I was tempted and I expect you were too. But we didn't. We left, and then what? One of us came to Toby's room afterwards and stabbed him in cold blood?'

'Yes.'

'I didn't mean to agree,' Aaron said. 'I mean, you are claiming that's what happened.'

'But you do agree, don't you?'

'No,' Aaron said through his teeth. 'No, I do not. I don't think either Nicky or Prue stabbed Toby in a fit of thwarted passion. I don't know any reason either you or Hugo would have wanted him dead, though you might have felt he deserved kicking. And it wasn't Ella or myself.'

'Because you were together?'

'Because we were together.'

'You're a better liar than you used to be.' Jem was quite impressed, in a distant way, with how level his voice sounded. 'But you still aren't marvellous.'

Aaron's deep brown eyes were very steady on Jem's. He didn't speak. They looked at each other in silence, the moment stretching almost unbearably, and then Aaron rose. 'I think you should go.'

'I'm not accusing you,' Jem said. 'I'm not accusing anyone yet. But one of us is a murderer, and it's past time we knew who. So I'm asking.'

'And what if you ask us all and find no answer? If you upturn this rock and expose everything under it to the light, will you be happy?'

'I haven't been happy in ten years. Are you happy not knowing?' He glanced at Aaron's left hand, ringless. 'Are you happy now?'

'Happier than I was when I was refused a dozen posts because I was all but known as an unconvicted murderer,' Aaron said savagely. 'Do you think you're the only sufferer here?'

'Then why don't you want to know the truth?'

Aaron strode to the door and jerked it open. 'Please leave. I shan't charge you for my wasted time but don't repeat this. And I strongly advise you not to pursue this business, Jem. It will do no good to anyone.'

Jem made a somewhat shamefaced exit from the surgery and went to the nearest public house to scribble down what little he'd gleaned in his notebook. He wasn't sure what to make of that conversation; he wasn't even sure how he felt.

What if you ask us all and find no answer?

He didn't want to consider that too closely. He had a goal for the first time in years. He wanted to pursue it because he had nothing else to do, and when it ended and left him with nothing to do again, with one more failure to his account... Well, perhaps it would just make things worse, but he would rather make things worse than do nothing any longer.

Jem had cut himself off from caring about anything, because an empty existence had seemed preferable to a pale shadow of his lost past, his lost future. Talking to Aaron and Hugo again, even so awkwardly, had been like a splash of water on the drought of his life.

He wondered what it would be like to talk to Ella. Jem had never been sure the Seven Wonders would have been the set of friends she'd have chosen for herself, with the raucous exchanges and constant bickering and foolery. Ella was the only one of them who hadn't set to anything except work. She hadn't been interested in sport, or university politics; hadn't joined societies or taken up hobbies; only did *Cymbeline* because Toby insisted. She'd always been at a little bit of a distance, happiest in the lecture rooms or the laboratory, or talking quietly to Aaron. Jem had never had a heart-to-heart with her.

She'd rarely spoken to Nicky.

CHAPTER 7

Trinity Term, 1893

It was the summer of their first year when Jem really noticed the gap between Nicky and Ella. His first term had been a giddy blur of work, play, drink, chaos; of starting a new life and—self-consciously, awkwardly, unstoppably—remaking himself in a new form. He worked on his vowels, losing the dragging weight of his Midlands accent; he learned hierarchies and statuses and the vocabulary that marked him as one of the group; he went from humble, incredulous gratitude to a heady determination to enjoy every minute. He joined a couple of clubs, the sort where one talked rather than drank because he couldn't afford more dissipation than he already had. By contrast, Toby was in the Bullingdon, which was exclusively for rich thugs, and Nicky belonged to something called the Peacock, for aesthetes, which Jem felt he would do well not to ask about.

By Trinity term, he was firmly an Oxford man. This was his life, these people were his friends, and it was not going to be snatched away.

It was a week before Mods started. The others were all out, leaving Nicky and Jem at a loose end after Hall. Jem thought they might perhaps have a quiet drink in his room. He was wrong.

'Come on,' Nicky said. He had on his gown over his jacket, a bottle of wine in his hand and a glint in his eye that made Jem's heart stutter. 'We're going to indulge in a view. Have you been on the roof yet?'

'The roof? What roof?'

Nicky led the way to the library in Old Quad. The golden light of the summer evening lit the ancient stone, which seemed to glow responsively from within; it caught Nicky's hair and made the pale strands sparkle. Jem followed, as he would follow Nicky anywhere: into the great dark room, through the ranks of shelving and the rows of desks, into the back rooms and through a door that read No Admittance, and up a plain set of narrow stairs, their feet clapping noisily on the worn wood.

'Ought we to be here?' Jem hissed.

'Not at all,' Nicky murmured. 'We'll be in terrible trouble if we're caught. Want to run away?'

'I was just asking,' Jem said, and kept climbing. He disliked putting weight on his club foot, so he led on each step with his left foot, which meant his left knee and thigh rapidly began to complain. Nicky climbed the stairs in a casual, lounging sort of way as though he wouldn't have wanted to go at any other pace, and Jem gritted his teeth and plodded on.

There were occasional small windows as they went up, none at the top landing, which was extremely dark. Jem stood, feeling the burn in leg and foot and trying not to breathe too heavily, as Nicky did something with metal that rattled. Evening light flooded over them as he opened a door, and Jem looked out onto a rooftop.

'Good God,' he said. 'You meant it.'

Nicky made a courtly gesture, inviting Jem to go first, and shut the door behind them. Jem came out warily. The roof sloped up to the centre of the building but had a wide flat area between the slope and the ornamental parapet, which seemed very low, considering. The flat space was, he had to assume, designed to be walked on. He went forward in a cautious way, making sure of his footing, before he turned and looked.

They were facing south, looking over Front Quad and Broad Street and towards the main spread of Oxford, and the setting sun turned everything before him to glowing rose gold. The domes and spires rose like masts from the sea, like prayers to heaven, a glory of human brilliance in stone, and Jem stared, and stared, because he couldn't look away.

Something hard and smooth nudged his hand. 'Here.'

Jem raised the wine bottle to his lips and swigged a mouthful without looking. Nicky took it back off him. 'Worth the climb.'

'God, yes. God.'

'One can do this lawfully elsewhere, of course, but there is a dreadful likelihood of encountering *people*. I thought you'd prefer solitude. There's a perch here.' He led Jem further along to where a square piece of brickwork allowed them to sit and see the view. It was a little close for two. Jem sat to rest his leg and foot; Nicky propped his arse on the remaining space, sitting sideways to give Jem more room, their backs and hips just touching.

'Do you often come up here?' Jem asked at last. 'Why haven't we been before? Or do you—' He cut that off. He was not going to ask if Nicky and Toby had been regularly together in this forbidden eyrie. He was here now.

'I come up now and again. It gives me perspective,' Nicky said. 'I had the key off a fellow who left last year. It's not to be abused. I don't suppose we'd get more than a stern talking-to for trespass if we were caught, but I should have to hand over the key and I'd rather not.'

'Is that why we haven't had a party up here?'

'Good Lord, dear boy, imagine trying to prevent Toby from hurling empty bottles over the parapet.'

Jem grinned and took another swig of wine. It was the college hock, rather sweet for his developing tastes. 'It's marvellous. Thank you for bringing me.'

'I thought you'd appreciate it. Not everyone would.'

'Oh come. Anyone would appreciate this view.'

'Nonsense. Toby would be finding out what the echo's like, and Ella would be counting spires or working out mathematical ratios for more efficient load-bearing.'

'I say,' Jem protested. 'Is that fair?'

'Neither Feynsham twin has an aesthetic bone in his or her body. And it's not about artistic appreciation, anyway. It's about whether one imagines the world exists to serve one's needs, or whether one is open to its wonders, a vessel into which the world may pour its beauty.'

'I'm fairly sure I'm not that,' Jem said somewhat warily.

'Oh, of course you are.' Nicky passed him the wine. 'It's the difference between thinking, *That is a beautiful thing*, and *That is a beautiful thing, so I must own it*. Or, in Ella's case, demanding an analysis of what constitutes beauty, in triplicate.'

'That *isn't* fair. Why don't you like Ella?'

'Who says I don't?'

'Well, you.'

'I did not.'

'Did.'

'My God, you child. I don't dislike the woman. It is simply that it doesn't do to be *too* important in one twin's life; it risks putting the other's nose out of joint, and we can't have that.'

Jem stared out at the spires. The sun was set now, the remaining light briefly turning the gracious stone blood-red. 'I don't think Toby is possessive, is he? He strikes me as extremely generous.'

'Those aren't opposites. Are you familiar with the Feynsham family?'

'Of course I'm not.'

'I mean Toby's position.'

'Well, his grandfather's a marquess, isn't he? And Toby's his heir.'

'No, not precisely,' Nicky said. 'Toby is, if I may so describe it, the heir presumptive to the heir apparent.'

'I have no idea what that means.'

The bells started then, chiming the hour all over Oxford. The distant boom of Old Tom in Christ Church, the lighter peals from St Mary Magdalen, Balliol and Trinity, antiphonies, scales and cadences and pure single chimes, with Anselm's own brassy chapel clock so loud up here that Jem gripped his stone seat, fearful of being jolted off by the force of the noise. Nicky took his wrist, as if to steady him, and kept hold of it, and they let the glorious cacophony wash over them until it was indisputably agreed to be nine o'clock.

'Can't hear yourself think,' Nicky said. 'What were we talking about?'

'Toby.'

'Of course we were. Well. The Marquess of Grevesham had two sons. Toby's father was the younger. The older son, Viscount Crenshaw, is a childless widower and notorious drunk. If he dies without issue, the next heir will be Toby.'

'Isn't that what I said?'

'*If* Crenshaw dies without issue. Which he well may: he's over sixty, and the marquess has started taking Toby round the estates and doing the speech about *One day, my grandson, all this will be yours*. But Toby has no claim at all on the marquessate or its riches until the sozzled old fool expires. And if Crenshaw marries on his deathbed, the title could still be lost to an unborn child. Do you see? You and I can reach for our glittering futures. Toby has no way to achieve his except to wait for someone to die. Which, you may imagine, preys on the nerves.'

'Maybe he should settle to something else in the meantime, then.'

'Don't be ridiculous. Can you imagine Tobes working?'

It sounded like everything Jem had read in satirical novels about the upper classes. 'What happens to Ella when Toby becomes a marquess?'

Nicky shrugged. 'She will become Lady Petronella.'

'Lady *what*?'

'Didn't you know Ella's baptismal affliction? It would have soured my character too. Why was I talking about this?'

Jem tried to remember, a task made less easy since they'd got a fair way through the bottle. 'Possessiveness?'

'That's right. You and I don't look upon the world as a mass of *I could have that*, or *I should have had that*, and if we think, *I want that*, we don't expect it to fall into our hands for the wanting. And the corollary of that, of course, the reward for our denial, is that we can see beauty without resenting that we don't own it. A poverty of the flesh, a richness of the spirit.'

'What utter rot. Anyone can appreciate a lovely view if they care to look. And talk about the spiritual benefits of being poor is something you never hear from the poor. Only from the rich giving reasons why it's not in anyone's interests to raise wages.'

'Bloody socialist.'

'*And*,' Jem went on, 'you're as rich as anyone. Aren't you? You went to Winchester!'

'My father is reasonably well lubricated,' Nicky agreed. 'It doesn't mean I can have everything I want.'

Jem stared ahead, at the white cupola of the Sheldonian Theatre, faint and orange-tinted by the gaslights of the street. He thought he could feel Nicky's breathing, the tiny added pressure every couple of seconds to the connection where his body and Jem's rested against one another. He was aware he was slightly drunk, and that he had to say something, and that he didn't know what.

He didn't know if he was permitted to say, *Do you want Toby?* or whether he could bear it if Nicky said yes.

'I don't think—I don't think, whatever the reason you can't have something, I don't think it's a good thing,' he managed. 'I mean, if it's something other people could have because of their birth or their—their nature. I wouldn't be here if I was happy to look at the dreaming spires and think, well, that's not for my sort. I took the scholarship examination to get this for myself. I don't *want* to admire things from afar.'

'Nor do I, Jeremy,' Nicky said, and his voice sounded harsh. 'Sodding hell. Nor do I.'

He tipped up the bottle, then passed it to Jem, who drained the last mouthful. Toby probably would hurl it over the parapet, he thought. He could almost understand the urge. Just to see it rise and arc and tumble and fall. Just for the thrill of it, before the crash.

He didn't, because he was Jem who thought about things like broken glass in the quad below and the danger of hurting someone. Because he feared consequences. So he didn't throw the bottle, and he didn't ask Nicky what he wanted in case Nicky asked him that in return, and it was a relief—he was sure it was—when his companion rose.

'Come on, it's dark. Let us grope our way downstairs and try not to be caught.'

After two days trying to make an appointment to see Ella, or discover her address, Jem gave up. She guarded her privacy, clearly, and, even if he took her by surprise, she had always been one of the most self-possessed people he knew. And if Aaron was protecting her still, if they were maintaining their fiction of an alibi, might he not even have written to warn her?

He looked up the trains to Hertfordshire instead.

The village of Aldbury proved to be a mile from Tring station. Jem arrived at around eleven on a bright, cold November day, and walked the distance for the sake of the sparkling-fresh air, even if he'd be aching later. It was bitterly cold, with the grass and leaves in shadow still rimed with the night's frost, and his breath steamed out in front of him in feathery plumes.

He thought of Prue as he walked. The girls had been close ever since they'd roomed together in the first year, but he had sometimes wondered if Ella had selected her as a friend because she was there. Prue had given Ella a woman to talk to; Ella had given Prue the chance to be more than another bluestocking.

Toby hadn't seemed to resent that friendship at all. He'd encouraged Prue's ambitions, insisted on her trying for the starring role in *Cymbeline*, and lavished her with the irresistible charm that had them all following more or less helplessly in his path. Naturally, she had fallen in love with him, with the sort of hopeless adoration that had made Jem flinch away because he didn't want to see it. Had Ella considered that as a disloyalty from her sole female friend?

Toby hadn't reciprocated Prue's affections, and she'd doubtless have grown out of those feelings in time, but she'd undeniably loved him. How had she married so quickly after his death?

Jem's thoughts kept him distracted as he walked what proved to be a country mile to Aldbury. He had always been good at immersing himself in study to the exclusion of outside distraction and bodily need, but he regretted it as he reached the village green and realised that his hip was aching with a steady beat of pain. He'd walked too fast, or it was the cold. He'd need to find a conveyance back.

He stopped in the centre of the little village to look around. It was entirely unimproved by modernity, with a cluster of low red-brick or Tudor-beamed cottages around a central pond, next to which stood an actual set of stocks. Jem's ankles hurt just looking at them.

Prue lived, he knew, on Toms Hill Road; he would have to find that but felt in need of a sit-down first. There was an antique-looking public house facing the pond, a Georgian building called the Greyhound Inn; he went inside, relishing the enveloping blast of heat from the blazing fire. He ordered a half of ale and perched on a stool, the better to talk to the woman behind the bar, whose air of authority suggested she was the landlady. She gave him directions to Toms Hill Road, which was apparently just round the corner, and added, 'Any particular reason, sir? You're not from these parts, I think?'

'I live in London. I'm looking for Mr and Mrs John Warren.'

'John Warren? Oh, dear, sir. Were you a friend of his?'

'Uh, no. He's dead?'

'I fear so, sir, four years or more. Lockjaw, it was, terrible thing. Poor Mrs Warren, she's had a great deal to bear.'

'This is Mrs Warren who was Miss Prudence Lenster?' Jem said. 'I am extremely sorry to know it. Will I find her at home, do you think?'

'In another half an hour or so, sir. She's the schoolmistress here, did you not know?'

Jem had not. He thanked the landlady, and sipped his ale, thinking of Prue, eyes shining, centre of them all in *Cymbeline*, or shrieking and kicking after being elected treasurer of the Women's Association, as Hugo lifted her onto a plinth in the gardens. A widow teaching in a village school.

He'd wondered once if he could be happy with Prue. She had adored Toby, but in those last days of his life she had been white-faced and desperate, as though she'd finally understood the impossibility of her dream, and, since Jem had been just as desperate in his own way, he'd given serious thought to proposing as a way of escape for them both. *Let's pretend it never happened,* he'd wanted to say. *Let's escape from this damned place where neither of us is wanted, let's make a sane life, a reasonable one, without grand passion.*

It probably wouldn't have worked, but perhaps he should have tried, because ten years on he still hadn't escaped Oxford's terrible pull. He wondered if Prue had.

He set off for Toms Hill Road when the clock struck and the landlady nodded to him. He walked slowly, almost reluctantly, and wasn't sure why. He was quite sure that Prue, of all of them, was not the guilty party.

She might have had the time to kill Toby, and even the desire. She had returned to Anselm Hall via Park Road, and would have had plenty of time to slip through the garden gate to Toby's room. She wasn't the sort of woman that people noticed in a crowd, not like Ella, who several people had seen. She'd loved him, and Jem knew all too well how easily love could curdle into hate. But he simply didn't believe that such a short woman could have driven that knife up through Toby's flesh to pierce his heart. She might have had the moral force; she lacked the physical.

Her cottage was small, and not smart. It didn't betray severe neglect, but Jem's mother had been houseproud, and he knew what a listlessly kept home looked like because he lived in one now. The brass on Prue's doorstep was unpolished, the rosebush left to straggle, the windows dusty.

He knocked and, after a few moments, the door opened.

'Yes?' Prue said.

She'd aged. That was the first thing Jem thought. She'd aged so much that he wasn't sure he would have recognised her. Her hair was greyed and pulled back tight; her faded dress was plain and shapeless to the point of aggression. Jem didn't know about women's fashions, but he knew a don't-look-at-me appearance when he saw one.

This wasn't Prue, the laughing young woman out to conquer Oxford. This wasn't what should have happened.

'Yes?' she said again, and then her face changed. She stared at Jem, eyes narrowing to a squint in a painfully familiar way, and he managed a smile.

'Hello, Prue. It's me.'

'Jem.'

'May I come in?'

CHAPTER 8

Prue's cottage was no better tended inside than out. It wasn't cluttered, but that seemed to be more because it didn't contain much than because of tidiness. There was a chair by the fireplace in the little parlour, and another by the window, its back turned. There was nothing on the mantelpiece. The dresser showed the bare minimum of crockery: two plates, two side plates, two bowls, two cups. There were four framed photographs on a little table, and nothing else.

'What are you doing here?'

'I wanted to talk to you,' Jem said stiffly. The clenched bare misery of Prue's living space was appalling. Was this what people saw when they looked at him? 'Could we sit down? Please?'

'Tea?' she said, as if the word was forced from her by propriety.

'Please.'

She nodded, didn't move for a second longer, still studying his face, then turned and walked out.

Jem went over to the table to look at the photographs. There were four cabinet frames, and each one showed a child. The first image showed Prue, looking solemn as everyone did in posed pictures, with a child of toddling age on her lap. The next three showed a stubby-legged child growing into a lanky grinning urchin. There was no image of the deceased Mr Warren or of a wedding day, just four pictures of a boy. Was Prue an aunt? A mother? This house didn't feel as though it held a child.

Jem contemplated the images a little longer, then sat, feeling rather chilled by the chair's cold wood through his trousers. Prue came in with the tea tray. They went through the ritual of how Jem took it, and finally Prue sat, stiff-backed, and said, 'So. Did you just drop by for a chat?'

'No. I wish I had. I should have, a long time ago. Are you all right?'

Prudence looked around the cold little room, one long sweeping gaze, and back at him.

'No,' Jem said. 'Nor am I. I never sat Finals, I was unwell. They called it a breakdown of the nerves.'

Prue's lips tightened. 'Are you here for sympathy?'

He hadn't thought of sympathy. He *had* thought empathy, that she was the one of them who might understand.

'I'm here because someone sent my superior at work an anonymous letter accusing me of Toby's murder and I lost my position as a result. I've asked around, and Hugo and Aaron had them too. Identical wording. Hugo's was sent to his fiancée and Aaron's to his partners in his practice.'

Prue opened her mouth slightly, as if she were about to speak, then snapped it shut.

'Three of us have had the same letter, aimed to stir up trouble. And I'm cursed if this will be the rest of my life. Going through all the work of finding employment and starting in a new position and waiting for the next person to find out and write *Murderer* across my blotter again. I've had enough.'

'So you want to know who wrote the letters? That's why you're here?'

'I don't care who wrote the letters. Perfectly respectable men and women, I expect, hiding the fact that their minds are a slurry of malice by vomiting it onto strangers. Did you get one?'

'To the school. *Prudence Warren is a murderer. She killed Toby Feynsham. Ask her why.*'

'Prudence Warren,' Jem repeated. 'So the writer found out your married name.'

Prue blinked. 'Well, yes. I suppose they must have. What about the others? Ella?'

'I haven't seen her yet. She's difficult to get hold of.'

'I wouldn't know,' Prue said. 'And, uh—'

'I haven't seen Nicky, no. He's still at Anselm's. Senior lecturer.'

'He must be mad. How could he stay?'

'Why did you leave?'

Prue gave him a long look. 'Why do you think?'

'I don't know. I thought I knew some things, and I chose not to know the rest, and I think all that was wrong. One of us killed Toby.'

'Yes,' Prue said.

'And we all knew, and we didn't say.'

'Yes.'

'And we colluded in an alibi, which—'

'Yes,' she said again. 'I agree with all of that. So?'

'I want to know who it was. I want to know what happened to us.'

Prue's face distorted. It was just a brief second of something uncontainable, her mouth opening into a wide, ugly, agonised shape like a theatre mask of tragedy, and then her features smoothed again.

'I can tell you what happened to me, Jem. The people I had thought my best friends were monsters, and I ran away. I came back here. I married John. I tried to forget everything about Oxford, every lie it told me about who I was and what I might be and who my friends were. I was *happy* here.'

'Is that your son in the pictures?' Jem asked.

Prue's mouth tightened. Jem could see the pulse beating in her throat. 'He was.'

'Oh. What—what was his name?'

'Joseph. Joe.'

'When—'

'Last November. He was climbing a tree and fell. He loved to climb trees.'

'I'm so sorry,' Jem said. 'Oh, Prue. I am so sorry.'

'He was the one good thing—' Prue stopped short. Jem could see the sheen in her eyes. 'He was my boy. All mine. He was marvellous in his lessons, and so good at sport, and he wasn't even nine yet, but he said he'd soon be taller than me and he'd be able to help more then. He was looking forward to that. And then he climbed the willow over the brook, and he must have lost his grip. He hit his head on a rock and drowned before anyone was there to help. Nobody's ever there to help.'

'Prue…' Jem reached for her hand. She jerked it away.

'It's true.' There were tears trickling down her face that she made no effort to stem or conceal. 'We thought we had such wonderful friends, didn't we, you and I? Didn't we believe they cared? Didn't we believe we were more than pets to the rest of them, with our funny little voices—'

'That's not true.'

'After what Nicky did to you? Did you really think he cared for you, or for anyone except Toby? Do you think Ella cared for anyone at all? Even Aaron—he lied for her, and she still wouldn't marry him, not in the end. She never—she didn't—We were all lied to, Jem. It was one great foul game they played, telling us there might be something different. I wish I'd never left Aldbury. I came back here, and John married me. He was decent and kind. I loved him. He loved Joe. We were happy for a little while, and then—I could have had more if I'd never tried to leave. I could have had more children, more time with John, *better* time. Oxford took it all away. I hate it. I hate them all.'

Jem sat poised on the edge of his seat, muscles tight. Prue sat, equally tense, for a second, and then flopped back as though her strings had been cut, and hunted for a handkerchief. She wiped her eyes. Jem didn't dare move.

'Well, that's what I think,' she said at last. 'I lost my wonderful, interesting future and my so-called friends and my husband and my child. I don't have anything left. I dare say I'll keep going to school and coming home to this for another thirty years. That's something to look forward to, isn't it?'

'You could move, perhaps?' Jem ventured to suggest. 'If you're not—'

Her eyes blazed. 'Don't give me that *now you're free* rubbish. Don't you *dare*. Joe wasn't an encumbrance to me, he was my son!'

Jem couldn't imagine who had said such a thing to a grieving mother, even if it held a kernel of truth. Doubtless an Oxford-educated widow without a child could find a better post than that of village schoolmistress, but if anyone in this village had been so damned crass as to say so—well, frankly, it supported the argument that she should indeed move away, which he wasn't going to offer twice.

'I'm sorry you've had so much to bear,' he said. 'I've never married, and I can't imagine losing a child. I, uh…'

'You want to talk about who killed Toby,' Prue said. 'You came here for that, not me. You might as well get on with it.'

Jem cringed internally, but she was right: he was here for that, and to leave now would be a waste of money he couldn't afford. 'I'd like to know what you meant about Ella and Aaron,' he said. 'You think he lied for her sake? Not the other way around?'

'I think he lied for her. I think he'd have done anything for her, and she'd have taken it as her due.'

'Hugo thought she lied because that racialist police investigator was determined to blame Aaron.'

Prue's mouth tightened. 'How generous of him. How kind, absolving them both from blame. How very like Hugo.'

Jem felt slightly sick. He hadn't wanted to believe that he was the only one of the Seven Wonders to be destroyed by Toby's death; he'd taken a kind of unpleasant satisfaction in seeing that the others bore wounds, but Prue's bitterness was unspeakable.

'What do you think, then?' he asked. 'Why do you think they lied?'

'I expect Aaron thought Ella did it because Toby was going to prevent their marriage,' Prue said calmly. 'She adored Aaron. I didn't know she was capable of it. I don't suppose she did kill Toby, but I promise you, she will have wanted to.'

'But how could Toby have stopped them?' Jem asked. 'She wouldn't have to break off with Aaron just because her brother disapproved.'

She shrugged one shoulder. 'You saw Toby that night. He meant Aaron nothing but ill. And Ella didn't care about anyone else then. Not Toby any more, and certainly not me.'

The hurt was audible in her voice. Jem shifted uncomfortably. 'But I can't believe she killed him, even so. She was his *twin*.'

'Nor do I, really,' Prue said. 'But not because she was incapable of it. Just because it's obvious who did.'

'Who—'

'Oh, come on, Jem,' she said testily. 'Who's tall, good with a blade, and hated Toby as much as he loved him?'

Jem's throat dried. Prue gave him a look composed of what felt like pity and contempt. 'Nicky was monstrous that night. He used you like a, a *thing* and threw you aside because for those people, the Nickys and Hugos and Tobys and Ellas, there are the people who matter and the people who don't, and you and I never mattered, not really. Well, that night, Nicky understood he didn't matter to Toby either. It was about time he noticed.'

'You think it was Nicky?'

'Yes,' Prue said. 'I think it was Nicky, because he loved Toby, and Toby was hateful to him.'

Jem could taste bile in his throat. He swallowed and took a gulp of the now-cold tea, controlling his stomach. 'I…don't want to believe that.'

'Don't you?' Prue asked. 'Really, after everything? Oh, come, Jem, you used not to be a fool. If you don't think it was Aaron or Ella, and I suppose it wasn't me or you, then it was Nicky or Hugo, and Hugo was the only one of the seven of us who *didn't* want to commit murder that night. Or maybe he did. He was denied, after all, and Hugo never heard *no*, did he? He didn't know what the word meant. I can't see why he'd have killed Toby for it, but, looking back, I don't understand anything of those times at all. It was gilt slapped on lies, and I'm glad it's over.'

'That's not true,' Jem said. He wasn't sure where this fierce defence had come from; he ought to be agreeing, since it was how he'd felt for years, but hearing it aloud made him need to deny this awful picture. 'I remember all of you on the banks, screaming like fools as I brought the boat home. I remember how we celebrated when Hugo and Nicky got their Blues. When you became Treasurer and Hugo put you on that pedestal—' Prue's face convulsed, and she flung a hand up as if warding off a blow. 'Prue?'

'Don't,' she said. 'Don't ask me to remember all the golden times and how wonderful it was. It's such a lovely lie, and it makes everything worse now. Stop dreaming about the spires. It was a dreadful place and those were dreadful people, and you and I got caught in their games and paid for it. And you may not want to remember how much we hurt each other, but Toby is rotting in the ground to prove it. I think you should go. I don't have anything else to say. Leave me alone.'

Jem was shaking as he set off back along the road to Tring station. He ought, he knew, to find a ride, but he couldn't bear to sit and wait. He needed to move. He needed to think.

I think it was Nicky, because he loved Toby.

It was vile. Prue was vile for having those thoughts, and Jem was vile for listening.

He knew the narrative of the rejected, hysterical queer too well. One heard the stories, hinted at in newspaper reports full of euphemisms or discussed in undertones—or worse, with brash, vulgar laughter, in the pub with no women present—and it always sickened him. As though the fact that Nicky looked at Toby rather than Ella made him a slave to his emotions.

That sort are, people would say, and it made Jem's stomach twist horribly. *That sort.* Nicky's sort.

Not Jem's sort. He wasn't flamboyant, or louche, or emotional; he didn't drawl or make a fuss. Not under usual circumstances, he thought, refusing to consider that awful time after the murder, at home, curled on his bed, crying and raging. But that had been an illness. Nervous exhaustion. The doctor had said so. He wasn't like that.

And yet.

CHAPTER 9

Hilary Term, 1895

Jem had always watched Nicky. He wasn't even sure why. Nicky wasn't conventionally handsome, and his bony features could be almost ugly in the wrong light, or when animated with the wrong thoughts. He didn't have Toby's exuberant joy, or Hugo's charm, or Aaron's comforting strength. And yet, as the weeks and months passed, it was Nicky that Jem watched. Nicky's long-toed bare feet as he fenced. The way he lounged, the way he kept up the constant facade of world-weary decadence, the tiny twitches that betrayed his real thoughts, the rare, sweet smile. Jem knew all those because he watched Nicky all the time. Toby knew them as well because he was Nicky's best friend.

It stabbed Jem sometimes, at little odd moments. Toby knew how Nicky felt and never pushed him away. He couldn't give Nicky more than friendship, but he gave him that and kept him always at his side, and surely that was enough. To be valued for who one was, and not to be rejected because one wanted too much: that was kindness and caring. Toby couldn't help it if he didn't want Nicky, just as Nicky did no injury to Jem because he had eyes only for Toby.

Jem told himself that repeatedly. It still hurt. It would, he thought, hurt less if only Toby returned Nicky's affection. If only Nicky was happy.

He wasn't happy. He drank too much, and he was still drinking too much in Hilary term of their third year, on the day everything changed.

Finals were starting to loom. Jem was well ahead with his studies; Toby was not. He didn't need to be, of course, with his gold and velvet future as a marquess, but he had reluctantly conceded he ought to do some work, so Jem was slightly surprised to see a mop of red-gold hair at the other side of the buttery as he came in for his own well-earned break. He made his way over to where Nicky and Toby sat, and his cheery greeting died on his lips as he saw Toby's face. It was red, in an oddly patchy way—blotchy, as though he'd been crying, and set in a grimace that distorted his features. Nicky, by his side, looked drawn.

'Toby? Are you all right?'

Toby looked up at him, and there was something so unfamiliar and savage in his gaze that Jem recoiled.

'Toby?'

'Just—fuck—off.' Toby enunciated the words with extreme precision. 'Just fuck off and leave me alone. Just fucking—' His voice rose as he spoke.

'Shut up, Tobes. It's not you, Jem,' Nicky said. 'Not at all, but best to…' He made a brushing gesture. 'And if you see any of the others, head them off for me? Until we're thrown out. *Go.*'

'Yuh, do that,' Toby said, and Jem realised quite how drunk he was. 'Sod off. Run away. Hop away—'

'Shut *up*,' Nicky told him. 'Leave him to it, Jem, for God's sake, he's unfit for human company.'

Jem went, turning on his heel and walking out, as though they had the right to ban him from his own college buttery, and didn't realise that he was shaking until he got out into the quad.

Neither Nicky nor Toby was present at Hall that evening. Jem sat with a couple of mathematician friends, hurt and bewildered, and retired to his digs in Broad Street afterwards, huddling with a book until there was a knock on the door and his landlady informed him he had a visitor.

Nicky was waiting outside, looking dishevelled, unhappy, and ashamed.

'Nicky?'

'Can I come in?'

Jem stepped back. Nicky came in, sat in the one armchair, slid straight out of it, and curled up into himself on the floor. 'Jesus Christ. Oh Jesus, Jem.'

'What on earth is it?' Jem demanded, seriously alarmed. He lowered himself to a knee by Nicky. 'What's *happened*? Is Toby all right? Did something happen to Ella?'

'God, no. No. It's Toby's uncle. He's had a son.'

That seemed so astonishingly trivial that Jem spent a couple of seconds examining the words for double meaning, as if it might be a piece of unfamiliar slang, and then realised. 'You mean, his uncle the heir?'

Nicky uncurled enough to thump the back of his head against the seat of the chair. 'The marquess's heir, who now has a fine fat healthy legitimate son.'

'But he's not married.'

'Oh yes he is. It appears that some five months ago, the barmaid he was tupping informed him his labours had borne fruit and the degenerate old fool made a private marriage. Now his child is here, and the misbegotten brat is a boy. Eight pounds in weight, five months after the wedding, and who knows if it is even Crenshaw's, but the wretched thing was born in wedlock, so there is no more to be said. The barmaid—I beg your pardon, Lady Crenshaw—is apparently wonderfully well, and, since she is not much older than you and me, it seems plausible that she will go on doing her wifely duty as long as Crenshaw can raise his flagpole. Toby's out of the succession.'

'Oh, good Lord,' Jem said. 'Oh goodness, I am sorry. That must be the most awful shock for him.'

'You understate it considerably. He's devastated.'

'He was certainly drunk.'

'Don't mind what he said.' Nicky's posture was unusually youthful, sitting on the floor with arms wrapped around his knees, but his face was weary, the bones of his skull accentuated by the shadows of the gaslight. 'He tends to take things out on the people he loves; he wouldn't have spoken like that to any passing college man. And it was worse for him that you saw him at such a low ebb. He didn't want you to see him like that. I'm sorry.'

'It's not your fault,' Jem said, biting back the observation that, if Toby had not wanted to be seen, he should not have been in a public place. 'What happens now? With his inheritance, I mean?'

'He has no inheritance. Only what remains of the little his father left, plus an allowance from his grandfather, which Crenshaw is unlikely to continue once he succeeds. The property is entailed. He'll get a pittance at most. It's all gone.'

There was so much pain in his voice. Jem ached for him aching for Toby, even while he tried to push down a rebellious thought that this mourning for lost expectations far exceeded any sympathy Nicky or Toby tended to show for people who'd never had anything to begin with. Nicky didn't need an argument now. He looked wretched beyond belief.

Jem lowered himself all the way to the floor, so they sat shoulder to shoulder. 'Is it just that?'

'Isn't that enough?'

'Well, you look awfully upset. Is that all about Toby's problems?' Something belatedly occurred to him. 'Was he unkind to you?'

A half shrug was all the answer. Jem glared at the floor. 'That's not right, Nicky. I'm sorry he's disappointed—'

'He's more than disappointed, he's ruined.'

'Nonsense,' Jem snapped. 'He's got more than most of us start with. He's got a perfectly good brain when he chooses to use it, and he will have a degree from Oxford—'

'Will he? You must have noticed he hasn't precisely been applying himself,' Nicky said. 'And yes, even if he crawls out with a poor Third, he has the family connections to find a place, but for Christ's sake, he never expected to have to drudge for a living. He thought he was going to be a *marquess* and he's had it snatched away.'

'We all have hopes,' Jem said. 'I understand this is a bitter disappointment, but it isn't a tragedy.'

'He's got debts.'

'What?'

'Debts. He lives well, he's been living on the expectation. Oh, come, Jem, you know how generous he is. How much of his champagne have you drunk? How often has he taken us out, that trip to Boar's Hill? Didn't he settle your buttery bill in the second year?'

'I never asked him to.'

'You didn't have to. But those debts are in his name, and quite a few more. He likes to play, you know. Horses.'

Jem did know that. Toby and Hugo had gone to Ascot together, returning flushed and laughing about their misfortunes on the turf. 'Does he owe a lot?'

Nicky propped his elbow on a knee in order to support his head with one long-fingered hand. 'Enough that this won't be a pleasant conversation with his grandfather. The old man's already in a towering rage about his new heir. Toby will have to resign from the Bullingdon.'

Jem wasn't listening. Nicky's cuff had fallen back a little with the movement of his arm, and Jem could see marks on his wrist, red and darkening. Nicky's pale skin bruised so easily, as Jem knew from watching him fence, and from the occasional scuffles he had with Toby or Hugo. 'Did Toby do that?'

'It's nothing.' Nicky shifted to pull up his cuff.

Jem grabbed his arm. 'It's not nothing. Those are finger marks. I don't care how disappointed he is, he isn't entitled to maul you!'

'I was trying to haul him out of the buttery. Don't make a fuss.'

'You don't have to defend everything he does.'

'Do you have *any idea* what a disappointment this is for him?' Nicky demanded. 'He's just had his entire life pulled out from underneath him!'

'No, I don't know,' Jem said. 'Nobody ever offered me untold wealth, so I don't know how it feels to have it snatched away. But you said that the inheritance wasn't a sure thing. He relied on it coming off and it hasn't. That's not your fault.'

'He didn't want to—'

'He didn't want to face facts,' Jem said savagely, unsure where his anger had come from, but filled with its bright flame. 'His uncle's got every right to marry, and I'm very sorry, but if you depend on a system of primogeniture and inheritance, you have to accept it when it doesn't work for you, as well as when it does. It's not fair for him to take this out on you.' He was gripping Nicky's arm too hard, he realised, but he didn't want to let go altogether because he could feel Nicky's misery dripping through his defences.

He released his grip and shifted his hand up, skimming Nicky's bruised wrist, clasping his hand. Nicky was very still for a second, then his other hand came up, covering Jem's.

'You deserve better than this,' Jem said, softly, urgently. 'It's not right. I know he's your friend, I know you care for him, Nicky, but I wish—'

'You wish what?' Nicky's voice was tight, and his hands were tight too, holding on. Jem could feel the gentle pulse of blood. He wasn't quite sure what he should say, what he was permitted to say out loud.

'I wish he cared more for you,' he said, speaking as plainly as he dared. 'And if he can't, then…I wish you cared for someone who would.'

'So do I,' Nicky said. 'Oh, so do I, dear Jem, but I fear I don't quite see how that's to be achieved.'

'Nicky.' Jem shifted awkwardly, to face him, wanting to say something to stem the unhappiness with which Nicky had trusted him. If he'd had the power to compel Toby's love on the spot, he would have; he almost hated the man at this moment for his inability to understand. He brought his other hand up so all four hands were together. He was holding Nicky's tightly. 'Nicky…' he began again, and realised he had no idea what to say now. 'Can I help? Can I do anything? If there's anything at all…'

'My dear little innocent,' Nicky said through his teeth. 'I shouldn't offer that if I were you.'

It was the kind of remark he sometimes made when people got too close: a warning off. Jem usually scuttled like a startled rabbit. He wasn't going to this time; he would not look away. Nicky's eyes were very brown in the low light, and he wasn't looking away either. Jem didn't know what he was doing, or what was happening. His chest felt tight; the air was full of *something*, as though it was thicker and the light somehow more saturated with colour, and he wasn't going to pull away or run away or any of those things.

'Jesus,' Nicky said, so low it was almost a whisper, almost a plea. 'Jem…'

Jem opened his mouth without knowing what he was going to say, and left it open because Nicky's gaze had gone to his lips, and he didn't know what to do, but he tugged again. Pulled Nicky forward, closer, just a little, and that was enough. Nicky leaned over, slowly, eyes back on Jem's, leaned in without releasing his hands, and kissed him.

Jem had never been kissed in his life. At home, he'd been too unimpressive before Oxford; now he was too much of a known face in a small town to play the fool with girls even if any had wished to play the fool with him. He'd never dared to look at another boy; it had never been imaginable until Nicky, bright and slim and supple like a foil, had come to fill his furtive thoughts. And now Nicky was kissing him. His mouth, tasting of beer, his lips oddly soft, his skin barely bristled. Jem had no idea what to do, how one managed lips moving against lips, and even as he registered that Nicky's mouth was more open than his, Nicky pulled away.

'Jesus,' he said again. 'You really are innocent, aren't you?'

'I won't be if you show me,' Jem said, with a boldness that deserted him a fraction after the words came out. He wanted to take them back immediately, with a wild moment of terror for whatever the devil he might have just asked for. He didn't.

Nicky contemplated him for a couple of seconds, or months, and then said, 'Do as I do. Open your mouth.'

That sounded absurd. Jem opened his mouth—to argue, to query—and Nicky's lips met his again, and he was right. It was different.

Nicky was kissing him, and Jem kissed him back, fumbling, nervous, wanting so much, daring to move his own tongue because surely that was right. Nicky disengaged his hands and Jem felt them on his face, on his hair. Nicky's touch on his skin, cupping his jaw. Nicky.

It was the stuff that Jem's dreams were made on, and he couldn't do anything but follow. Nicky unbuttoned his shirt and Jem let him; Nicky kissed and stroked, and Jem did the same to Nicky's bare, smooth chest with fingers that shook, but swiftly grew in confidence. Lying face to face on the rug, kissing and touching, and then Nicky's hand roamed below Jem's waistband, and he couldn't help the hiss of shock. Shock and shame, too, because he was aroused to the point of fearing he might disgrace himself, and he hadn't even dared to consider if that was acceptable.

Nicky pulled back slightly, one brow raised. 'Tell me, dear boy, how much innocence are you hoping to lose tonight?'

'I don't know,' Jem said, or whispered, because his voice wasn't quite working. 'Uh, what should I do?'

'You should do precisely what you want. It would help if you knew what that was, of course, but I dare say we'll muddle through. Suppose you tell me what you like, and mention anything you don't, as we go.'

'All right.' Which wasn't much of a way to convey what he felt, the sheer terror and gratitude and impossible joy of it as Nicky's long fingers brushed downwards, and Jem felt the top button at his waist give way.

Much later he came to understand how gentle Nicky had been with him that night, what he might have done with Jem's hopeless inexperience and willingness to please. He encouraged Jem to explore with fumbling touches and gave instructions in a way that made Jem laugh rather than wince, and let him sprawl over his long, pale body afterwards, feeling his warm chest rise and fall. Naked together, or mostly naked. Jem hadn't been able to take off his stocking. He hadn't wanted Nicky to see his foot.

They lay together in silence, Jem not knowing at all what to do but happy to let Nicky dictate, until the clocks of Broad Street struck their various tens, and Nicky shifted to sit up. 'Curse it. I must go. Morning tutorials demand overnight essays.'

Of course he couldn't stay, not with the landlady downstairs. 'Oh, well, good luck,' Jem said, trying to match his casual tone, but watching as Nicky dressed. He wanted to ask, *What happens next?* and didn't dare, in case the answer was, *Nothing*.

Nicky pulled on his coat, hesitated at the door, then turned, a slight smile on his lips, at the door. 'Thank you for your innocence, Jemmy,' he said softly. 'I shall treasure it.'

He came back to Jem's room four more times, between the last day of February and the murder, and dealt with the remnants of Jem's innocence very thoroughly indeed. He'd taught him words and tutored him in acts, and though he couldn't offer more than pleasures of the body, well, at least he'd offered those in full measure. Jem had never believed he could supplant Toby in Nicky's affections, so he didn't let himself think thoughts to which he wasn't entitled.

He'd let Nicky use him, that last time. Or he'd begged Nicky to fuck him, or he'd longed for Nicky to make love to him. He still didn't know which was true; perhaps all of them. Afterwards, he'd wept in Nicky's cradling arms for no reason he could voice, and felt his tears kissed away without shame.

He hadn't known it would be the last time then, of course; it was just their fifth time, a Sunday night that was not yet the Sunday before Toby's murder, and Nicky hadn't come to him for a week. Of course he'd been busy with work, as they all had. Jem had tried not to think more of it, but he hadn't been able to hold back his rush of pleasure and excitement when Nicky had knocked on his door. They had kissed hard and wordlessly, almost desperately, as though Nicky had been as hungry and lonely as Jem, and they'd… fucked, made love, whatever it was, and Nicky had kissed him again when he cried.

Three days later, Nicky had betrayed him utterly and cruelly, and the worst part was that Jem still cherished the memory of those Judas kisses, like deadly nightshade flowers pressed between the pages of a book.

CHAPTER 10

When Jem returned to London, there was still no reply from Ella. He sat in his rooms, knowing what the next step had to be, and dreading it.

He'd calculated that he had enough put by for two months, if he lived frugally. That meant, really, a month before he ought to start searching for a new position. It didn't allow for a great many railway fares, but he'd have to pay for one to Oxford, because he had to go back to Anselm's.

The thought made him feel sick. He curled up in his chair, trying unsuccessfully to persuade himself it wouldn't be so bad. Would the same porters still work in the lodge? Would they recognise him and stare? They'd all remember, everyone there would, down to the newest students. Doubtless Toby's room would have been repainted, the floorboards sanded or carpeted to hide the stain of his blood, but they'd all know that was the murder room.

And Nicky had stayed. He'd been arrested; he'd emerged dry-eyed and hard-faced, gained one of the top Firsts in the university, and now he was a senior lecturer at Anselm's. Why would he stay in a place where every flagstone, every room, every building would remind him of the man he'd loved?

Maybe that *was* why. Maybe Nicky had loved Toby so deeply that walling himself up alive with Toby's memory had been the only way.

Maybe something else.

I think it was Nicky, because he loved Toby, and Toby was hateful to him.

Trinity Term, 1895

Jem didn't see as much of his friends as usual in Trinity term of their last year. All of the undergraduates were working hard, or at least claimed they were, although as far as Jem could tell Toby was always at one or another of his societies, the life of the party, showing the Bullingdon Club what it had lost. Jem didn't mind exactly. He missed the carefree days, but he had a First to secure, and studies he enjoyed, and he was looking forward to the examinations in a perverse way. It would be the end of a wonderful chapter in his life, but he had quietly, steadily built up his ambitions for what he would do next.

He was, nevertheless, glad when he had a note from Toby inviting him to a private room at the Mitre Hotel on Wednesday of Fourth Week. Undergraduates were not permitted to go to public houses, hence all the drinking clubs, and Toby had frequently taken a room when he wanted a gathering of the seven of them.

Jem walked up Turl Street, a narrow path between high stone walls, wondering who would be there. He hadn't seen Nicky since that Sunday night, and the thought of meeting him now in public clenched Jem's heart and tightened his gut. He wasn't sure what it was: fear, shame, excitement; something more, something worse. He was terrified that Nicky might behave as though nothing had happened between them; he was terrified that he might behave as though something had. How did one face a man who'd taken one's—one's *virginity* without betraying the fact? How did women do it? What would Nicky want to do now?

Elegant, upper-class Nicky might be able to wear his heart on his sleeve, even though he pretended it was a posture; Jem could not. He had to be just as usual, but his blood was pounding in his ears as he pushed open the door of the small private room in the Mitre to see the others. He was, it seemed, the last to arrive.

Toby was there, frowning, red in the face, as though he'd had several drinks already. Hugo was by him, with the slightly studied smile he wore when he was taking charge of a situation. Jem's heart sank a little. Prue was at the other end of the long table, looking down at her hands. She didn't greet Jem, though he hadn't seen her in weeks; Nicky did, with a casual, uninterested nod that Jem would have liked to believe was aimed at throwing the others off the scent, but feared meant no more than it seemed.

Ella and Aaron sat together, side by side, and the second Jem looked at them, he realised something. He couldn't have said what, only that it was something he wouldn't have seen or recognised before Nicky had taken his innocence, and, even as he realised that, Aaron smiled at him in greeting with an odd combination of happiness and uncertainty, and Jem knew.

The last free chair was on the corner, next to Nicky. Jem tugged it a little further away as he pulled it out from the table, and caught a flicker in Nicky's eyes.

'Well, we're all here,' Toby said, like a jovial host. 'And how are *you*, Jem?'

'Oh, you know. Drifting around, doing nothing, living the life of leisure.'

Hugo and Toby both laughed at that, too loudly. Nicky didn't. Jem could feel the tension coming from him without looking. Was Nicky afraid Jem would expose him? Did he fear Toby discovering his infidelity? Jem had not let himself think of it in those terms—surely where love was unrequited, there could be no betrayal in turning elsewhere—but he had a sudden sinking feeling that neither Nicky nor Toby might agree.

'Well,' Toby said. 'Aside from those terribly tedious examinations, how are we all?'

Jem felt his lips curve in anticipation of whatever clever observation someone was about to make. Nobody did.

'Uh, well…well,' Hugo said at last. 'I dare say we're all submerged by study.'

Jem nodded, wanting to add something that would get the conversation flowing as it should, but couldn't think of a thing to say. Prue was silent at the end of the table, Nicky sat unspeaking, and Jem had a growing sense that something was terribly wrong. These were the best friends he'd ever had, and they felt like strangers.

'Oh, come on, Nicky,' Toby said. 'Surely you must have a story to share with the rest of us? Haven't you done anything dreadfully amusing recently?'

'The only amusing experience I have had involved a particularly off-colour double entendre in one of Shakespeare's sonnets. And since grasping the humour would require a basic understanding of not only Shakespeare but the English language, an explanation could take *months*.'

It was the kind of thing he always said, and Toby always laughed, but his jaw was set now. 'I'm sorry we're not bright enough for you, Nicky. I dare say it's marvellous to be so very much cleverer than everyone else.'

'Oh, come,' Hugo said. 'It was a joke.'

'Of sorts,' Nicky said. 'If the dunce's cap fits…'

'*Nicky*,' Jem hissed.

'Why not? Why shouldn't he call me a dunce? It's precisely what he thinks,' Toby said. 'You all think it, and I'm a little tired of being taken for a fool.'

'Nobody's doing that, old chap.' Hugo looked exquisitely uncomfortable.

'Are they not,' Toby said. 'Drinking on my shilling while you make a mockery of me and betray everything I thought we had? Sneaking behind my back, rutting like animals—God damn you!' His hand hit the table with force, making the glasses rattle. 'I thought you were my friends!'

There was a chorus of voices. 'Now, wait,' from Hugo and a distressed, 'Don't—' from Prue, her first utterance, and 'God's sake!' from Nicky. Aaron's face was set in an expression of such preternatural calm that he looked like a statue. It was the face he wore on the track, as though he couldn't hear what the rival supporters were shouting at him. Jem couldn't breathe, let alone speak, his chest tight with terror and anticipated shame. *He doesn't know*, he told himself. *He can't know. Nicky wouldn't have said anything.*

Ella shut her eyes for a long moment, and then opened them again. 'This isn't a wise way to go on, Toby. If you've something to say, it would be better done privately.'

'How could this be more private?' Toby demanded, voice rising. 'Just us, all friends together, aren't we? Such *very* close friends.'

'Yes,' Nicky said. 'We are all friends, and I suggest you and I take some fresh air in order to keep it that way.'

'Why?' Toby demanded. 'Because I'm at fault? Because I'm drunk? *I'm* not the one who let us all down, like some slobbering sot—'

'Toby!' Jem protested. 'Stop it. Please. You don't mean this, and I'm sure you'll regret it in the morning. Look, why don't we call it a day? It's awfully close to Finals to be drinking.'

'An excellent idea, Jeremy,' Nicky said. 'Let us disperse.'

'God, listen to you,' Toby said. 'Mr and Mrs Rook, cawing in harmony before they fly back to the nest. All that hopeless pining paid off in the end, eh, Jem?'

Jem's throat clamped shut, so hard he couldn't breathe. He heard a couple of inhalations, but he didn't look round. He didn't want to look at his friends for fear of what he might see on their faces and what they might see in his. He knew he was scarlet; he felt dizzy and slightly cold.

'Toby,' Hugo said carefully. 'That, uh—'

'Oh, come on,' Toby snarled. 'Nicky's taken little Jemmy to bed; has that surprised anyone except Jem? I hope you didn't violate his provincial virtue too painfully.'

'Fuck you,' Nicky said, the words clipped and shocking. Prue gasped aloud, and Hugo began a furious protest to which nobody attended.

'Thanks awfully, I'd rather not,' Toby said over him, tone vicious. 'Which is why you had to turn to Tiny Tim here. I wish you'd done it earlier and spared me the endless histrionics. Congratulations, Jem, you finally got his attention. You won't keep it long, of course, whatever promises he may have made. Which is lucky for you. He's not precisely discreet, and you two wouldn't want to be caught, I suppose.'

There was a second's endless, awful silence, then Nicky spoke, with appalling calm. 'The histrionics here seem rather one-sided to me. You are making quite the mountain out of a *very* insignificant molehill, Tobes.'

Jem couldn't help the tiny gasp that escaped his painfully tense throat. Nicky went on steadily. 'You entirely overestimate how much importance I might place on really quite trivial pastimes. No offence, Jem,' he added. Jem thought he might have looked round; he couldn't see, with his gaze locked on the table and tears swimming in his eyes that he refused—absolutely refused—to let fall. 'I am, I think, permitted a *little* self-indulgence, with examinations on the way. We all need a diversion occasionally.'

This was the precise, surgical horror of a nightmare. Jem wanted to leap up and flee from the shame and exposure and agony of loss, but he couldn't do that, and he couldn't bear to heave himself up and hobble out, with his face red and wet, with the people who had been his friends staring at him. He didn't know if it would be worse if they offered comfort or if they didn't.

'You are a damned cold-blooded swine, Rook,' Hugo said savagely. 'A disgrace. How you presume to call yourself a gentleman—My God.'

Prue made an inarticulate noise. Nicky began a response and Aaron said, '*Enough,*' his deep voice thundering out over them all. 'Stop this at once. Apologise, Nicky. Now.'

'You pack of hypocrites,' Toby said. 'Why shouldn't Nicky dip his wick as he pleases when everyone else does? I simply think people should know their place in these matters and understand their positions. Don't you?'

He sounded like that was addressed to someone; Jem couldn't look up. Prue shoved her chair back from the table. 'You're *horrible.* Foul. You're all hateful and cruel, using people like toys, you're all—all—'

'On the contrary,' Toby said over her. 'Some of us have decency. Some of us consider what our actions might do to others. Some of us don't want to disgrace our names, our families—Are you not going to say anything, you bitch?' he roared, making Jem jump. '*Nothing?*'

'I'd rather talk in private.' That was Ella's voice, very calm.

'Well, I don't want to talk in private!' Toby shouted. 'Are you going to do it all in private? Marry in private? Breed a nursery of half-caste brats in private?'

'Go to the devil,' Ella said, voice no longer composed. 'Damn you, Toby. How dare you?'

'How dare *I*? With you sneaking and whoring behind my back?'

'You may not speak to her like that,' Aaron said at some volume. 'Mind your tongue.'

'I'll speak to my sister how I choose!' Toby shouted. 'She's *mine*!'

'I am not,' Ella said. 'I am not yours to withhold or bestow. I never have been. Aaron and I will be getting married, and you have no say in that at all.'

'A Feynsham,' Toby said through his teeth. 'A Feynsham, of our blood, our family, degrading herself—'

'Watch—your—mouth,' Aaron said, and his tone was far from his normal measured speech. He took a deep breath, stretching his clenched fingers out. 'Let us calm down. We intended to speak to you, Toby—'

'Liar. You didn't even tell me! I had to find out from Prue!'

Prue gasped. Ella shot her a truly vicious look. 'We were waiting for a time when you might be able to think of someone other than yourself. We hoped you might care what made your friend and your sister happy.'

'Friend?' Toby said savagely. 'Is that what I'm supposed to call a man who seduces my sister? Did you seriously imagine I'd give my blessing to anything so grotesque? For God's sake, you're a Feynsham, not some East End barmaid spreading her legs—'

Aaron lunged. Ella and Hugo both grabbed him; a chair tumbled backwards as Toby sprang to his feet. Nicky caught it. 'For God's sake, Toby. Stop.'

'I will not permit this,' Toby panted. 'I won't have my sister deflowered by some bloody savage, still less married to one.'

'Ah, British friendship,' Aaron snarled. 'Tolerance as long as everyone knows his place; but God forbid your subjects should declare themselves your equals.'

'You can't seriously think yourself my equal,' Toby said.

'No.' Ella's voice was coldly vicious. 'He's a scholar, a Blue, and a gentleman, whereas you'll be lucky to get a Third after three years of drink and self-pity, you greedy whining child. We're going.'

'I will stop this,' Toby said, teeth set. 'I will not allow it. You'll ruin everything. Isn't it bad enough Uncle Crenshaw marrying that whore? I will not have you make our family an object of contempt and ridicule as well. I *will* not have it.'

'You have no say in the matter. None.'

'That's what you think!' Toby shouted. 'I can deal with him for good, and I will!'

Ella inhaled sharply. 'Stop it,' Hugo said before she could speak. '*Stop*. Wait. Ella…'

'What?' she snapped.

He straightened up, handsome face serious. 'As your friend, I must tell you, this isn't the way. I mean no insult to Aaron, and God knows if things were otherwise I should wish you well, but they are not otherwise. An Englishwoman of your family—it simply isn't done. You'd be a pariah. Consider your children, the hardship they'd face. Please, Ella, think.'

'You know, Hugo, I really do fail to see how this is your business,' Nicky remarked.

Hugo shot him a look of intense dislike. 'Because, unlike some, I care for my friends. I cannot stand by and observe this—Ella, marry me.'

Prue gave a shrill gasp. Ella said, '*What?*'

'Forget this,' Hugo said. 'We'll all keep it quiet. I can give you what you want, support your studies, without making you the object of ridicule or contempt. My name—'

'You're proposing to my fiancée,' Aaron said, anger roiling underneath the incredulity. 'You are proposing to my fiancée in front of my *face*?'

'She's not your fiancée,' Toby said.

Ella shook her head. 'I'm leaving. *We're* leaving, and every one of you may go to the devil.' She turned on her heel, ignoring Toby's angry shout. Prue stared after her as she and Aaron left, mouth open as though she might weep, then stood and stumbled after them without a word.

'Jesus,' Nicky said into the silence.

Toby slammed his hands on the table. Hugo said, 'Well, I tried, Toby. I can't help it if she won't come to her senses.' His eyes darted over Jem, with Nicky next to him; he shook his head slightly and went without another word.

Jem pushed the chair back. He levered himself upright, and put on his coat, fumbling at the sleeves as he walked out of the room. He didn't speak to Nicky and Toby as they sat in silence; he didn't look at their faces. He simply left, with just one aim in mind: that he would not let either of them see him cry.

CHAPTER 11

That dreadful night cemented that he'd been a fool. Toby meant more to Nicky than all Jem's hopeless pining ever could. Toby would always be the sun to Nicky's star, and Jem a mere earthbound clod. He'd known it from the beginning; that night branded the message on his soul.

It had felt like the end of everything, and then the next day Toby was dead, and everything did, in fact, end.

Jem stared at the blank wall, trying to breathe through the remembered tightness in his chest, to make himself think about it.

That was the problem. The night in the Mitre had been so excruciating his mind still flinched from the memory. None of the others had discussed it later. And none of them had told the police about it either.

Jem hadn't precisely set out to conceal information. Probably he'd have made himself answer if they'd asked him directly. But he couldn't have offered the information, not at gunpoint. *Toby told everyone that Nicholas Rook and I…*

He'd prayed that his friends wouldn't betray him, wouldn't turn Toby's death into some sordid illegal love triangle, and, in that hope, he hadn't offered the police any other details of what had been said. *We were all drunk. Pointless bickering. Toby was upset about his inheritance.* They had all kept quiet, and he hadn't realised until far too late that their mutual silence had allowed Toby's killer to walk free.

'Think it through,' he told himself aloud.

Toby had known that he and Nicky were—not lovers, but something of that shape. Had he simply guessed? Or had Nicky let something slip, or even deliberately told Toby to provoke a reaction? If so, he'd succeeded: it was painfully clear that Toby had been jealous.

He'd exposed Nicky's goings-on. That might be a motive for murder for some men on its own, and he'd spoken vilely to Nicky, but Nicky had cared only to regain Toby's good opinion at Jem's expense. It hadn't been a motive for murder. It was just one of their rows.

He'd also attacked Ella and Aaron. Aaron was a deeply proud man and Toby had grossly insulted him, but Aaron wouldn't kill for an insult, as proven by the many other insults Jem had seen him ignore. Although, they had not come from men he thought his friends.

Toby had expressed his intention of blocking the proposed marriage, but Jem was fairly sure he couldn't have done so. The twins had turned twenty-one, and Ella could surely marry without anyone's consent. Jem remembered her white face, though, her cold fury when Toby had made his threats. Had she taken them seriously? Had Toby had more power than Jem knew?

And Hugo. At the time, Jem had barely considered how bizarre it was that Hugo had offered Ella marriage. He'd never seemed attached to her, and Jem couldn't in the slightest see how her reputation had needed saving, given nobody else had known of the engagement. And if Hugo had been pining over Ella, he'd got over it well enough. Still, it was odd.

Prue had been decidedly odd too, first silent and then shrill as though the words had burst out. That had come when Toby made his remark about people knowing their place. Jem had assumed that was directed at himself. What if it was at Prue? Had Prue hoped that Toby would marry her, perhaps been free with her favours, and been devastated to understand that he would not stoop?

It seemed unlikely. She'd been a provincial like Jem, of the virtuous working class who obeyed the laws and polished their doorsteps and waited for marriage. She wouldn't have lifted her skirts for Toby. It would have gone against all her principles, never mind the risk of unwanted consequences that women ran.

Then again, Jem had made a bonfire of his conventions for Nicky, with the risk of two years' hard labour, inevitable humiliation, and no chance of happiness at all, because he'd wanted him. Might a woman do the same? *Could* Toby have talked Prue into bed? If he'd made promises that he'd never intended to keep, and she'd believed him…

Jem sat up straight. He reached for his notebook and had to stretch uncomfortably to retrieve it from the floor, then flipped through the pages with urgent fingers.

Prue had married John Warren on the third of August 1895, and her son had been 'not yet nine' in November last year, when he died. That surely suggested he'd been close to nine, otherwise she'd have said 'eight'. But a child conceived on the wedding night wouldn't have turned nine until early May this year.

Jem might just go back to his old workplace before he went down to Oxford.

The return to the Registrar-General's Bureau was a little daunting, after having left so abruptly, but Jem was surprised and a little touched by how ready his ex-colleagues were to assist him, and how much quiet sympathy he was offered. He took full advantage in looking for what he needed.

There was no record of Ella Feynsham marrying privately, which he'd toyed with as a remote possibility, and nothing in Toby's father's will to give his son any power over his daughter's marriage, but his third guess was a success. There was a birth certificate for Joseph John Warren, son of John Alan Warren and Prudence Matilda Lenster, born on the twenty-first of January 1896, which was six months after her marriage, eight months after Toby's murder. She'd fled back home not long after, and perhaps she'd met her husband, been smitten at once, anticipated her vows and given birth early. But the odds were that she had been in Oxford when her son was conceived.

Jem wished he'd looked harder at the photographs in her home. All he recalled was a monochrome image, which naturally didn't show Toby's red hair, although Prue's son might have had her colouring anyway. He hadn't noticed any resemblance to anyone in the slightly blurred, childish features, but he was never very good at that.

What would it mean if Prue had been carrying Toby's child and he'd refused to marry her? Would she have known she was pregnant by then? Jem had no idea, but he knew a man who would, and he accordingly made a second appointment to see Dr Aaron Oyede, under his own name this time.

Aaron didn't look overjoyed as Jem halted in.

'Your foot looks painful,' he observed in lieu of greeting. 'Are you seeing someone?'

'I have a doctor,' Jem temporised. 'I've been walking a great deal recently.'

'Sit down. I don't suppose that's what you came to me about,' Aaron added with a glimmer of humour.

'I'm afraid not.'

Aaron massaged the broad bridge of his nose. 'Jem…'

'I know you think I should let sleeping dogs lie. I can't. Did you know Prue had a son?'

'I haven't heard from her since she left Oxford.'

'She did. He died a year ago. He was born on the twenty-first of January 1896.'

Aaron's blank look took about a second to change. 'Really.'

'Yes. I saw the birth certificate. She married in August. I, uh, wondered how soon a woman might know if she was with child after the, the act.'

'It depends,' Aaron said. 'Some don't find out until they deliver. I'm entirely serious, you'd be amazed. The generally recognised sign is cessation of the menses—the monthlies,' he added at Jem's questioning look. 'Oh, for heaven's sake, man. Women usually realise within two to six weeks of conception, assuming their systems are regular and they are knowledgeable about the facts of life, but there is always variation. Some become aware of their condition within a few days of conception.'

'So could she have known?' Jem said. 'If she was expecting, I mean. At Oxford.'

Aaron gave him a look. 'Do you feel it right to speculate on this?'

'No. It's a gross intrusion and Prue's affairs are none of my business, but you must see that if she was carrying Toby's child that night—'

'I do see,' Aaron said. 'It's perfectly possible that a woman would know about a pregnancy on the fifteenth of May for a child she went on to deliver at the end of January, but…Well, what then?'

'How do you mean?'

'Suppose Prue was indiscreet with Toby. Do you propose to shame her for a decade-old weakness, or to suggest that as a motive for murder?'

'I went to see her. She's bitter. She was widowed, and then she lost her only child. He was eight when he died.'

Aaron winced. 'Poor Prue.'

'And she's angry,' Jem said. 'I didn't really understand quite why she was so angry, because it seemed to me that she'd chosen to go home and to marry—but if that was forced on her by necessity, wouldn't one be angry?'

Aaron's brows drew together. 'There are other means of dealing with the consequences of indiscretion.'

'You mean…abortion?' Jem almost whispered the word. 'You can go to prison for that.'

'For life. It is an extremely serious offence, for both the practitioner and the patient. And yet women seek abortions nonetheless, because they need them. They put themselves in the hands of quacks and liars and ignorant old wives operating in filthy conditions; they poison themselves with God knows what concoctions ordered through the newspapers, or bleed to death from botched procedures, and yet they do it every day, because they feel the need. It should be a purely medical issue: it is criminal that the law makes it criminal.'

'I'm sure,' Jem said uncertainly. 'But Prue had the child.'

'Indeed.' Aaron settled back in his chair, relaxing his shoulders. 'I merely intended to observe that women deal with unwanted pregnancies in many ways.'

'If she'd been prepared to break the law and risk her health.'

'And if she knew she was pregnant then, and indeed if she actually was. Have you any reason to believe that the child was Toby's?'

'No. But she loved him, and she didn't have a gentleman follower, did she?'

'I wasn't aware of one. But there are alternative explanations.'

'Such as what?'

'For God's sake, Jem,' Aaron said irritably. 'An outrage—a stranger, a fellow student. The notion that children are only conceived through pleasure has been entirely exploded, sad to say. Or a simple indiscretion. It is hardly unusual to turn elsewhere for comfort when one's affection is not returned.' Jem tried not to wince at that. 'The parentage of Prue's son might well be a deeply distressing topic to her even if it is in no way relevant to Toby's death. You should tread exceedingly lightly.'

'I realise that.'

Aaron hesitated, then went on, carefully, 'And Prue is not the only person who might want the dead to bury their dead. Who might resent you digging up old scandals from a decade ago. To be quite honest, I'm astonished that *you* want to do that.'

'Toby is dead,' Jem said, reddening. 'Surely that matters more.'

'Maybe. But someone resented Toby enough to kill him ten years ago, and that person has a great deal more to lose now. If you must proceed with this business…' He hesitated, then shrugged. 'You should probably let someone know where you're going.'

Aaron's words stuck in his mind all day. *A great deal more to lose.*

He hadn't quite faced that until now. He would be pitting himself against someone who had been driven to kill Toby, and who now also had a murder to conceal. Someone who killed people. He was provoking a killer.

He was frightened, and, once he recognised that, he realised he'd been frightened for a very long time, at a level so deep he hadn't known it. One of the people he most loved had become a murderer, and he'd never trusted anyone again.

He sat in a park for a while, nerves prickling, unpleasantly aware of everyone who passed. A tall dark man in the corner of his eye made him think, *Hugo*, and look round with urgency that cricked his neck. Of course it wasn't. Nobody was following him.

Only, he'd told three of them that he was going to find out who did it.

He hadn't told Nicky or Ella yet, and it was their names that kept coming up. Nicky and Ella, who had loved Toby and hated him. Speaking to them would make this irrevocable.

He had time to stop. He could say he'd changed his mind, let the others know he was sinking back into silent obscurity and…

And what? Sink and be silent, for the rest of his life?

No. He was not going to run away; he'd done that too often. Toby was dead and Jem was barely alive. He'd had ambition once; he'd intended to make a splash in the world. Well, this would be the splash. He'd just have to be careful.

Let someone know where you're going. He couldn't think who; there was nobody who'd care. Well, Aaron or Hugo might care, unless one of them was actually the killer, a plausible liar who'd pretended to the old friendship…

The old friendship: that was the answer. He'd write to his former friends. Four of them would care because they had loved each other and Toby. The fifth would care because he or she had killed him.

'Four out of five isn't bad,' he said aloud, and almost laughed.

He would write to them all—no, he would write to them all except Nicky, and tell them what he was doing. He'd talk to Nicky in person. No point warning him.

Was this stupidly reckless? Perhaps. Then again, unlike Toby's murderer, he had nothing to lose. If he wanted some kind of end to ten years of emptiness, he had one chance, and no choice.

Dear _____, he wrote, a template that would go to four people.

As I have told you, I am determined to discover what truly happened to Toby and who was responsible. Next week I will visit St Anselm's, where I hope to speak to Nicky Rook. I will share what

I learn from him with you all, as I will share what I have learned from you all with him.

One of us knows what happened to Toby. The others can, I believe, find out. It is my intention to do so, no matter the consequences. Should anything happen to me—

He stopped there, staring at the paper. It looked at once an absurd, melodramatic thing to write, and of such significance that his hand shook.

He spent a moment composing the words in his head and began again.

Should anything happen to me before I discover the truth, I hope one of you will take up the challenge and succeed where I have not. I think we owe that to ourselves, to each other, and to Toby.

Yours,
Jem

CHAPTER 12

A few days later, Jem sat in a second-class carriage, watching through the grimy window and the billows of smoke for the first sign of a spire. It was cold and bright. The sun always seemed to shine on Oxford.

He tried his best not to think as the train drew in, or as he waited for one of the horse-drawn trams that still ran up from the station. Thinking meant the past, which was overwhelming, or the future, which was terrifying. He focused on his foot instead. It hurt more or less continually at the moment, between the cold and the unaccustomed amount of walking he'd done, saving omnibus fares and trudging further to cheaper markets. It was pennies, but he had more time than money, and pennies would soon count.

Nevertheless, he paid his twopence for a place on the tram rather than limp along with his bag, and he sat and looked out of the window at the foreign, familiar streets as they jolted up St Aldgate's towards the Broad, and Anselm's.

There were motor cars in Oxford's streets now—just a few, stinking and rattling along, though the tram-horse didn't seem to care. They seemed wrong, a London intrusion into the dreaming golden city he remembered.

They turned onto Broad Street, and passed the medieval walls of Balliol, then Trinity with its blue iron gates, students and dons hurrying past, inside and out. And then he was at St Anselm's.

Anselm's looked smaller, somehow, and lower than he recalled. It had seemed huge on that first day. He'd been so nervous and so hopeful. They'd been so young.

He walked through the arch into the porters' lodge. It, too, was smaller, its pigeonholes crammed with papers and the odd stray black gown. Jem approached the desk, and the elderly porter looked up.

'Ah, Mr Kite. Nice to see you, sir.'

The Head Porter's memory for students past and present was legendary. 'Good afternoon, Moffat, how are you?'

'Oh, mustn't grumble, sir, mustn't grumble. Just passing through?'

'Er, no, I'm here for a week. I reserved a guest room.'

Moffat licked a finger to flip the pages of his blue-covered ledger, which looked exactly like the one he'd had in Jem's day. 'So you are. Bascomb Stair, second floor.' He handed over a key.

'Thank you. Is Dr Rook in college?' He tried to ask it casually, and knew he'd failed. He knew Moffat would be thinking of the crime, and Jem wondered now if their personal crimes had gone as unnoticed as he'd assumed with the ignorant confidence of youth.

'Dr Rook? Yes, indeed. I dare say he's teaching now, but you'll find him on the ground floor, Staircase Thirteen, Old Quad. Is there a message, sir?'

'No. No, I dare say I'll see him. Thank you.'

The porter nodded, shrewd eyes examining Jem's face. 'Very good, Mr Kite.'

Jem made himself walk out at a casual pace, like any gentleman of leisure returned to the scene of his youth. He stopped to take in Front Quad—the impeccable lawn, the great old shading oaks, impossibly youthful students wandering by, and the whole quad dominated by the library. The winter sun was already low in the sky, and its rays coloured the ancient stone warm butterscotch.

It was beautiful, and gracious, and its familiar elegance put a hard lump in his stomach that made him feel for a moment as though he might be sick.

Jem forced himself onwards to the open gateway at the far right corner of Front Quad, next to the Master's lodgings, and went through to Bascomb Quad. Most of the quad's building was administrative. The only accommodation was Bascomb Stair, a narrow building three floors high overlooking what was farcically called Bascomb Wood: thirty slender, crowded beeches in a small patch of ground.

Jem had never actually been in Bascomb Stair before: it was reserved for visitors. He was glad of that. He wouldn't have wanted to stay in a familiar room.

The climb up the steep and narrow stairs to the second floor was as tiresome as stairs always were. Jem set his teeth and plodded up, and let himself in to a small room. Bare walls, narrow bed, a chair, a desk, a faded and slightly stained rug. It felt like home.

He dealt with his few clothes and sat on the bed, breathing deeply against a feeling of worry that was not very far off panic. What insanity had made him imagine he, an entirely unqualified clerk, could solve a decade-old mystery by returning to the scene of the crime? What if Anselm's believed he intended to revive that old and terrible scandal?

What would Nicky think?

There was a small mirror above the sink. Jem didn't want to look into it because he knew what he'd see. A little man with a pain-marked face, looking older than his thirty-one years, brown hair already sprinkled grey, eyes of that indeterminate colour his mother had called hazel. Nothing wonderful. Nothing remarkable. Nothing at all.

What would Nicky think, he wondered again, and this time it hurt.

He sat on the bed, contemplating his hands, for a few moments more. Then he got up, and made his way downstairs, out and along the path that ran by Bascomb Wood, round the back of the walled Master's Garden, and into the formal gardens. The lawn looked bare, its fringe of shrubbery dead and brown. He limped resolutely along to the double garden gates at the end, then turned.

Summoner Quad stood proud in front of him, the pale stone of the solid Georgian buildings glowing at the top, already stained by reaching shadows at the lower levels. Toby had died in the right-hand ground floor room; Jem could see his window on the end wall. He'd hopped out of or into it, over the low sill, so many times. It ought to be open; the weather ought to be summer; Toby ought not to be dead.

The quad was mostly empty since it was ten to four and many undergraduates would be in tutorials or lectures still. A few black-gowned figures hurried by, none of them casting more than a cursory glance his way.

Jem went to the opening of Thirty-One and looked in. Toby's door was shut. It wasn't the same door; that had splintered under the force of a porter's shoulder.

He stood all the same, as though the closed door of an undergraduate's room held any answers, then he turned on his heel and went out into the quad again.

A long, low archway separated Summoner from Old Quad. It had been built at the same time as Summoner Quad, but in a dramatically Gothic style with gargoyles to match Old Quad's hunched medieval walls. Nicky had called it the Bastard Arch.

Jem stood there, waiting till the chapel clock chimed four with its familiar clamour, and then came out into Old Quad. The name board in Thirteen told him Dr Rook had Room Two, the right-hand ground-floor room. Jem retreated, and waited where he could just see into the entrance of Thirteen, until a powerfully built youth emerged, looking somewhat dazed.

Jem gave it a few minutes in case Nicky came out or another student went in. Neither happened, so he approached, chest heaving hard.

He was going to see Nicky again. After everything, after how they'd parted, after ten wasted years in which Jem had dwindled to a shadow of himself. After Toby's murder.

I think it was Nicky, because he loved Toby, and Toby was hateful to him.

Someone resented Toby enough to kill him ten years ago, and that person has a great deal more to lose now.

He didn't want to do this. He wanted to run again, away from Oxford, except he had nowhere to run to.

Or he could knock on the door, and see Nicky again, and demand answers to the questions that had ruined his life, of which 'Who killed Toby?' was just one.

He rapped at the door labelled *Dr Rook.*

'Yes!' Nicky shouted from the other side of the door, the truncated greeting absurdly familiar. Jem turned the handle and went in.

It was a don's room. The old-fashioned arsenic-green wallpaper was barely visible for the bookshelves that covered every available vertical surface. Books formed a knee-high border wall and made towering heaps on the desk. There were no pictures on the mantelpiece, no knick-knacks, nothing but books, and a chair by the fire, and a long-limbed, fair-haired man in a grey tweed jacket and spectacles scribbling irritably on a sheaf of paper that he held on his knee.

'If you've returned to beg for mercy, Mr Jefford, spare me,' he said without looking up. 'I *said* have it done by tomorrow morning, and I prefer not to repeat myself.'

Nicky had become one of *those* tutors. Jem wasn't even surprised. He cleared his throat. 'Hello, Nicky.'

Nicky's writing hand stopped dead. He looked up, a frown forming between his eyes, and his mouth dropped open. 'Jem?'

'Me.'

'*Jem.*' He put the papers on a pile and his spectacles on top of them, and rose. He looked as he would probably look when he was sixty, Jem thought, and could see the elegant older man Nicky would become, alone in his book-lined room.

He held out his hand, without thinking. Nicky came to take it, almost cautiously. Their fingers touched, and Jem had a momentary vision, lasting a fraction of a second and so real he could taste it, of Nicky pulling him close, and striking upwards with Toby's stiletto clasped in his bloody hand.

He didn't do that. Their hands clasped lightly, flinchingly, and parted.

'I must admit to surprise,' Nicky said. 'It's been a long time.'

'It has.'

'For a good reason. What are you doing here?'

'Did nobody tell you I was coming?'

'Who?'

'The college staff?' Jem suggested. 'Or one of the others. I'm here for a few days, in Bascomb.'

'The others,' Nicky repeated, ignoring the rest. 'The *others*?'

'I've been to see them. All of them, except Ella. I wondered if any of them might have written to you.'

'No. What are you doing, Jeremy? Oh Christ.' He stepped back. 'Tell me you aren't intending to revive that business.'

'If by *that business* you mean Toby's murder, yes. I'm looking into it.'

'You've joined the police force?'

'Hardly. No, I've lost my position, actually. I was a clerk at Somerset House—'

'A *clerk*?'

'People like me rarely get one chance, certainly not two. I did a job in an office, and then there was another letter, and people calling me a murderer again, and I lost my job. I'm tired of suspicion, and not knowing. Has there been a letter recently, by the way? About you?'

'Dear boy, there's a pigeonhole especially for them,' Nicky said. 'Not so many as there used to be, so I'm delighted to learn you intend to dig it all up again: that *will* be fun. Do you seriously intend to play Sherlock Holmes over Toby's death? Is the idea to avenge your lost position, or your lost hopes, by unearthing a killer?'

Jem had forgotten quite how unpleasant Nicky's smooth scorn could be. 'I want to know who killed my friend and ruined all our lives. You might care about that too.'

'Is my life ruined?'

'Are you happy?'

'That's an entirely different question. Who else's life is ruined? I thought the more resilient of us seemed to be doing rather well.'

'Hugo is.'

'He would be.'

'Aaron has a medical practice. Ella works at the University of London. But they never married, each other or anyone else. Prue is widowed, living in a village. I'm…this.'

'I'm not sure what *this* is meant to convey,' Nicky said. 'You seem to me still to be Jeremy Kite, a state of being to which I rarely found reason to object. Is Prue unhappy? Beyond widowhood,' he added, making it sound like a trivial inconvenience.

'She lost her son,' Jem said. 'She had a child and he died.'

'I'm sorry to hear it.'

'He was born a little over eight months after Toby's murder.'

Nicky took a second, then his eyes widened sharply. '*Post hoc, ergo…?*'

Jem's Latin had never been good and was mostly forgotten, but he knew the tag: *After that, therefore because of that.* 'I'm just stating facts. And the fact is, one of us did it. We all had reasons to be angry, and it seems that most of us were hiding secrets. Secrets that Toby knew.'

'Toby,' Nicky repeated, and Jem was quite sure he was stalling.

'How did he know?' He wanted to push Nicky, unbalance him. He hadn't realised how much he needed the answer until he'd asked the question. 'How did he know about you and me, Nicky? Did you tell him? Were you trying to make him jealous?'

'Jesus wept,' Nicky said. 'I didn't tell him a thing, you fool. You did.'

'I did not!'

'Oh, you did. You have remarkably expressive features to one who knows you, and Toby could be observant when it suited him. He worked it out all by himself, I assure you. But I question the relevance of this. I assume you didn't murder him?'

'No,' Jem snapped, since he felt a little foolish now.

'And he'd known I was queer since I knew myself, so that wasn't so much a secret as a fact of life. Why would it become something to kill over?'

'Because he exposed you,' Jem said. His mouth was dry. 'We all knew, but we didn't say, did we? Not aloud, never aloud. And then Toby did, and I suppose he might have done it again.'

Nicky's jaw hardened. 'So I killed him? Is that your suggestion?'

Their eyes met and held. Jem swallowed. 'Did you?'

'No. But I would say that, wouldn't I?'

He hadn't lost his knack for irritating people, Jem thought, and took a stupid comfort in that. 'I didn't come here just to accuse you. I want to know what happened and I think, between us, all of us, we can find out. I hoped you'd talk to me—about the others, and that night, and Toby.'

'About you and me?'

'There was no *you and me.* You made that abundantly clear at the time.'

Nicky's eyes, such a warm brown for such a cold man, were steady. 'Yes. I did. What do you want to achieve, Jem? To see one of us hang: Aaron, or me, or Prue perhaps? The judge putting on his black cap and the walk to the gallows?'

Jem had to lick his lips to answer. 'I don't want to see any of my friends hang. But whoever killed Toby wasn't our friend.'

Nicky considered that without expression. Finally he said, 'I suppose we should talk. But I need a period of mental adjustment. Tea?'

'What?'

'Tea. The beverage that cheers but not inebriates. Take a seat and let us have some sort of normal what-have-you-been-up-to conversation over a cup of tea, as old friends do after a decade.'

'Why don't we talk about it now?' Jem said flatly.

'Because I'm not sure I trust you,' Nicky said equally flatly. 'You aren't the only one who's thought about Toby since his death.'

Jem looked at him, alone in a room of books. He took the chair.

They didn't speak as Nicky busied himself with the kettle. Jem looked around, searching for something that spoke of memories or happiness or relationships, seeing none. He did, however, notice a stack of monographs on a table. *Riddling the Romance: a new interpretation of 'Wulf and Eadwacer', by Dr Nicholas Rook.*

'You've published.'

'Repeatedly. It's the done thing, you know.'

'What did you do? After, I mean.'

'From then till now?' Nicky shrugged. 'I took my Finals, with some success, and went to All Souls, where I achieved my doctorate. I was offered a position here as senior lecturer under Professor Hartley three years ago.'

It was a bare-bones account of a spectacular rise. Jem didn't bother to congratulate him. 'Why here?'

'Because I didn't choose to leave. And Anselm's has the best Anglo-Saxon department in Oxford thanks to Hartley.'

Jem remembered Professor Hartley, an intimidatingly odd man with eyebrows like marching caterpillars. 'Is he still here? Not retired, I mean?'

'Not yet. I trust he'll go on for another decade, enraging the Master and sublimely unaware of it. He was my strongest advocate during the period after it all happened; couldn't see why people were giving me so much trouble. I occasionally wondered if he was actually aware of the business.'

Jem couldn't quite laugh. Nicky spooned tea into the pot. 'And here I stayed. What about you?'

'Wait a moment. You must have done something in ten years apart from Anglo-Saxon.'

'Such as what? Marriage and children?'

'You might have met someone,' Jem said a little breathlessly.

'I might have,' Nicky said. 'I didn't. I think I have learned my lesson as to intimacy.'

'Yes. So did I.'

'I thought you might have married.'

'I've nothing to offer a woman. And I haven't cared to try.' Not women, not men, not anyone. He'd had a few desperate, anonymous encounters in dark rooms; anything more had horrified a soul that clung to isolation as its only defence. 'I've nothing to offer anyone.'

'Jesus,' Nicky said. 'We really did ruin your life, didn't we?'

They fell into silence. Nicky watched him, stirring his tea mechanically, not drinking. The spoon clinked against china.

'You were always the best of us, damn it,' Nicky said at last. 'Your place was here. If there was anyone who didn't deserve it—Ah, God. You were probably right about not having this delightful little chat.'

'We can't talk to each other as we did, because we're not as we were,' Jem said. 'I've spoken to everyone except Ella, and it has been horribly wrong every time. We're all still suffering for what one of us did.'

'And who do you think did it?'

'You tell me.'

Nicky leaned back in his chair. 'Hugo had no reason to kill Toby. Aaron is a gentleman. He might act with violence when pushed—and by God he was pushed—but he wouldn't have let the rest of us live under suspicion, and in my case arrest. I feel sure he would have confessed rather than be a coward in his own defence. Ella...' He paused. 'I am not persuaded by her committing a crime that left her and Aaron in such an invidious position. She's ruthless but not stupid. Prue *might* have found the physical strength required for the blow, but I'd need to see it to believe it.'

'That leaves me,' Jem said.

'It wasn't you,' Nicky said. 'Of us all, I'd say you are the only one not capable of murder. Your response to insult is to castigate yourself for what you must have done wrong. If you had attacked anyone that night, it would, and should, have been me, but it didn't even cross your mind to throw your beer in my face. It wasn't you.'

Jem couldn't find a response. Nicky drained his cup and put it down. 'So: all of us could have, none of us would have, one of us did. It resembles one of those immensely tiresome riddles.' He stood, towering over Jem in the chair, all lean hips and long legs. 'Were you fool enough to commit yourself to dinner at High Table?'

'No.'

'Good. Come on. Get your coat.'

CHAPTER 13

He followed Nicky into the library, through the painfully familiar dark walls, weaving between the desks and the pools of gaslight, to the door at the back, and was at once incredulous and barely surprised when Nicky produced a key.

'I can't believe you still have that,' he hissed, once the door was safely shut behind them.

'I'm now authorised.'

Let someone know where you're going, Aaron had said. He was going up to a rooftop with a murder suspect far fitter and nearly a foot taller than himself, in the dark, and nobody knew that at all.

It was insanely reckless. But then, everything to do with Nicky had been that, always. So he didn't stop, but he did leave a couple of steps between himself and Nicky, as though that might do any good.

Nicky opened the door at the top with a scrape of metal, and shut it again behind Jem. Jem stood, breathing more deeply than he'd have liked. It was almost dark now and very cold. He sat on the stone perch, huddled in his coat, and stared out over Oxford. Spires black against the near-dark sky, the yellow glare of gaslight rising from streets or streaming from bright rectangles in the dark mass of stone. A swooping movement in the sky told him the bats were out.

Nicky sat by him, not as close as last time. Not touching. Jem was still vividly aware of him, the warmth of his long body, engulfed in a heavy chesterfield with a velvet collar.

'You don't wear the fur any more.'

'Long gone, I fear.' He rapped something hard against Jem's arm. 'Here.'

Jem uncapped the flask he'd been handed and took a sniff. 'Scotch?'

'It should be wine for a fully nostalgic experience, but I'm too old to drink wine from the bottle.'

Jem took a mouthful of the smoky spirit and winced at the burn. 'Thanks.'

Nicky took it back and Jem heard him swallow. 'Gah. Well.'

'Why are we up here?'

'Because it's too hard to talk down there,' Nicky said. 'Do you remember coming here before?'

'Of course I do. You told me about Toby's family and how he wasn't necessarily the heir.'

'Do you know what happened with Lord Crenshaw afterwards?'

They both used *afterwards* in the same way. There was no need to specify; there would never be any other event from which time was measured. 'No.'

'His baby, the heir who supplanted Toby, died of croup. Crenshaw sued for divorce on the grounds of adultery, and Lady Crenshaw contested it on the same grounds, with photographs. It was all over the society pages for months. Toby's grandfather died, I assume in self-defence. His uncle got his divorce, became the marquess, and now resides in a sanatorium, where he is drunk from dawn to midnight. If Toby had lived, he would once more be poised on the brink of his expectations.'

'Good God. Where does that leave Ella?'

'Nowhere. When the new marquess drinks himself to death, the title will descend to some cousin or other, who must be thanking his lucky stars.'

'You aren't suggesting—'

'Of course not. If this chap had decided to Macbeth his way to the marquessate, he'd have started with Crenshaw and the baby. No point in killing anyone lower down the line of succession.'

'I suppose not. So Toby would have got the title after all. But if he hadn't thought he was out of the succession…'

'Quite.'

'A lot of things wouldn't have happened.' Jem's throat felt tight. He could see Nicky, curled up and cradling his blood-raw heart, those brutal finger marks on his wrists.

'Perhaps.' Liquid sloshed softly in the bottle. 'Jem, I owe you an apology.'

'You don't.'

'Of course I bloody do.'

'You don't,' Jem said, 'because it makes no difference if you apologise or not. It changes nothing. You said what you said. I made a fool of myself—'

'You behaved with extraordinary dignity, while I was a coward and Toby a brute,' Nicky said. 'I don't expect to change anything, and I'm not asking for your forgiveness: I don't merit it. I simply need to tell you that—well, I made a number of poor decisions a decade ago, and if I was given the power to change a single one, I would choose not to have said those things. I'm sorry. I lied to you, or about you, and I threw your honesty and generosity back in your face, because I was afraid.'

'Afraid,' Jem repeated. 'Of what?'

'Oh, Jem. My god was a jealous god, and he did not choose that I should worship except at his altar.'

Jem sat, staring ahead. 'Do you mean—Were you and Toby—'

'Oh, heavens no. Toby kindly permitted me to suck him off once or twice, but he had no real use for anything except my devotion.

He did, however, expect that. He was amused by dalliances that didn't matter; he was not amused to learn about you. Not in the slightest. We argued, afterwards.'

'In the Mitre?'

'Once you'd all left. He—ah well, it doesn't matter now.'

'I think it does.' Jem felt airless. 'You argued with Toby over me?'

'He was disinherited, failing his exams, discarded by his sister, and, to top it all, his most faithful worshipper was guilty of infidelity. And with *you* of all people, a man without his looks or his birth or his God-given right to be adored. He was more than angry. He was humiliated.'

'I never presumed I could compete with him,' Jem said stiffly.

'Well, you did, and he lost,' Nicky said. 'Not that I'm much of a prize, but there we were. Toby was no longer the centre of the world, to Ella or me or anyone, and he hated it.'

'What happened?' Jem asked. 'After the rest of us left the Mitre, I mean. You two stayed longer, didn't you?'

A whisper of cloth suggested Nicky's shrug. 'We spoke. Toby made his feelings very clear on Ella and Aaron and you and me, all in predictable terms; on Hugo's ineffectuality at securing Ella's hand, as if that would ever have happened, and on Prue, even.'

'Prue?'

'He spoke of her with startling contempt,' Nicky said. 'I don't know why. He described her as a whore, which finished off my remaining shred of patience, so I called him several fairly trenchant things in return and left. I went to your digs, but you weren't there, so I went back to mine, thence to Anselm's to get a book I needed from Hartley, returned home, and got back to work. I had Finals in mind.'

He tapped Jem's arm gently with the flask. Jem took it, swigged, and licked his lips. 'Why did you go to my digs?'

'To apologise, I hope, if I wasn't too much of a coward or a fool. Probably to seek comfort. I expect I should have ended up bemoaning my broken idol and demanded your sympathy for having sacrificed you on his altar. I expect you'd have sympathised.'

'Probably. I mostly did what you told me, didn't I?'

'Untrue, Jeremy.' Nicky shifted, a jerky motion. 'Ah, God. Toby was excruciating that last term. You don't know how bad; you had your head in your books. He'd become suspicious of Ella's loyalty some time before that night—she hadn't mourned his lost prospects enough, was spending too much time with Aaron. And he was angry at you, well before I gave him reason to be.'

'Why? What did I do?'

'You came here with your club foot and your provincial accent, and triumphed. You weren't meant to outstrip him, Jeremy, any more than Aaron, or anyone else in his collection.'

'What do you mean?' Jem said, but he had a hollow feeling he knew.

'Look at us all. The women, the queer, the black, the commoner—'

'Hugo's none of those things.'

'Hugo and Toby both had a very good understanding of what they wanted from Oxford,' Nicky said. 'Hugo's intention was to emerge as a progressive Liberal, a wealthy man with the common touch. If we hadn't so inconveniently plunged him into scandal, I expect he'd be citing you and Aaron in the House now. *My friends from across the Empire. I have spent a deal of time with the working classes.*'

'But—no. He was my friend. We liked one another. I *like* him.'

'He's terribly likeable,' Nicky said. 'And so was Toby, with his marvellous gift for friendship, his disparate, wonderful group, so interesting and modern. He was noticed because of his friends—'

'He'd have been noticed anyway.'

'I *know*. He was handsome and charming and exciting, and when he walked into a room, it was as though one had turned the gas to full. I adored him, even when I hated him, in his careless wonder. But…Oh, Jem. How many of us men took Anselm's to sporting victory?'

'All of us, except Toby.'

'How many of us were on for Firsts, or the women's equivalent?'

'All of us, except Toby.'

'Whose performance would one have praised first in *Cymbeline*? Toby?'

'You or Prue, but—'

'Who was elected to university positions? Prue had the Women's Association, Hugo was chair of the Liberal Club, and what did Toby have? Secretary of the college JCR. He was the least of us, Jem. In the first year, it was all "Feynsham's set". By the third year, he was only notable because of us. And he didn't like it.'

'But he always *said* he wasn't a sportsman or a scholar. He made a joke of it.' Jem huddled into his coat. 'Until it wasn't a joke, I suppose.'

'He liked to be the golden lad. He liked to be surrounded by exceptional people who found him wonderful, and while he was a marquess in waiting, of course, he *was* wonderful. And then his uncle spawned the brat, and instead of wealth and a title, he was looking at a poor degree and debts. The lame dogs he'd picked up were outstripping him at every turn, and then his most loyal lieutenants betrayed him, Ella with Aaron, I with you.'

'That wasn't the same at all,' Jem said. 'They were getting married. We were just—'

'What were we?'

'I don't know. How should I have known? I'd never so much as been kissed in my life, and you were in love with Toby!'

'Yes,' Nicky said. 'I realise that I am a cold-hearted prick and no gentleman, but would you please accept my assurance that I would never have risked our friendship as a matter of casual diversion?'

'You said—'

'I know what I said. I thought, in a desperate sort of way, that I might turn the tide of Toby's wrath if I assured him you didn't matter. You need not tell me that was disgraceful, cowardly, and doomed to fail. I was afraid.'

'Of what?' Jem demanded. 'Losing Toby's good opinion because that counted more than my humiliation? Doesn't that rather prove my point?'

Nicky began to speak, stopped himself, restarted. 'I promised myself I wouldn't make excuses for my conduct. But I wish you would believe that I was thinking of you, even if it was through a glass darkly. I thought I was going mad that wretched term. I had Toby ranting and raving at me nightly. His uncle, his sister, his treacherous friends, the unfairness of it all. It festered and burst out, again and again, and Ella declined to take the brunt any longer. She avoided him, and I can hardly blame her. He talked to Hugo a little, but mostly to me. And it made me angry.'

'On his behalf?'

'On mine,' Nicky said. 'I had a top First to secure and he was wasting an hour or more of my life *every single day*, over the same bitter ground again and again, demanding endless sympathy, of which my stocks are limited at the best of times. Have you ever fallen out of love?'

'I haven't had the opportunity.'

Nicky paused at that. 'I am sorry to hear you say so. Probably. It did me no good, I'll tell you that. I was desperate to get away from him, and of course he could tell. Those nights with you—I went out sometimes, walked up and down Broad Street just to be out of Anselm's, and to see the light in your room. I looked and saw you were there, and it was a beacon of sanity, Jem. "This way lies that which is good, and clean, and healthy."'

Jem was sitting straight upright. 'Nicky…' He wasn't sure what to say, against the tumbling confession or the old remembered pain.

'And perhaps it would have been all right in the end,' Nicky said. 'Perhaps he might have pulled himself together and faced his disappointment with grace if there had only been *time*, but he ran out of time, didn't he? Or if I'd told him not to be a prick. I wonder that, sometimes. All the years I agreed with him and soothed his wounded self-esteem. What if I hadn't?'

'I don't know. It's not worth considering. You were who you were because he was who he was.'

'Never inflict a sentence like that on me again. I can't remember where we started with this. Only that he felt all of us had hurt him, one way or another, and he reacted accordingly.'

'You hurt him by spending time with me,' Jem began.

'By fucking you and caring about it. Let us not mince words.'

Jem was glad of the darkness that enveloped them now, and of the cold that soothed his burning cheeks. He didn't know how to talk about this; he wasn't ready, here and now on a rooftop, to hear that Nicky had cared. What that might have meant. What they might have had. What he'd lost.

He pushed on desperately. 'He saw you and me, Ella and Aaron, as betrayers, I grasp that. What did Prue or Hugo do to offend him?'

'I don't know. But you suggested she was expecting? If he wasn't the father, if yet another of his worshippers had succumbed to someone else—'

'Oh God. He'd have been spitting feathers.'

'Indeed he would.' Nicky paused. 'Jem, must you do this? Toby was not who we loved, not the man he should have been, in those last days. He was bitter, and it made him cruel. He did harm, he *intended* harm. I think he was killed because of what he intended to do.'

'Does that mean he deserved to die? That the murderer should get away with it?'

'If the alternative is digging up everything that was buried with Toby? Yes.'

They sat in silence after that. There was, really, nothing else to say. Oxford was a dark plain ahead of Jem now, studded with yellow lights that shone but didn't illuminate. 'It's cold,' he said. 'We should go down.'

CHAPTER 14

Jem woke the next morning to the sound of the chapel bell, wondered if he had a tutorial, and had to blink at the ceiling for a few seconds as reality settled back into place.

They'd come down from the roof in silence, each heavy step burning in Jem's foot. He'd thought that would be it, but instead Nicky had said, 'Come on,' again, and Jem had followed. Again.

They'd gone to Seal's, where he'd been dragged to meet Ella and Prue that first morning when the world was young. Jem decided not to read anything into it; Nicky probably didn't remember. Far more likely he'd chosen it as the closest eating house. He was careful of Jem's foot; he always had been.

They'd talked about other things. Russian political developments, Irish independence, the works of Joseph Conrad and Arnold Bennett. It had been surprisingly easy conversation, given that Jem had nothing to show for the last decade and reminiscence was impossible, but Nicky had never found talking difficult, and it felt as though no time had passed at all. They lingered over one glass of wine more than Jem needed, for the pure pleasure of it, as though everything that lay between them were covered with the tablecloth, the plates, the glasses, and they'd walked back to Anselm's together, and—

And Nicky had asked him if he'd come back for a cup of tea.

He couldn't swear that Nicky had been suggesting more than tea. It would be entire madness for him to do so or for Jem to take up the offer. But Nicky had raised a brow, and Jem had opened his mouth, smiling, to agree.

And then he had caught his breath, and stopped, and the warm, laughing light had gone out in Nicky's brown eyes like the gas cutting off as they both remembered.

Refusal had been the only possible response, but it hadn't made a night alone in this cold, bare cell any more enjoyable.

He got up and washed. It was a Tuesday, and Nicky would be teaching, or lecturing. Jem wondered briefly if he could slip in to listen, hear Dr Rook at work, rather than his old friend Nicky. Probably not, and Anglo-Saxon had never appealed anyway. Nicky had waxed lyrical about its stark, rough beauty, but none of them had been convinced.

Jem went to breakfast in the Hall, since it was included in the cost of the room, solitary amid the chatter of black-gowned students. The undergraduates looked childishly young, far younger than he'd been, he was sure. Half of them probably weren't shaving yet. How could anyone of that age commit a murder, or incite one?

A hefty young man sat with a thump on the other side of the long bench. Jem recognised him as Nicky's erring student from yesterday.

'I say.' He found himself leaning over. 'Excuse me. You study here?'

The youth looked a little surprised at the question, as well he might since he was sitting in the Hall at breakfast wearing a gown, but responded courteously enough. 'English.'

'Do you have Dr Rook?'

'For my sins.'

'I was up around the same time as he was.'

'Oh, were you?' The youth's ears pricked. 'Did you know the one who was killed?'

'Toby Feynsham. Yes.'

'That must have been extraordinary. A murder here, and unsolved! It must have been marvellous. Well, dreadful, but awfully good fun even so. What did people think at the time, as to the culprit? Dr Rook was arrested, wasn't he? I shouldn't put murder past him, I must say: you should see what he writes on my essays.'

Jem had no possible response to that. The young man rattled on. 'College made the room into storage for three years because they thought nobody would want to live there, and of course when they reopened it, people positively fought over the ballot. Apparently, the first man who took it held a murder party and got rusticated for it.'

'A murder party,' Jem repeated.

'Yes, everyone in fancy dress as the suspects, you know. I wonder if we could do something like that now. It would be an awful lark. No offence meant, of course.' The young man was watching his face with a dawning expression of alarm. 'It was just an idea. Probably poor taste. I say, sir—'

'Excuse me.' Jem pushed his chair from the table and left, appallingly conscious of his limp, braced for a shout from behind him. *You there, are you Kite? The cripple?* He wondered if someone had attended the murder party with a crutch. Someone would doubtless have applied boot polish to go as Aaron. He was shaking.

It was cold and damp outside, making a walk uninviting even if his foot had been up to it. Jem took the second-best option and headed for Blackwell's Bookshop, just down Broad Street.

'I'm looking for local history,' he told the counter clerk. 'I wondered if you had a book on the St Anselm murder.'

Jem had been approached by writers twice, and burned both letters, and he had a vague idea that Hugo had mounted legal proceedings against one at some time. He hoped for a look of disapproval, a *We don't stock that rubbish*, but the clerk directed him without comment to an extensive local history section.

The St Anselm Murder was little more than a pamphlet. *Murder at the University* was the larger book, casebound, with a plate section. Jem opened it to that, and was confronted with the picture of *Cymbeline*. His own youthful, happy face; Nicky's hooded eyes; Toby's striking good looks. He clapped the book shut, feeling horribly self-conscious, as though everyone else could see what he was reading.

He didn't want to buy either work, but particularly not the expensive one. He made a note of the author of *Murder at the University* so he could borrow it from a library, resentfully purchased *The St Anselm Murder*, and took it to Seal's, where he ordered tea and waited for his drink to brew before he opened the vile thing.

Just holding it made him feel breathless, as though the air no longer held sufficient oxygen. He didn't want to read this, didn't want to know what the text might hold. He wanted to drop it all and walk away, to go back to the impenetrable shell in which he'd hidden from life for a decade.

He'd spent the night in Anselm's and sat on a roof with Nicky, drinking. He could read a pamphlet.

He opened it and ploughed through competent copy introducing the college and the cast of characters, though when he saw himself described as 'the club-footed son of a factory hand, attending Anselm's through charity', he did have to look away for a moment. The pamphlet offered variously offensive summaries of them all, concluding with the Feynshams, and the upheavals in the family.

The next page was headed *The Night of the Crime*. 'I can't,' Jem said under his breath. 'I can't.'

This was what he was here for. *You can*, he thought fiercely, and read. A necessarily vague account of the evening in the Mitre. A map of Summoner Quad, and an explanation of Summoner's

Gift. The testimony of the fellow who had come to borrow ink and been sworn at by Toby.

Jem turned the page and was confronted with a photograph of the murder scene. He slammed the pamphlet shut, heart thudding.

The photograph didn't show Toby, thank God; he couldn't have borne the indecency. It was only the scene after the body had been removed. Even so, when he opened the pamphlet again, it was at the next page. He didn't care what he might miss: he couldn't look at that.

There was a summary of their movements after the row. Aaron and Ella had on their own account been together; everyone else had wandered around Oxford in miserable solitude, attracting no attention. Nicky had come back to college to borrow a book from his tutor, and Hugo to see Summoner's Gift, as they had both freely admitted. Jem and Prue could very easily have been there, unnoticed.

Aaron had been arrested immediately, mostly on grounds of race, and freed very quickly when Ella intervened. The pamphlet was careful here, presumably with libel laws in mind. Nicky's arrest had come a little later, probably when someone at college had presented him as pining, jealous, queer. They'd had to let him go too. There was no evidence at all.

The pamphlet moved on to the coroner's inquest, with its verdict of murder by person or persons unknown. The coroner had speculated that a stranger might have entered the college during Summoner's Gift for purposes of theft and murdered Toby when caught in the act. The pamphlet gave this short shrift, pointing out that this supposed sneak thief had ignored banknotes to the value of £40, jewelled cufflinks, and a gold watch, all left in plain view. *Or are we to believe that the murderer was a passing homicidal maniac who seized upon this single undergraduate for no reason but to slake his bloodlust?*

Jem didn't think much of the passing-lunatic theory either, but it was all too obvious that the author's objection had more to do with the shape of the story it created. A murder needed a villain, and a satisfactory denouement, and the author had evidently been determined to find a conclusion that would satisfy the reader while avoiding the laws of libel.

His solution, which Jem read with bewilderment and then anger, was Anglo-Saxon. The pamphlet concluded with a depiction of Nicky sitting alone in his digs on the night of the murder, translating *Beowulf.* There was an artistic passage on *one student writing in a dead tongue as another's tongue was stilled for ever*, and then a few lines:

The man's mouth was silent. It spoke
No more, it had declared all it might disclose.
He would slumber in softness soon. His soul
Fled his flesh, and flew to glory.

An Anglo-Saxon quotation as the conclusion. No wonder the students believed they could call Nicky a murderer.

The pamphlet said it. Prue said it. Apparently, everyone felt able to say it, and spiky fear coalesced in Jem's lungs as though he'd been running in the cold.

He headed back to college and Staircase Thirteen, from which an Indian man emerged wearing the browbeaten expression that Jem assumed to be common to all Nicky's students. Jem let him pass and knocked, a double tap and then a third. It was the way he'd habitually knocked here a lifetime ago, and Nicky opened the door with a smile already dawning.

'Jeremy.' He stepped back to let Jem in. 'I wasn't sure if you would return.'

'I need to talk to you. In private. Can we—?'

Nicky moved to lock the door, then stepped over to the shutters and closed them. There was already a lamp burning, since the ground floor windows let in little light at this time of year, and he went over to turn up the gas. It was suddenly rather close, as intimate as their dinner had been last night, or their evenings a decade ago before someone had put a knife in Toby's heart.

Someone. Maybe Nicky.

He was locked in a room with a man who might be a murderer, who might resort to anything to conceal his crime. Too many people had implied or said freely that they thought Nicky had done it; Jem couldn't in truth have said, *I don't believe it was you*. What he did believe, somehow, was that Nicky wouldn't hurt him.

No. That wasn't right, because Nicky had hurt him badly, before. What he believed, the reason he was here now, was that if Nicky would kill him to protect himself, then the world was too bleak to be borne.

He swallowed. 'Listen—'

'Me first,' Nicky said. 'Are you going to tell me you've changed your mind about looking into this?'

'No.'

'Then I don't want to hear any more. I don't want you to do this. It's a mistake, and it might be a dangerous one.'

'Aaron said that.'

'Aaron is a bright man. Look, you know as well as anyone what Toby was capable of. He let the others know you're queer for no better reason than spite, and I'd wager none of them had realised till then. He was waving a threat of two years with hard and personal ignominy in your face—Jem?'

'Nothing. It's nothing.' Jem felt a little dizzy. 'I didn't expect you to say that.'

Nicky looked, for once a little unsure. 'I assumed your tastes hadn't changed since college. Am I wrong?'

'No. No, you—I'm sorry. Only I've never really had anyone say that to me, that's all. It just sounded a little…' The simple word out loud, applied as a description and not an insult. It had seemed to shake everything like the beads of a kaleidoscope and make it all settle in different patterns.

'Ah,' Nicky said. 'Still innocent?'

'More or less.' Jem managed a smile.

Nicky was watching him, eyes steady, a little frown behind them. Jem shifted. 'What?'

'I don't know. I thought you might have found some horny-handed son of toil, or perhaps a fellow arithmetician. Some quiet, comfortable chap to smoke a pipe with. You always seemed to yearn for a peaceful hearth.'

Jem shrugged awkwardly. He'd long ago given up thinking of more than a chilly rented room.

Nicky stepped forward, bringing his fingers very lightly to the side of Jem's jaw, a brush rather than a touch. '*Fastened in fetters your inmost thoughts*—How much have you lost to this wretched, sordid business, Jem? How much of your life did it lay waste?'

'All of it. I'm tired of this twilight existence, Nicky. Everyone keeps telling me the killer might want to keep me quiet, but I've been quiet for ten years and I'm sick of it. What the hell have I got to lose, Nicky? Tell me that. What have I to lose?'

Nicky stared down at him, brown eyes very dark and deep in the dim light. He leaned in, without speaking, and his mouth came down on Jem's. Jem didn't—couldn't—move for a few seconds. Nicky's mouth was extraordinarily alien and very familiar, his lips light but their effect overwhelming. Jem hadn't been kissed since Nicky had bidden him farewell, that last time, and he'd forgotten what to do, he didn't know what he *ought* to do—

Then Nicky drew away a little, with a questioning frown—Nicky who had locked the door and might be a murderer—and Jem reached up for his fine, soft hair and pulled his head back down.

Nicky's bedroom was as filled with books and bare of personality as his study. There were no photographs or paintings, no records of his prizes and achievements, nothing that looked like him except for several foils in an umbrella stand.

Jem lay on his back, looking up at the ceiling, Nicky's arm over his chest, skin to skin.

For all the urgency that had swept through him, and that he'd felt once again in Nicky's almost painful grip, they hadn't rushed things. They hadn't talked about them either, both relying on touch and silence and a locked door to keep everything at bay. It had been tender and gentle, and it had felt at once utterly alien after so long of nothing but knees on cold floors and the hard hands of strangers, and as familiar as though they'd never stopped.

The chapel bell struck one, long and loud.

'Send not to know for whom the bell tolls,' Nicky muttered. 'I've a tutorial at two. If I didn't, I'd suggest a long and alcoholic lunch. How about dinner?' He paused at Jem's silence, and propped himself on an elbow to examine his face. 'Is something wrong?'

Jem didn't know if it was, and he didn't know how to express any of it. 'I wrote to everyone,' he blurted out. 'I told them all I was coming to see you. Aaron told me that someone should know where I was going and I didn't know who I could trust, so I wrote to them all.'

'Someone should know where you were going,' Nicky repeated. 'In case, as Toby's murderer, I took the hump and stabbed you?'

'In case of that, yes.'

'Does your presence in my bed indicate that you have decided on my innocence?'

'No. No, it doesn't. Sorry,' Jem added, and then realised quite how ludicrous that must sound.

'I…see. Could I suggest *not* going to bed with people you think might be homicidal maniacs?'

'I don't believe you're that.'

They looked at each other. Nicky's expression might have been called quizzical by someone who didn't know him well enough to see the tiny lines of strain, the bleakness. Jem refused to drop his eyes.

'Well,' Nicky said at last. 'That's nice. Marvellous. Now what?'

'I don't know. I'm going for tea in the Master's lodgings this afternoon.'

'Do you propose to tell him your plans to make St Anselm's the centre of national scandal once more? I only ask so that I can prepare my curriculum vitae in anticipation of having to find another position.'

'Maybe we could do that together.'

Nicky smiled sourly. 'Touché.'

'I don't know what I'll tell him,' Jem said. 'But if he doesn't like scandal, maybe he should ask Blackwell's not to stock books about us.'

'Try and stop them: they've made a fortune. I trust you haven't—no, of course you've read them.'

'I read the pamphlet. *The St Anselm Murder*.'

'Ah, yes. Hugo's father had lawyers all over that. I trust you liked the delicate hint at the end?'

'Mmm. Why do you think the author implied it was you?'

'Because Hugo and the Feynshams would have sued, and to accuse Aaron would be to call Ella a liar. You and Prue are tediously plebeian, and it would be *so* disappointing if it was a passing lunatic or sneak thief after all. Thus, me.'

'Yes, I suppose that covers it.'

'Don't read the book,' Nicky said. 'It's more of the same, but this time you learn how many of our fellow students were prepared to share memories with a muckraker. There is a full chapter on *Cymbeline* alone. *Quite* unflattering.'

He sounded as light and sardonic as he always did; that cool, uncaring manner that never displayed hurt or shame. Jem didn't want to know the depths it masked. 'I'm surprised you read it.'

'I had a copy prominently displayed on my shelves for a while,' Nicky said. 'In the nature of a warning, you understand. If you insist on reading the bloody thing, you may have it. Throw it away when you've done. I suppose we should dress. One never knows when a student may appear; the place is infested with them.'

Very light, very amusing, no feelings. Jem propped his elbows on his knees and his head on his hands. 'Nicky, I should love to have dinner with you tonight, and to talk to you, and to come back here and—I don't know, whatever elaborate Restoration comedy way you have of saying *go to bed*. I missed you too. But that's why I have to keep asking questions, to find an answer. And I'm sorry if the person who killed Toby did it for good reason, but he is *dead*, and I can't imagine a reason good enough for that.'

Nicky swung his legs off the bed and stood, long and lean. 'Do as you must.'

He tossed Jem his clothes. They dressed in silence, Nicky disappearing into the study before Jem started to work the surgical stocking and built-up shoe back onto his foot.

He checked that he looked respectable rather than ravished, finger-combed his hair into some sort of order, and emerged. The shutters were open, and Nicky was back in his chair with his reading glasses and a pile of papers, just as Jem had first seen him. Jem looked at the pallor of his hair, the prominent bone structure, and quite suddenly he saw an old man, alone for a lifetime in a room of dead words.

'Nicky…'

'Lovely to have you visit.' Nicky spoke with deliberate, dry insincerity, and then looked up before Jem could react. 'Sorry. I didn't mean that. Jem—' He stopped there and put up a hand. 'Well. Off you go.'

'Um, the book?'

'Of course.' Nicky put down his papers and went to the bookshelves. Jem followed and noticed a shelf with several stacks of monographs. The *Wulf and Eadwacer* one he'd seen before, and one that looked older, the cream cover faded with sun or time. *The Wife's Lamentation: a new translation and consideration. Dr Nicholas Rook.*

'Can I have one of these?'

'Are you taking up a course of study?'

'I'm just interested.' He wanted to see how Nicky turned an ancient language into poetry, but it felt like too much of an admission to say so.

'Help yourself. It's never too late for education. I hate to hurry you, but—'

'Tutorials. I know. Goodbye, Nicky. And, well. Thanks.'

Nicky was still for a second and then gave a tiny shake of his head. 'Dear boy…you're welcome.'

CHAPTER 15

Jem wasn't looking forward to tea in the Master's lodgings. Dr Earnshaw had been an intimidating and superior figure even in the days when Jem had been a star of the college and invited to drink champagne. He wasn't keen on meeting him as a failure.

The Master welcomed him with a handshake that betrayed age. He was smaller than Jem remembered, almost completely bald. An old man in a room that looked like a museum exhibit of the mid-Victorian era.

'Well,' he said, as they sat with china teacups, after the inevitable enquiries as to his parents' health and his occupation, and the inevitable awkwardness at his answers. 'And what brings you back to Anselm's, Mr Kite?'

'For one thing, I wanted to see Dr Rook.'

'You were always great friends.'

'We were.'

The Master was watching his face with eyes that were clouded with age, but sharp for all that. Jem sipped his tea.

'It was a terrible business,' the Master said eventually. 'Poor Mr Feynsham's affair, that is. I know all of you suffered; the college suffered greatly too. We have weathered much over our history, and will doubtless weather more, but blood is a stain that is hard to wash away.'

'Yes.' Jem turned the thin, delicate porcelain teacup. The handle was angular and uncomfortable to hold. He'd never seen the point of posh china. 'I loved my time at Anselm's, until the end. I learned a great deal more than mathematics here. Things like intellectual honesty and the pursuit of truth.'

The old man set down his cup and steepled his fingers. 'Are you here to pursue the truth?'

'If I can. Yes. I want to know what happened to Toby.'

'And how do you propose to discover that, when the police could not?'

He chose his words carefully. 'I don't feel entirely certain that the police had all the information.'

'That is a potentially serious accusation.'

'I mean the details. The little interactions day to day that are meaningless, forgettable, normal, and which might have seemed too trivial to remember or repeat.'

The Master's lips thinned. 'If they were forgettable ten years ago, why would they be memorable now?'

'Maybe our ability to remember changes with our desire to do so.'

They watched each other in silence for a moment. Jem had the sudden, distinct feeling that he was in a tutorial. The book-filled room, the old photographs, the old man asking sharp questions.

'I see,' the Master said at last, taking up cup and saucer once more. 'But, Mr Kite, any investigation inevitably turns up private matters. Your little clique had those, didn't you? Affairs that might not be relevant to this matter, but that you would certainly not wish to be disclosed.'

'I suppose everyone's got those,' Jem said as steadily as he could. His heart was thumping unpleasantly. Surely the Master couldn't know. Had anyone peered through the cracks in shutters, heard noises? 'I don't want to intrude into anyone's privacy. But Toby's dead, and I've never known why. I just want the truth.'

'I'm quite sure you do.'

Don't you? Jem wanted to demand. The man was twitchy, and he thought he could guess why. The rest of them had had those letters sent to their workplaces, after all: Nicky would not be exempt.

'I know about the anonymous accusation,' he said, and the Master's cup tinkled violently against the saucer.

'You—' Dr Earnshaw's mouth worked slightly. 'Mr Feynsham told you?'

Jem's first, bewildered thought was that the old man was senile. He opened his mouth to say, *I'm afraid Mr Feynsham's dead*, but some part of his brain, working faster than the rest, cut in. 'He told me a great deal.'

'Did you inform the police of what he had said?'

'I don't put any stock in accusations from people who aren't prepared to use their names,' Jem said, feeling his way.

'I told Mr Feynsham the same thing. I told him, if he or anyone had evidence of a crime, or reason to suspect one had been committed, he should go to the police. The college could not launch an investigation into a complaint if the complainant refused to stand by his allegation.'

Toby had been considering a formal accusation, something perhaps worthy of the police. Jem's stomach plunged. 'And you didn't tell the police what Toby had said to you,' he hazarded.

The Master tapped his cup, hands restive. 'Mr Feynsham simply asked how the college might proceed if it received an anonymous accusation that one of its students was guilty of a serious offence. It was a theoretical enquiry. Naturally, if he had told me anything of substance, I should have repeated it. Naturally. I had nothing of substance to repeat.'

'He spoke to me on the subject in Trinity term of 1895,' Jem tried. 'A couple of weeks before he was murdered.'

The Master pressed his lips together, which was sufficient confirmation. Toby had let him know there was trouble at Anselm's, and when he was murdered shortly afterwards, the Master had kept quiet rather than risk opening a can of worms, and never mind that Toby's enquiry might suggest the killer was an Anselm's student. Anything to protect the college. He'd probably put pressure on the coroner to suggest the passing-lunatic theory too. Oxford colleges did not like scandal.

'So Toby didn't confide anything worth repeating to you,' Jem said, and tried to keep the contempt out of his voice.

'Nothing. I consider the matter quite irrelevant. I have always believed that poor Mr Feynsham's death was the act of an intruder, abusing the hospitality of Summoner's Gift. I hope everyone now accepts that.' His rheumy eyes were fixed on Jem. 'I hope you do, Mr Kite. It would be most distressing to have this business stirred up again. It is unconscionable and Dr Rook would be the greatest sufferer.'

'Yes, sir,' Jem said. 'I quite understand.'

Jem left the room in a state of some mental disarray and emerged into fog. It was light, just enough to brush his skin and blur the light of the lamps that were being lit against the enclosing twilight, but chill and clinging.

Back in his bare room, he summarised the conversation in his little notebook, feeling like a first-year student once more. He recorded the specific words the Master had used as best he could, thinking around the implications as he did so.

Toby had asked what would happen if an Anselm's student was anonymously accused of a serious crime. Once, Jem might have assumed he was simply concerned about Nicky's safety. He wished he could think that now.

It seemed all too likely that Toby had intended to make trouble. For Nicky? Or for someone else? The others had all been law-abiding so far as Jem knew, but then, they'd probably thought the same of him. He was beginning to think he'd known a great deal less about his friends than he should have.

He wondered how he'd find out more, and decided he might as well ask.

Dear ______

As I wrote to you before, I am now staying at St Anselm's. I have had a number of informative conversations here. In particular, I have learned that, before his death, Toby enquired about the possibility of laying anonymous accusations of a certain serious offence against a fellow student.

I need not say more, I think. I shall not put the specific details of the accusation on paper.

I have no intention of dragging up private matters if they are unrelated to Toby's murder. But I need to be sure they are unrelated. I hope you will agree to talk to me about this at your earliest convenience.

Yours,
Jem

He read his note over with some disgust. It seemed horribly like a blackmailer's letter. Well, it was one. If any of them had been harbouring a secret, they would have to assume Jem knew what it was. And then, perhaps, he might have a chance of actually finding out.

It felt vile and intrusive, but he had no idea how else to get what he wanted, so he copied it out four times, one for each former friend. He'd speak to Nicky in person.

He addressed the envelopes as 'Strictly Private and Personal', and stared at them, a cold feeling growing in his stomach. An innocent person who received this letter would be angry and disgusted. Someone with a secret would be angry and afraid. And someone who had killed Toby to keep him quiet might be angry enough to kill again.

But what choice was there? He needed to know, if anything more urgently than when he'd started on this path. He needed to know if—

Oh God, just face it. He needed to know if it was Nicky.

Nicky had had a motive to kill Toby, and the opportunity too, though they'd all had that. It was said criminals returned to the scene of the crime; Nicky had barely left it. Nicky had loved Toby, and hated him, and people killed the objects of their love and hate. Jem knew that too well: ten years ago he had loved Nicky, and hated him enough to kill him too, and he had no doubt Nicky knew that. He would have found it very easy to say, *Forget the murder, forget the past.*

Was that what Nicky had wanted to achieve by reaching for him? Wasn't it a great deal more probable that he'd wanted to manipulate greying, limping Jem than that he'd desired him?

Manipulate or, of course, simply have something on him. You got two years for gross indecency, with hard labour if the magistrate was unsympathetic. If Nicky was the murderer, if he said *I'll tell if you do—*

'Christ,' Jem said aloud, and dropped an arm over his eyes.

*

It was dark when he went out to post the letters, and the fog had thickened noticeably. It was only a wet mist, nothing like the choking stew of a London particular or the rolling black clouds of his industrial home, but it was freezing and clammy and it bit. Jem stood at the base of the stair, bracing himself for the weather. The ghostly white birches of Bascomb Wood loomed opposite as though he were in a forest, not an Oxford college. He tied his muffler with chilly fingers and fumbled his gloves out of his pocket.

He wondered as he walked if he would stand at the pillar box hesitating, if he'd walk up and down, plagued by doubt and fear and second thoughts, but in the end, it was too damned cold, so he just dropped the letters in.

He found a small café for a cheap meal, ordered, and looked for something to read. He checked his coat's capacious pockets, and found Nicky's pamphlet, *The Wife's Lamentation.*

The poem was a mere fifty-three lines according to Nicky's extremely erudite introduction, and was the lament of a woman separated from her lord, first by travel or exile, then by the malice of others. Toby had once described Nicky's beloved Anglo-Saxon poetry as 'a lot of chaps wailing and waiting to die', which seemed fair. Jem leafed through the pamphlet, unable to see what on earth the appeal of this ancient rambling was, until he turned a page.

There are friends on earth,
lovers living who lie in bed,
while I walk alone in the dawn light
under the oak tree and through this cave of earth,
there I must sit the summer-long day;
there I can weep for all my woes,

my many miseries; and so I may never
flee from my grief of heart,
nor all the longings that have snatched my life.

Jem stared at the words, his food untouched. He flicked to find the poem's date. The tenth century AD, it said. A millennium ago, yet the pain at loneliness and its injustice were raw on the page to the point that Jem had to squeeze his eyes shut.

How could Nicky have borne to translate this? Maybe it had been cathartic, except there was no hope or relief to be found in the poem, not even the relief of an ending.

Sorrow be to those who live
in longing for those they love.

CHAPTER 16

Jem barely slept that night. Partly he was hungry—he hadn't been able to finish his meal, with a nausea at the idea of food that was all too familiar from his days of nervous prostration. He'd got too thin then. He'd need to be careful now, to make himself eat, but—that damned poem.

The damned poem, the damned letters.

The letters ought to arrive today; he could hardly expect any response for at least a day or two, if he got any at all. He didn't, in the cold light of morning, entirely believe they would have any effect. Was it really plausible that someone in their group had committed a crime worth reporting to the police? That they had a secret worth killing over?

It had to be plausible, he reminded himself, because one of them had done it.

He thought it through as he lay awake and alone and hungry in the dark, and, by the time he finally drifted off to unsettled sleep, he'd had a couple of ideas.

The next morning, he got hold of a directory of Anselm Hall's faculty in Blackwell's, then walked up Park Street to save a penny on the bus. The newspaper-sellers all shouted about the tottering government; Jem couldn't summon the energy to care. It was a misty morning again and the air was cold and wet. He hunched his shoulders against it, knowing he would look like a drowned rat by the time he got to the Hall.

He hadn't tried to make an appointment; it wasn't as though he knew what he was doing anyway. He'd simply play the cards as they fell.

Anselm Hall had been a new building in his day. The bright, patterned red brick had weathered over the last decade, but it still stood out, glaring in its modernity. Jem put in a request at the Lodge to see Miss Keele, and, somewhat to his surprise, was informed she would see him in an hour. He wasn't permitted to roam around the women's college unaccompanied, so he retreated to wait in the Natural History Museum down the road, to avoid the rain rather than out of thirst for knowledge.

He'd forgotten the beauty of the museum's interior, with its slender, soaring columns. He'd used to meet Prue here, to wander around the Pitt Rivers anthropological collection, squinting at African masks and Indian musical instruments and Sussex witch bottles, talking about mathematics and books and anything else that came to mind. He wished, so hard it felt like a blow, that he could have wanted Prue as a man ought to want a wife. If they'd only been able to stand together, they could have stood, he was sure. But Prue had loved Toby, and Jem had loved Nicky, and there had been no more to be said.

Miss Keele gave him tea in her room. She had been Ella and Prue's 'morality tutor', there to provide wise guidance in case of trouble. All the women had had one. There hadn't been any such thing for the men.

She looked almost exactly as she did in his memory, a thin woman with her hair in a bun and thoughtful eyes. A little greyer now, more lined, still upright, as though she couldn't risk relaxing by a single degree.

'I'm pleased to see you again, Mr Kite.' She poured tea and offered him a biscuit. 'It's been many years. Is this your first return to Oxford?' She nodded along with him. 'One can see why you might not have wanted to, ah. Yes. I have often thought of the business, naturally. One sees Feynsham's name in the scientific journals. I have followed her career with interest. A remarkable woman.'

'Have you heard from either of them? Ella, or Prue Lenster?'

'No. Lenster left before sitting the Examination of Women, of course. I understand her, ah.' Her reluctance? Her reasons? Miss Keele had always had that trick of not actually voicing the final word. Jem had a sudden vivid memory of Prue reducing them all to hysteria with an imitation in which she replaced every word except *and* and *the* with *ah*. He had to bite his lip against an unexpected bubble of laughter.

'But Feynsham was a credit to the Hall and remains so,' Miss Keele went on. 'One should have liked her to remain more involved with us. Perhaps in time she may become able to look beyond the, ah.'

'The murder?' Jem suggested.

'The unhappy past.'

'Do you remember much of that time, Miss Keele?'

'Naturally,' she said somewhat drily. 'It sticks in the mind.'

'Do you…' Jem tried to feel his way. 'As the morality tutor, did Prue speak to you? For advice?'

Her face closed up. It wasn't a dramatic change of expression, but the muscles froze, in the way Nicky's face sometimes did. It was the reaction of someone who was used to thinking, *I mustn't show what I feel.* 'If she had done so, about any matter, it would be very wrong of me to discuss it with anyone else.'

'Did you tell the police about it?' Jem asked.

'Certainly not. Discussions with students are confidential.'

Jem felt his nerves quiver, knowing he had to play this just right. 'But, with Toby's murder—'

'Lenster was not suspected of the murder at any time, nor should she have been. The idea is absurd.'

No *ah* while she was defending her student, Jem observed, and felt a rush of warmth towards the woman. 'I wasn't suggesting otherwise,' he said. 'Of course she didn't kill Toby. But—confidentially—I have reason to wonder if the, uh, the other business might have been relevant.'

'How?'

'I can't disclose that,' Jem said. 'I'm sorry, but you understand, the last thing I want is to spread gossip. But I've heard something recently that worries me and—'

'Why don't you speak to Lenster directly, in that case?'

'I have. I went to see her a few days ago.'

'How is she?'

'Not marvellous,' Jem said. 'She's a village schoolmistress now. Widowed.' Miss Keele tutted. 'And her son died last year, an accident.'

'Oh,' Miss Keele said slowly. 'How did she feel about that?'

Jem blinked. The obvious response was, *How the blazes do you think?*, and he felt a furious urge to shake this bloodless woman into some semblance of human sympathy. 'Distraught, of course. Devastated.'

'So she loved it. A son, you say. She loved him.'

'Of course she did!'

'There's no *of course* about it,' Miss Keele snapped, with such unexpected force that Jem recoiled. 'Don't give me pap about maternal instincts, when you will never have to deal with an unwanted child foisted upon you by the curse of biology and the injustice of law.' She jabbed a finger at him. 'Women are not all mothers in waiting, Mr Kite, and maternity is *not* our highest or only destiny.'

'No, of course—'

'The expectation that a woman *must* be a mother, must *wish* to be a mother, must embrace motherhood willingly in any circumstances—oh, if men bore children, they would sing a very different song.'

'I couldn't—'

'I may as well tell you that I am a proud member of the Malthusian League. I support the legalisation of birth control and education of women in family planning, across the nation, in all walks of life.'

'So do I,' Jem said. 'Absolutely.'

'Really, Mr Kite?' She gave him a deeply sceptical look.

Jem cast about for something to make his assertion more convincing and found it. 'I was speaking with a doctor just the other day on the subject of, uh—' Was it indelicate to mention abortion in front of a woman, or would Miss Keele eviscerate him for using euphemisms? 'Of abortion,' he rushed out. 'I don't pretend to any great knowledge of the subject, but I cannot believe the current situation of illegal procedures dangerously carried out is the best way for the health of the nation, or of its women. And I should be very interested to learn more about the Malthusian League,' he added shamelessly.

'You are quite right.' Miss Keele put down her teacup with an enthusiastic chink. '*Quite* right. One sees women reduced to shadows by excessive childbearing, struggling to feed a family that could have been quite happy with two children but is ruined by ten. Women with marvellous futures reduced to mediocrity. Look at Lenster. She had so much to offer, and—what did you say, a village schoolmistress? Not that teaching is ever less than an honourable profession, but Lenster could have done far more, and wanted to. She had ambitions. The waste enrages me.'

Jem nodded slowly, not entirely sure of his ground. 'I don't think she thought it was a waste. She loved her son very much.'

'I'm glad of that.'

'It must be a terribly hard thing, though,' Jem said, unobtrusively crossing his fingers for luck. 'For an unmarried woman to find herself expecting, with so much to lose. I would have quite understood if Prue had not wished to have, or keep, the child.'

'Oh, indeed. The consequences for unmarried women are shame, ignominy, a hasty, ill-judged marriage or a blighted future, while the swine responsible for her condition goes unpunished. I should have supported her absolutely in whatever course she decided to take.'

So Prue had indeed been expecting at Oxford. That opened up a number of questions, most of which Miss Keele couldn't answer.

'And abortion is very dangerous,' he tried, attempting to build on the sliver of common ground he'd established.

'Unnecessarily so. It could be a hospital procedure—it is considered a quite usual form of family planning for married women in France, carried out by doctors—but British law has never been concerned for women. They die in their hundreds every year, at their own hands or those of backstreet abortionists, because the law denies them safe medical treatment in hygienic conditions.'

'That seems quite unjust,' Jem said. 'But Prue didn't—that is, she had the child.'

'Indeed. She made her choice, and I am glad to know she loved the child, despite everything.'

'Yes. I suppose all this would have been around the time that Toby was murdered.'

'Poor Lenster. It was devastating for her,' Miss Keele said, picking up the teacup again and turning it in her hands. 'To lose a friend so terribly, paired with Feynsham's extraordinary behaviour…'

'What did Toby do?'

'Not Toby Feynsham. Ella.'

'What did *she* do?'

'One should not rush to blame her,' Miss Keele said. 'Her twin brother had been murdered. And it is grotesque that she was subjected to public scorn because she did not faint, or weep, or have hysterics, as though women must express their grief in only the approved manner. Nevertheless, she was shockingly cold to Lenster, turning her back on the poor child in public. She was not an easy woman. She lacked the gift for friendship.'

Yes: Toby had got all of that for the pair of them. 'It was a terrible time for us all,' Jem offered.

'I dare say. And if Lenster's child gave her comfort, I am very pleased to hear it.' Miss Keele tipped her head. 'Perhaps, now she is no longer, ah…now she no longer has domestic responsibilities, she might wish to resume a life of the mind. Perhaps you could give me her address? I should like to write to her.'

Jem did so, with a little uncertainty. He hoped Miss Keele would phrase her letter tactfully. She obviously cared for Prue, though, and God, he'd have liked it if someone from Anselm's had ever held out a hand to him.

He thanked Miss Keele and set off back down Park Street, mulling over what he'd learned.

Suppose Prue had considered finding an abortionist to deal with her unwanted child. Procuring abortion was punishable with anything up to a life sentence, for the woman and for the abortionist. That was the kind of secret he'd imagined lying behind Toby's death, some threat so huge that murder was the only answer. Suppose Toby had gone to the police and said…

Said what, though? *I hear Prudence Lenster of the women's hall is considering an abortion*? Surely not. That would be truly, deeply foul, and surely Toby had had no reason to be so vile to her. Unless he really thought she'd betrayed him by loving another man…

Or, of course, unless the child had been his.

Had Ella stopped speaking to Prue after the murder because of an affair with Toby? What would Toby have done if Prue had been carrying his child? Wouldn't he at least have helped her financially? Except, of course, he'd lost his inheritance and had gambling debts. Presumably his grandfather wouldn't have been pleased about an illegitimate child, but surely he wouldn't have abandoned her to choose between the shame of being an unwed mother and the dangers of abortion?

It was a dreadful place and those were dreadful people, and you and I got caught in their games and paid for it.

Jem came up short against a motor car, and realised he'd reached Broad Street. He hadn't even noticed the walk down, lost in his whirling thoughts. He'd have liked to keep going, but his foot was painful, and it was damned cold, though the claggy, drizzle-filled air was almost a relief, chilling a face that was reddening with anger and near-tears. The atmosphere was thickening with the promise of fog, and he wanted to sit down and think.

He went back into Blackwell's since the prospect of his bare guestroom was uninviting. It had always been possible to treat the cavernous shop like a library; he found a seat and picked up a book at random to hold as if he were reading it.

Suppose Toby had learned Prue was carrying his child and intended to procure an abortion, and he had threatened her with the police. He hadn't turned on her particularly that last night, but perhaps that in itself had been a punishment, or a demonstration of how little she meant.

If Prue had been desperate enough to consider abortion, with all the attendant risks, to what other extremes might she have been driven? Suppose she had gone after Toby and confronted him, slipping through the crowds at Summoner's Gift unnoticed.

Suppose he'd spoken to her with the sort of words he'd used on Jem, and the stiletto had been to hand…

Suppose all that, what would Jem do about it?

Nicky had said he wanted the murderer to get away with it. Right now, Jem could see his point. He wondered what Nicky knew.

He sat there, looking at the shelves without seeing, until his lower back protested at the immobility. When he eventually left, the street lights were already lit against the encroaching darkness.

He still couldn't face his little bare cell and another lonely evening, aware of Nicky a few staircases away. Maybe he would go to the chapel; the medieval wood and stone and the heavy silence of centuries in its walls made it a good place to think. Maybe if he sat there, the God to whom he had long ago lost any connection might vouchsafe him a revelation. Divine inspiration had to come to someone, so why not Jem?

Or maybe he'd sit on the hard benches amid cold stone while his life ticked away.

Sorrow be to those who live
in longing for those they love.

He should go to the chapel and pray for the sense he was born with, but instead he headed to Staircase Thirteen, and when he knocked, Nicky let him in.

CHAPTER 17

Jem buried his head in Nicky's chest as the chapel clock chimed seven in the evening. Nicky's shutters muted the clamour of Oxford's bells for the most part, but the chapel clock was almost above them and nothing could keep out its piercing brassy notes. 'God above. How do you sleep through it?'

'Habit makes anything endurable. We're missing Hall. Or at least will be too late for it; nobody could *miss* it per se.'

Jem had missed Hall, when it had meant the chatter of friends ringing off the ancient polished wood, but he couldn't summon up any urge to dine among callow youths and strangers, and especially not in Nicky's company. There would be stares, and Jem did not think he would be able to ignore stares.

Nicky had let him in wordlessly and locked the door without looking away from his face, and Jem had followed him to the bedroom. Jem didn't think either of them had spoken a meaningful word for an hour or more, excepting Nicky's repeated questions of, 'Is this good?' and Jem's gasped or muttered answers. They'd lain in silence in between, in Nicky's monastic cell of a bedroom, listening to one another breathe. It was the longest Jem had ever spent making love in his life, and he had no idea what to do now.

Falling back into Nicky's bed once might have been an understandable mistake, but twice was something else. Twice was a need that had never gone away, salve for a hurt that had never stopped aching, and a damned stupid way to go on. He couldn't even blame Nicky. It had been his own doing, start to end.

Where the devil did he go from here?

'If I offered you a penny for your thoughts, would I want my money back?' Nicky enquired.

'You'd certainly be overpaying. What are we going to do?'

'I had in mind Trafford's on the Cornmarket.'

'Not for dinner. In general.'

'I have no idea why you're asking me,' Nicky said. 'I sit in a litter of dead language, making myself unpleasant to students. I've done that for three years and, barring unexpected eventualities, will do it for another thirty. If you've another plan, please let me know.'

'I don't have a plan, except to keep asking questions. Nicky?'

'Here.'

'Suppose I found out who killed Toby.' Nicky's breath hitched, perceptible in the slight judder of his chest under Jem's head. 'Suppose it was someone who, well, who was provoked.'

'Whoever did it was provoked. None of us were given to assassination as a hobby.'

'But suppose one looked at the reason and thought, *I could not justify reporting this to the police.*'

'Have you found something?'

'It's a hypothetical question.'

'Possibly one you should have considered before you started on your stone-turning career,' Nicky pointed out. 'Are you asking me what I think, or what you should do?'

'Are they different?'

'Obviously. If you want to know whether *I* would tell the police the murderer's identity, the answer is no, because I don't want more harm done. Whereas you seem to believe that revealing the murderer would do more good than harm. Or are you changing your mind?'

'It's just speculation,' Jem said. 'Well. I found out something that might or might not have a bearing on things, but it's not my secret to tell you. Not unless I was sure it was relevant and maybe not even then. Sorry, I don't mean to be obscure.'

'Can you assure me you aren't going to point the accusing finger at anyone in the near future? Say, the next day?'

'I can promise you that.'

'Then let's talk about dinner,' Nicky said. 'Because I don't know what we're going to do, Jem, singly or together. I don't like any of the courses of action that seem right, and all the options I'd prefer to take seem wrong, and you seem to be in a similar state of moral suspension. Could we have the night to ourselves? Just us, without Toby's shadow?'

'We've had the afternoon.'

'And now I'd like the evening,' Nicky said. 'A meal in civilised surroundings where you and I can have conversations that don't pivot around the knife in Toby's heart as though we're a pair of compasses and that the spike. I want your company for a decent stretch of the evening, and that ought not to be too much to ask when other people get lifetimes. I wouldn't *dream* of asking for any such grace as is granted to most of the fucking country without question. I'd just like dinner with you.'

'Then we'll have it,' Jem said, because the sudden crack in Nicky's voice wasn't right. 'Let's do that.'

Nicky brushed a kiss over his hair, very light. 'Thank you. I'd like to say you won't regret it, but that's probably a promise too far.'

Jem didn't regret dinner, as such. The food was good, simple English cooking, of the kind he liked, rather that the French cuisine Nicky always praised. They talked, though not with the animation of that first dinner, because they'd moved beyond rekindling a friendship, into—Jem wasn't sure what. They'd had attraction and desire and uncertainty ten years ago, and not for very long; he had no idea what they had now.

I think it was Nicky, because he loved Toby.

Prue had said that, he reminded himself. Prue, who had her own bitter motive. Jem hung on to that as a lifeline, trying to keep fears and beliefs in a suspension in his mind, as though they could exist together. *Prue. Nicky.*

He didn't know what the devil he was doing, but Nicky had asked for the evening, and Jem felt he owed it, whether to his old friend or to his younger self. So they ate, and talked, and walked back to Anselm's together, and Jem slept well in his solitary bed, his skin sensitised with the memory of touch.

He felt rather less content the next morning. He couldn't afford more than a week at Anselm's; after this, he'd have to return to London, find work, give up. Or, worse, not give up, and become one of those obsessive little men poring over yellowed newspapers and coming up with contorted theories. He didn't want to do that. He wanted to be able to speak to Hugo and Aaron again, to stand friend to Prue, to knock on Nicky's door.

All of which depended on not suspecting any of them of murder, and he'd wasted an entire afternoon and evening that he could have spent asking questions. He got up, washed in punitively cold water, and wondered about his next move.

It was a frustrating thing, to want to be busy yet have no obvious task. Jem did his best, scrabbling around for other directions in which to explore. He requested a meeting with Hugo and Toby's old history tutor. Dr Trent was able to offer him a half-hour, which proved to be unnecessarily long, since all he did was complain about how many tutorials Toby had missed. 'I wished to impose a penal collection,' he said, the decade-old resentment clear. 'But his grandfather, the marquess, was of course a very generous donor to Anselm's. So, I may say, was Mr Morley-Adams' father, yet *he* did not require or seek special treatment. I really have nothing more I can tell you, Mr Kite. Mr Feynsham was not a memorable student to me, except in the wrong ways.'

He got no further in attempting to gossip with the Head Porter, who declined to be drawn on the subject of the murder, or the Seven Wonders, or anything else, and regarded him with what might have been hostile suspicion or just his usual charmlessness. Eventually Jem gave up, and found himself at lunchtime with no idea what to do next. Given the amount of money left in his wallet, he decided to skip lunch. He'd had a good meal with Nicky the night before, and his foot was feeling the effect of yesterday's cold trudge up to the Hall and back more than he liked. He'd be more refreshed by a lie-down than by food, he assured himself.

He made his way up the narrow winding stairs once more, flopped onto the bed of his little room, and lay there for five minutes before he could even make himself take his shoe off. He needed to go back to the doctor and couldn't afford it.

It had been a badly frustrating day, and it was nearly three o'clock now. He'd wasted a full twenty-four hours of his week's self-indulgence and dead ends. He'd have done better to sit and think. God knew he had plenty to think about.

Toby had intended to incriminate a fellow student. Prue had been expecting a child and had perhaps considered an abortion. The two facts must surely be related. Anselm Hall was up Park Street; Prue would have passed the open back gates as she headed back and you could see Toby's room from there, could even see if the light was on. It must have seemed like an invitation. If she'd gone in to plead with him, and been driven to fury…

It all sounded plausible, except that Prue was female and even shorter than Jem, and Toby had been frightening at that last meeting: drunk and savage and uncontrolled. Would she have risked confronting him?

And yet, and yet…

He jumped when a knock on the door startled him out of his tail-chasing thoughts. 'Who is it?' he called. There was no response, just another knock. Jem forced himself up, limped to the door, and opened it.

Aaron stood on his threshold, his expression set and very unfriendly.

'Aaron,' Jem managed. 'This is a surprise.'

'Why? You invited me.' Aaron stepped forward. Jem, perforce, had to step back, very aware that Aaron was a foot taller than him and several stone heavier. Aaron shut the door with force. 'You cannot have expected to write that letter and carry on undisturbed.'

'Do you want to sit down?' Jem suggested.

'No. This isn't a social call.' Aaron's gaze flicked, as if drawn, to Jem's foot, and he added irritably, as if forced, 'You sit down if you want to.'

And have Aaron loom over him? No thank you. 'I'll stand.'

'As you wish. What the devil did you mean by that piece of offensiveness?'

Jem locked his knees and straightened his back. 'What it said. You dropped everything and rushed down here to see me about it, so I suppose you know very well what I meant.'

'What the devil are you playing at, Jem?' Aaron demanded. 'What do you want?'

'I want to know who killed Toby, and why. Which seems a little more obvious now,' he added, giddily reckless, since bluffing had carried him all this way already.

'I did not kill Toby,' Aaron said through his teeth. 'Much though he might have deserved it. I wanted to marry his sister, damn it!'

'And he intended to stop you doing so by any means he could. Including, apparently, laying information with the police.'

'Ella would never have forgiven him,' Aaron flashed back. 'Have you thought of that?'

'I'm not sure he cared that night.'

Aaron didn't argue that. 'For heaven's sake, Jem, I was interrogated for hours and locked up for days. Do you not think the police would have found evidence if there was any?'

'Not with the dead man's sister swearing to your whereabouts.'

'Leave Ella out of this. In fact, leave us all out of it. Toby is dead and nobody is going to discover his murderer ten years on, least of all you. All you will do is cause far more pain and destruction to people who don't deserve it. I am warning you, Jem. Stop.'

'I don't think I can.'

Aaron looked at him, nostrils flaring slightly, and Jem had a sudden moment of panic. They stared at each other, Aaron's muscular bulk seeming to take up all the space in the room, Jem putting everything he had into staying upright. His foot throbbed under him.

'I can't stop,' he said again. 'I don't want to hurt anyone, but I can't just ignore what I've found out.'

'Have you taken what you know to the police?'

'Not yet.' Jem was aware the second he'd said it that he should probably have lied. At least he should claim he'd told somebody all about it, in the event of anything happening to him. He couldn't think of who he'd name, except Nicky, and wouldn't *that* open another Pandora's box, albeit one without any hope in it. 'I wanted to give you a chance to explain.'

'To explain,' Aaron repeated, almost incredulous, as though Jem had no right to ask that at all.

'I'd like to understand, that's all. If you want to tell me about it, I'll listen.'

'And if I don't choose to explain myself to you?'

Jem swallowed. 'Then I'll have to draw my own conclusions.'

Aaron's eyes narrowed. They looked at each other in silence that seemed to stretch endlessly. Jem was damned if he'd be the one to break it, or to shift uncomfortably under Aaron's gaze. His foot was aflame with pain.

'Fine,' Aaron said at last, as though exasperated beyond endurance. '*Fine*. Sit down, for God's sake.' He grabbed the chair, hauling it from the desk as Jem tried not to collapse too obviously onto the bed. 'Very well. What do you know, and who from?'

'I can't tell you.'

'For heaven's sake,' Aaron snapped. 'This isn't just about me, you pig-headed fool. It implicates others—people who could still be prosecuted, people who didn't know Toby from Adam, and who don't deserve to be caught up in your vengeance. I'd have thought you of all people would sympathise with the need to get around a damn fool unjust law.'

'I do,' Jem said, mind racing. 'Obviously. That's why I didn't go to the police.'

'I want to know how you found out,' Aaron said. 'This isn't trivial, Jem.'

Jem pressed his hand into the bedclothes to cross his fingers. 'I spoke to Miss Keele.'

'Ah,' Aaron said. That was all he said, but it wasn't *What the devil has she to do with anything?*, and Jem put together a number of things at a speed that reminded him of the days he'd been on for a First.

'Prue went to her to discuss her situation—that she was expecting. Miss Keele is a member of the Malthusian League. She said she'd have supported Prue if she'd sought abortion.'

'Good.' Aaron sounded vague, in the way of a man who was thinking hard.

Everything was falling into place: Aaron, speaking savagely of incompetent doctors and old wives' remedies. Aaron, who had belonged to progressive medical societies, and had often been out in the evenings in their last year.

Ella would have known, of course, as close as they had been.

Jem took a deep breath. 'What I wondered was, if Prue told Ella she was expecting and didn't want to be, whether Ella might have told her she knew a safe pair of hands. Someone who could carry out the procedure safely. Someone she could trust.'

'I will not confirm or deny any speculation about Prue, or about what Ella might have known. Absolutely not.'

Wrong angle of attack. Jem recalled again Toby's furious threat to Ella: *I can deal with him for good, and I will.* And he'd asked the Master about serious offences…'Fine. Were you carrying out abortions?'

'I was not.' Aaron tipped his head back and let out a long breath. 'Not personally. That was an established doctor, a man who knew what he was about, with a very experienced nurse. I acted as an assistant when required, not that the law or the Royal College of Physicians would regard that with any more leniency. I am well aware that what we did drove a coach and horses through medical ethics, but there are women alive now who would not be if they had gone to the back streets.'

A black man helping to procure abortions on, Jem would guess, mostly white women. The thought of what the newspapers and the judge would have said was eye-watering. 'God almighty. You could have gone down for life! What were you thinking?'

'I was thinking of women bleeding out,' Aaron said. 'Clutching their bellies and screaming, rendered infertile and damaged for life if they're lucky, dying if they're not. I have seen it happen too often, and if you intend to give me moral disapproval, you may first stand in a women's ward and wait for one of those cases to be brought in—it won't take long—and see what that particular hell looks like for yourself.'

'I'm sorry,' Jem said, holding up both hands against the barely controlled fury in Aaron's voice. 'And I'm not moralising. I don't know nearly enough about it to have an opinion. I'm just saying, it was a devil of a risk for you to run.'

Aaron subsided a little. 'I know. Good God, I know. But at the time it felt like the right thing to do. If you knew, if you saw… The nurse who led us was an inspiring woman, very like Ella in her way. She blazed. And she had seen too many deaths, and not one of our patients suffered complications, Jem. Not a single one.'

'And Toby found out?'

Aaron exhaled. 'Apparently so.'

'How?'

'I don't know. I had no idea he knew before that night. I didn't even know during the argument in the Mitre. He spoke privately to Ella before I arrived.'

'And what happened afterwards?'

'We left the Mitre, Ella and I, both furious. I asked her if she knew what Toby had meant when he said he could deal with me, and she told me he had found out somehow. You must realise that if he'd gone to the police, it would have brought down a lot more than me. The nurse and doctor, the people who sent women our way, the women who had had procedures. God knows what harm he could have done, purely to be rid of me.'

'Yes,' Jem said. 'And I'm sorry to say it, but that sounds like an awfully good reason for you to make sure he didn't talk.'

'Jem—'

'Hear me out. If Toby was threatening you with a life sentence, plus all the consequences to others, I can see how you might defend yourself. I could understand it if you did.'

'Well, I didn't,' Aaron said. He looked immensely weary all at once. 'We had the row in the Mitre, and I never set eyes on him again. Ella and I went off to walk and talk it out. We discussed what we were to do, and what might happen if Toby was cad enough to go to the police.'

'What *were* you going to do?'

Aaron's jaw tightened. 'I concluded that we had to let him win.'

Jem blinked. 'You broke off the engagement?'

'What else could I do? Hold fast to my beloved at any price like some damn fool romantic hero in a novel? Murder her twin brother? Don't be ridiculous. Of course we ended it. He'd won, and there was no course remaining except to hope he was magnanimous in victory.'

'What did Ella think of that?'

Aaron's face tightened. 'Leave Ella out of it.'

'That's not really possible, is it? Did you both agree that you had to break the engagement?' Jem couldn't imagine her acquiescing. She'd wanted Aaron, and she would not have backed down lightly.

'We discussed it. The conclusion was obvious.'

'Did she think so?'

'Ella understood the situation as well as I did.' His voice was stiff.

Nicky had once told Aaron, *If you must lie, confine it to single words. The more you speak, the more embarrassingly obvious it becomes.* Jem nodded. 'And she went and spoke to Toby? To tell him he'd won? And then the two of you—newly disengaged—spent the next hour or so walking in the Parks. It must have been difficult, spending that long together when you'd just decided to end things.'

'Naturally.'

'And Ella must have had a very difficult conversation with Toby too. How did she say it went?'

'He accepted her assurance that we would not marry and assured her he would take no action against me.'

'And she believed him?'

'Toby was a gentleman,' Aaron said, then held up his hands at Jem's look. 'All right, yes, but he gave his word all the same. He'd won. Why would he pursue the matter?'

Jem could think of several reasons, but they didn't matter because he didn't believe any of it. Aaron had been telling the truth about the abortion ring, he was sure, but none of this about Ella sounded remotely plausible. 'Why did you and Ella end things?'

'I just told you.'

'No, afterwards. Toby was no longer a threat. You could have married. Why didn't you?'

'That is none of your business.'

'But you must have considered it. You hadn't wanted to break things off, and once he was dead, you didn't have to.'

'You seem not to have heard me.'

'Ella said she was with you till ten, when the gates were shut. That gave you an alibi,' Jem said. 'Or, alternatively, it gave her an alibi. Which was it, Aaron?'

'She was with me all that time, and this conversation is over.' Aaron rose. 'And I'd advise you not to continue it with anyone. Who have you told about this?'

'Nobody. Nor will I unless I have to. I'm not trying to cause trouble for anyone except the murderer.'

'But you will,' Aaron said. 'You'll bring us all down, Jem. Stop.'

'Who killed Toby?'

Aaron gave Jem a long look, up and down. 'Do you know something? I really don't give a damn.'

On which he left, shutting the door with some force.

Jem flopped back on his bed to think. Suppose Ella had killed Toby. Suppose she had left Aaron while the back gates were still open, and returned to Toby's room, to confront the brother who had thwarted her love affair and intended to control her life. Suppose she had lied about her movements the next day, and asked Aaron to support that lie. He would not have refused her, Jem was quite sure, but he would have asked himself why she was lying.

And they had never married, and Aaron was still sticking doggedly to the alibi she'd forced on him.

Aaron would rather be suspected of murder his whole life than see Ella, and perhaps Prue, suffer. Jem considered that and, for a moment, his pursuit of some abstract truth seemed rather contemptible.

Toby, he reminded himself. Toby was dead. Jem was living in limbo. They *needed* the truth.

Even Aaron probably needed the truth because he thought it was Ella, and he'd never married anyone else. Did he still love her? Did she still love him? Had she killed her own brother for her lover's sake and found herself rejected, guilty, and alone?

'Christ,' Jem said aloud. His voice was a little raspy, and very small in the stark, cold room.

CHAPTER 18

Jem forced himself off the bed around six o'clock. He'd thought and fretted and, surprisingly, drowsed a little, and he was still entirely unsure what he should do.

He laced himself back into his built-up shoe, deciding that he would have an early dinner, alone, and an early night. He would sleep on what he'd learned and make a decision in the morning. He would not go to Staircase Thirteen to put it all on Nicky's shoulders. That wasn't fair, or right, or even sensible.

He had once read that very whimsical book by Mr Dodgson of Christ Church, published under another name because mathematicians weren't supposed to write nonsense. There was a character in it, the White Queen, who prided herself on her ability to believe six impossible things before breakfast. Jem wished he could do the same, because the mutually incompatible possibilities were jostling in his head now, all true, all false.

It was Ella, because Toby threatened Aaron.

It was Prue, because Toby got her pregnant and abandoned her.

It was Nicky, because he loved Toby.

There was a thin stream of gowned students coming out of Old Quad, from chapel or the library; he could imagine Nicky among them in full-length academic regalia, carrying it off as he had that absurd fur coat once upon a time. Jem kept his head down, just in case.

He went up to Seal's, for lack of better ideas. The icy air had thickened noticeably and had a sour muddy, chemical taste to it; there would be a full-scale pea-souper fog by tomorrow. He found a table and ordered beef broth as a cheap way to feel full. Students came in around him, shedding coats and college scarves, talking loudly. Jem leafed through a newspaper and ignored them.

He couldn't have said what made him look up. A slight hush, a voice not consciously heard, an instinct? He only knew that he raised his head and saw Aaron once more. With Ella.

Jem stared, barely believing it. Aaron had a hand under Ella's arm. Neither of them looked happy. But they were together.

Jem ducked his head. It was an instinctive response not to let them see him, and indeed they didn't, settling a few yards away.

He stared unseeingly at the table. He'd felt a single, agonising pang through his heart as they went by, which, he realised, was precisely because they hadn't seen him. They hadn't spotted him, called his name, swept him up as friends did, and the hurt of that was startling.

Of course they hadn't: it was ten years since that would have mattered. But what the devil were Ella and Aaron doing in Oxford, and one another's company?

Aaron had led him to believe that he had no contact with Ella. If that had been a lie, if they had remained together all along, in secret, away from the world's eyes…

That changed everything.

It would have been without benefit of marriage, but Jem was quite sure that Ella would count herself New Woman enough not to care. Aaron was far more conventional, and an honourable man—or so Jem had thought—but Aaron had claimed not to have seen Ella in years, and here they were together. After Jem had sent them each a letter claiming he knew their secret.

And Aaron was physically powerful, and Ella was ruthless, and if one of them was a murderer, then the other one knew, had always known. What if they'd been in it together from the start? What if they'd come after Jem now?

You're panicking, he told himself. He gripped his wrists, feeling the pulse in each with his thumbs, concentrating on his breathing. He wanted, urgently, to flee to Nicky for shelter, or support—to hide behind him, frankly, because he'd have given anything for a physically competent ally—but he'd have to pass them to reach the door. They might look round and see him, and then what?

He needed to calm down and pay attention. He glanced surreptitiously up at them, feeling absurdly like the jealous husband in a French farce. Aaron gave the waitress their order, and then turned to Ella and spoke in a low voice. Jem couldn't hear anything, to his frustration. According to detective novels, he should have slipped quietly over and concealed himself behind a handy pot plant to eavesdrop, but Seal's was as inadequate in the matter of pot plants as Jem was in surreptitious movement. He'd just have to sit here until they left and pray they didn't spot him.

He spooned broth into his mouth without tasting it, reminding himself to turn the pages of his newspaper occasionally, as though he could concentrate on the role free trade was playing in the imminent collapse of the government.

The logic of it was stark and clear. Toby had threatened to reveal their secret and had died. Now Jem had written a quasi-blackmailing letter, and here they were to deal with him.

His throat was closing, and the rich smell of broth made his stomach roil. He left half the bowl and sat trapped until a scrape of chair legs and ring of coins told him they were finally leaving. By the time he'd paid and made his way out between the tables, Aaron and Ella had long vanished into the crowds, or down one of Oxford's many curving side streets.

As long as they *had* gone. As long as they weren't waiting for him.

Jem hurried back to Anselm's as best he could, feeling his shoulder blades itch where someone might be watching him.

Moffat was manning the lodge. Jem asked without preamble, 'Is Dr Oyede staying here?'

'Dr…' Moffat began, reaching for his book automatically, then his mouth dropped open. 'Mr *Aaron* Oyede?'

'Yes.'

Moffat's mouth worked. 'But—Is he expected?'

'Is he staying in college?' Jem repeated. 'Can you please just tell me that?'

'Ah, I thought I recognised those tones,' said an impossibly familiar voice behind him. 'Hello, Jem.'

Jem turned. Hugo stood in the doorway of the Lodge, tall and imposing in an expensive greatcoat. Moffat made a stifled noise, as well he might. Jem couldn't forbear a glance back at him. The horrified look in his eyes appeared to demand, *Is this a reunion?*

'Good evening, old man,' Hugo said with a smile. 'What a stroke of luck. Have you eaten?'

They went to the Randolph Hotel for a drink since Hugo was staying there. The dining room looked exactly as it had ten years ago, when Toby had treated them all to wildly extravagant meals and they'd all laughed and argued into the night. Jem declined food but accepted a glass of wine. Once the drinks were poured, Hugo sat back and looked around.

'It hasn't changed, has it?'

'Not much. Nothing here does.'

'I miss it,' Hugo said. 'I didn't quite realise how much. I imagine we all simply tried to forget about it for sanity's sake, but since you came to me, I haven't been able to stop thinking about the old place, and my old friends. Don't think I'm grumbling: the Commons is the most exciting environment. But we had something special here, didn't we?'

Did we, really? 'Yes. I suppose so.'

'Well. I hate to say this, old man, but I think I must. What about that letter?'

'Uh…'

'I'm going to take a wild stab in the dark here,' Hugo said, 'which is that *you* were taking a wild stab in the dark. Was that just a fishing trip? Because if you have been fed a story about me, I should like to know what it is, and have the opportunity to defend myself. Slanders and nonsense are an inevitable consequence of being a public figure, but between us at least I should like a fair hearing.'

Hugo didn't sound angry, or accusatory, and his calm good sense sluiced down the hothouse in Jem's brain, in much the same way as a bucket of water to the face.

'All right, yes,' he said. 'I was fishing.'

Hugo sighed. 'Good. It really is an unnerving thing to receive a letter like that, you know, even if it is undeserved. One starts to wonder if one might have inadvertently embezzled a fortune and forgotten about it. Was that just sent to me, or to everyone?'

'Everyone.'

Hugo clicked his tongue. 'You can't just send people letters telling them you know what they did, old man. We can have secrets without being murderers. Well, on the night of Toby's death, we all learned of a serious offence committed by two members of our group.' He raised an eyebrow, not without sympathy; Jem felt his face flame. 'I don't think you could blame anyone for taking your letter badly, even if they were innocent of Toby's death. And if, God forfend, one of us is guilty, what do you imagine will happen?'

'I dare say I'll find out. I wanted to turn over some stones, to see what's under them.'

'Have you seen anything?' Hugo asked, then immediately held up a hand. 'No, I withdraw that. If you have good reason to suspect someone of Toby's murder, you may call on me for aid, but I don't want to know about my friends' secrets and peccadilloes. And if you have found out anything discreditable this way, I sincerely hope you will treat it in total confidence unless it becomes necessary to do otherwise.'

Discreditable. Jem almost laughed.

Aaron might have faced life in prison. Ella's brother forced the end of her engagement. Nicky hated Toby to madness. Prue was expecting a bastard child. There's too many secrets. I can't cope.

Hugo was frowning. 'Do you want my advice? Write to everyone, withdraw the letter, apologise before you provoke a reaction that might not be pleasant for anyone. I really think it would be best for everyone, including you. You look awfully run-down, you know.'

'It's been a hard few weeks,' Jem said with some understatement, and felt his throat close suddenly. He pressed his lips together.

Hugo's look of sympathy didn't help. 'Look, I'm here to manage a bit of business on the pater's behalf, so I'll be around tomorrow. Why don't you sleep on it, and we'll meet up and talk more? I am worried about you, Jem. I say that as your friend—I hope we can say we're still friends?'

'Yes. Yes, we can.'

'And as your friend, I'd like to be sure you're not running into trouble. I'll stand by you, old chap, but don't do anything else pig-headed. Are you staying at Anselm's?'

'Bascomb Stair.'

'Ugh,' Hugo said. 'They put me in there once as a guest of honour, which is why I always have my secretary book the

Randolph now. I shall find you there, since I will be in seeing the bursar, or you can leave a message for me here.'

Jem had only had a single glass of wine, but he felt its effects on his half-empty stomach as he walked into the darkness of Front Quad and headed for the far corner and the passage to Bascomb Quad. There weren't many students about, though gaslight glowed behind curtains. He passed what had been Nicky's set in the first year, with such a vivid memory of slapping the glass to attract attention that he could feel the wet chill on his palm.

He went on, under the archway. Bascomb Stair was unlit except for the gaslight leaking out the edges of the doorway, and the trees of Bascomb Wood loomed darkly out of the fog. There was nobody around, and the sounds of college life in the distance were extremely faint.

Silence, and shadows, and solitude. Jem hadn't considered himself an overly imaginative man before, but the shadows were very deep tonight, and he stopped because he was afraid to go on.

Nicky. Aaron. Ella. Prue.

He'd been briefly warm at the Randolph, in Hugo's understanding company. He was very cold now, and very alone. It was all too easy to picture some sinister form lying in wait for him, but he felt a momentary dizziness as he tried to give that form Aaron's understanding eyes, or Ella's cool grace, or Nicky's smile.

He couldn't go on like this, loving people and suspecting them at once. A human mind couldn't do that without breaking.

He couldn't just stand in the fog either. He set his teeth and made his way into the staircase and up the stairs.

It was awfully quiet, as was to be expected since Bascomb held only guests and visiting scholars. Jem would right now have appreciated a few rowdy undergraduates making their presence felt. It was also very dark since the gas was only lit on the ground floor. He felt his way up to the second floor, hearing his breath and his own footsteps, telling himself it was childish to be afraid of the dark. They ought to light the gas up here, though: it was unwelcoming.

There was an oddly chemical smell, too, and he wondered if the gas had simply gone out. He plodded up one more step, leaning heavily on the banister, and his good foot skidded wildly out and back from under him. He plunged forward, instinctively clutching the rail, pain from the sudden weight on his club foot stabbing up his leg, and his chest hit the edge of a stair with a thump that jarred the breath out of him.

He lay there gasping for a moment, splayed over the staircase, shocked and disoriented. There was something sticky and wet on his face and chest. He wondered for a panicked second if it was blood, if the pain of impact was masking something worse. His arm felt half wrenched out of its socket where it was twisted up behind him, still gripping the rail.

He had to get up. He put his other hand on the wooden stair, and felt it slide smoothly away from him. What the—

There was oil on the staircase. Some unbelievably irresponsible fool had spilled oil at the top of a stair and not cleaned it up. It could have killed someone in this damned steep narrow building.

Especially a man with a bad limp.

Jem lay there for a moment more, taking that in. Then he pulled himself to his knees, feeling the stairs for dry wood, edging up with excruciating care. His chest hurt where he'd hit the stair edge.

The gas fitting in his corridor was just visible in the gloom. He propped himself against the wall because his hands were shaking, reached for the matchbox, struck one, and lit the gas.

Light bloomed out and showed him he'd been right. A pool of oil lay at the top of the stairs and coated the first three steps down. He contemplated that for a moment, then turned to his door, bringing the key out of his pocket. He put it to the lock, only registering as he did it that something looked wrong; the door swung a little ajar under the pressure.

Jem pushed it all the way. He might as well. If anyone was waiting for him in there, he didn't stand a chance of getting away.

He lit the gaslight inside and looked around.

His clothes were thrown on the floor in a heap, and his bottle of ink had been upended over the bed. The room was littered with pages from *Murder at the University* and *The St Anselm Murder*, ripped out and flung around. Everything had been swept off the desk, except for one piece of paper, placed carefully in the centre. When he came closer, he saw it was a page from Nicky's pamphlet, the Anglo-Saxon translation.

'Well, that's a gentle hint,' Jem said out loud, his voice thin in the stark, ruined room.

He couldn't sleep in here, not with a broken lock and an ink-sodden bed. He vaguely wondered if he'd be charged for damage to the room: that was the last thing he needed.

Someone had tried to kill him.

He sat on the chair for a moment, gathering his strength, then he picked up his few vital belongings and the page of the pamphlet, and looked in the litter for his notebook, first slowly and then scrabbling through the drifts of paper and peering under furniture until he had to face the fact that it had gone.

Someone had ransacked his room, stolen his notebook and poured oil on the stairs. Jem wished with all his heart he had never put in his resignation, never left London, never done this bloody stupid thing in the first place.

He made his way back down the treacherous stair, with a pounding heart and a death-grip on the rail. He had to stop for a moment at the bottom, leaning on the banister, both because his foot was really hurting now and because he didn't want to go out in the cold and the dark where someone who had tried to kill him might be waiting. If he'd had anyone to ask—a stranger, a scout—he'd have begged them to accompany him outside, but there was nobody.

He took a single step outside into the darkness, and a voice said, 'Jem.'

He yelled aloud, whipping round and stumbling. A hard hand caught his arm. Nicky.

Nicky had been there, waiting outside Bascomb Stair, and the terror and pain and betrayal were so overwhelming he couldn't speak, couldn't try to run, couldn't do anything but think, desperately, *Not Nicky, not like this…*

'Jem? Are you all right?'

'No,' he managed. 'I'm bloody not.'

Nicky stepped into the pool of light from the door, brows snapping together. 'What in God's name has happened to you?'

Don't you know? Jem wanted to snarl. He felt himself lurch as his legs almost gave way, and Nicky's hand tightened. Taking his weight, keeping him up.

Nicky had always, always been careful of his foot.

'There's oil on the stairs,' he said. 'Lots of it. I fell. And my room's been vandalised, broken into, my books torn up, and I need to tell the Lodge but—but my foot hurts.'

Nicky hissed. 'Wait here. I'll go and look.'

'No!' Jem couldn't be left alone, not out in the dark. He saw Nicky's expression and moderated his voice. 'No, please. Could you—could you just walk with me to the Lodge?'

Nicky gave him a long look, up and down. 'No, you bloody fool. I shall walk you to my rooms, which are warm, dry and secure. I will then go and look at whatever's happened, and bring the porter to you before you know it.'

Jem wanted that, very badly, and resented the fear and the pain that made him want it. He stared up at Nicky, unable to agree or refuse.

Nicky sighed irritably. 'Do come on. It's freezing.'

If he'd wanted Jem in his rooms for nefarious purposes, he'd had plenty of opportunity before now. Jem gripped his arm, leaning heavily on him, and half-hopped three paces before Nicky said, 'Oh, for God's sake. Come here.'

'What do you mean?'

Nicky bent forward. 'Arm round my neck. Don't be stupid, I won't drop you.' His arms went round Jem, he straightened with a grunt of effort, and then Jem was off his feet, being carried past the Master's lodging at a briskly determined pace.

'Nicky!' he protested weakly, because Nicky couldn't just pick him up like this, and because he'd have liked to bury his face in Nicky's gowned shoulder. He hoped nobody was watching, and wasn't sure he cared if they were.

'You really do weigh an extraordinary amount.' Nicky strode through the arch, lean muscles tense with effort. 'You must have lead bones. Nearly there now. I very irresponsibly put the kettle on before I came out looking for you, so it should be boiling shortly.' He let Jem slip down, bracing him carefully, unlocked the door, and ushered him in. 'All right, let's have your coat. Good God, you're filthy. Sit. I will return with a porter, remember.'

Don't be waiting naked in my bed, Jem supposed that meant, though he had no intention of that. He let himself collapse into

Nicky's armchair in front of the fire, a filthy, exhausted mess, as Nicky went out and turned the key in the lock behind him.

That had been an attack on him, and the only question was by whom. Jem would have loved to believe it was a student rag, or that he'd been targeted by the sort of person who wrote anonymous letters. That would have been a comforting conclusion, given the alternatives.

Aaron, Ella, Nicky. Hugo, even, because, although he was far from likely, he was here. Maybe Prue had come to Oxford too and they had the full house. He almost laughed.

Nicky reappeared some time later with the duty porter, who looked decidedly harried, as people tended to when Nicky started in on them. He seemed to have persuaded the unfortunate man that Jem was on the verge of launching an expensive lawsuit.

'I'm dreadfully sorry, sir,' the porter said, several times. 'It's a shocking piece of spite. There's nobody else on that floor, but I'll go and put sand down at once. Do you need a doctor called?'

'No, no, I'm fine.'

'For now,' Nicky said. 'If his foot's playing up tomorrow, we'll naturally call one at the college's expense.'

'Er, yes, Dr Rook. I've seen to your things, Mr Kite. Was there anything missing that you noticed?'

'Notebook,' Jem said. Between the bad night, the warm fire, the shock, he was barely able to form words. 'Card binding. Did you find it?'

'Can't say I did, sir, I'm sorry. I'll have another look when I put the sand down. Was you wanting to call the police?'

'Uh…I don't know.'

'Probably not now,' Nicky said. 'It seems to be an extremely dangerous prank, or piece of malice, but it's past ten and I should rather consult the Master before making it a police matter. More urgent is the question of where he can sleep.'

'Yes, Dr Rook. Uh—'

'Your sofa's fine,' Jem said.

'My sofa it is, then, and he'll need a new room—which will be on the ground floor, I don't care what staircase—in the morning. Thank you, Drayton. I shall inform the Master tomorrow, but I think the priority now is ensuring nobody else risks injury. If I can leave that to you…?'

'Yes, Dr Rook.'

'Thank you.' Nicky escorted the man out and shut the door behind him, locking it. 'Christ alive, you look a state. Is there anything else I need to know before I put you to bed?'

'Did you see the room?' Jem managed.

'I did. You've got under someone's skin, my Jeremy. I did warn you.'

'So've you,' Jem pointed out but couldn't quite remember why he said it.

'I always do. You need to get those oily rags off and get to bed, you're half-dead. I'll lend you a nightshirt.'

CHAPTER 19

Jem woke up in a bed that smelled of Nicky. He sat up sharply and felt a stab of pain across his chest. He peered down into the billowing oversized nightshirt he wore and saw the beginnings of a nasty line of bruising.

He was alone. He looked around the dim bedroom, casting about for a clock, and saw that it was past nine. He got up, moving with caution, and rapped on the door to Nicky's sitting room, in case there was a tutorial taking place in icy silence; it seemed unlikely, but he wouldn't put it past Nicky. No answer came, so he helped himself to Nicky's quilted dressing gown, which was a rich mahogany shade and came down to his ankles, and poked his head round the door.

There was a fire, going very nicely, and breakfast things—tea, bread and butter, anchovy paste—laid out on the little table in front of it, plus a note. Jem picked it up.

Jeremy

Help yourself to breakfast and then go back to bed. I have sent your clothes for laundry. I will be back some time after eleven. Ignore any knocking; it will be students, thus unimportant.

Nicholas

He was trapped in a nightshirt. For heaven's sake, he had other clothes in his room in Bascomb Stair; someone might have thought to bring them. It was typical of Nicky. The whole note was typical, in fact. Jem didn't know anyone else who'd use semicolons in a brief scrawl, and he hadn't realised how much he'd missed that sort of thing.

He made himself a pot of tea and several slices of toast, lavishly spread with butter and Gentleman's Relish, which he hadn't had in years. It felt decadent to be lolling around in Nicky's nightshirt and gown. It felt like old times. It felt safe.

He felt safe in Nicky's rooms, and that was one more impossible, contradictory thing to add to the pile.

By the time he'd consumed his breakfast, cleared up, and had a wash, it was close to ten. He wanted to be doing something useful, and decided to make some notes, which gave him a squirm of worry about what had happened to his notebook. He had not, thank God, written up yesterday's conversation with Aaron, but there was enough in there about Prue's personal situation to make him feel exceedingly worried at it being in malicious hands.

He needed a bit of paper and a pencil. Nicky's desk was large and covered with stacks of paper, ordered if not precisely orderly. Essays, marked and yet to be marked; piles of books with bits of paper sticking out as bookmarks; what seemed to be a translation in progress, dark with crossings-out and scribbles. It was odd to see Nicky from this angle, ten years into his adult life and career.

There was a sheaf of what looked like blank paper with a large, battered diary on top. Jem lifted that off and saw the crumpled page from Nicky's pamphlet that had been left on his desk. Nicky must have found it in the pocket of his oily jacket. Jem picked it up, along with pencil and paper, and retired to the chair by the fire.

He made brief notes on everything he could remember of yesterday in the most obscure and unreadable manner he could achieve, then took a second piece with the intention of summarising everything he'd learned over the past week or so. He scrawled *Conclusions* at the top, underlined it, and then spent several minutes looking at the blank page.

Aaron. From what he had told Jem, a lot of lives including his own had hung on Toby's silence. Aaron had lied about his lack of contact with Ella, known where Jem was staying in college, and doubtless seen the notebook on his desk, full of incriminatory details.

Ella, so strong and determined. She'd had a powerful motive for Toby's murder, and, if she was still with Aaron, an equally powerful one to stop Jem's investigation in his tracks. She planned ahead. She was ruthless. He could imagine her pouring oil on a stair, in a way that seemed unlikely for Aaron.

Aaron and Ella collaborating. Would they risk it? Could they really give each other another alibi, after the last time? Then again, would they need to? If he'd broken his neck on the stairs, with no record of his investigations and findings, would the police have called it an accident? Would anyone—Nicky, or Hugo, or Prue—have agitated for a murder investigation? It was an uncomfortable thought, among many uncomfortable thoughts.

Jem screwed up the *Conclusions* paper and threw it into the fire. The pamphlet page fluttered off his knee with the movement; he slapped it against his leg to catch it.

Why had Aaron, or Ella, or whoever had wrecked the room, left that on the desk? It must surely be an attempt to cast blame on Nicky, but if so, it was a feeble one, akin to *The St Anselm Murder* with its sly quotation from *Beowulf*. It was spiteful, Jem thought, and that was another little niggle because, whatever else you could say of Aaron and Ella, they weren't spiteful. He could imagine Aaron killing if he felt it necessary; he couldn't imagine him upending a bottle of ink onto a bed.

But who else might it have been? It wouldn't have been Nicky unless the page was in the nature of a confession, which was both implausible and rather frightening to consider. Hugo would have had time if he'd gone to Bascomb Stair while Jem was trapped in Seal's, assuming he'd been in the college then: Jem wasn't sure if he'd been going in or coming out when they met in the Lodge. But why would he have taken such extravagantly unpleasant steps at all, still less invited Jem for a kindly drink afterwards? And that was everyone, unless Prue had arrived in Oxford, which would probably give Moffat an aneurysm.

Jem picked up the page and read the section of poetry.

I have very few people I prize in this land,
very few firm friends. And thus my soul is sorrowed:
That I found for myself a most marvellous man
though unfortunate and unhappy,
concealing his thoughts, plotting terrible crime,
with a blithe bearing. Often we gave our oath
that death alone could divide us,
Nothing else. But now that is changed—
now it is as if it had never been,
our broken bond. Both far and near, I must
bear the bitter hate of my beloved.

'God,' he said aloud.

It could have been written for Nicky and Toby, or by Nicky about Toby. *Unfortunate and unhappy, concealing his thoughts, plotting terrible crime with a blithe bearing.* Doubtless the translation would be faithful to the original, but the picture it drew of Toby in those last days was horribly accurate. Had Nicky thought of Toby as he wrote of a treacherous man and a broken bond of love? He must have done, surely. He'd translated this ancient cry of pain into words so raw that they jangled Jem's nerves, and then published the blasted thing as a pamphlet.

Might they have repaired their friendship, given time? They'd all forgiven Nicky for *Cymbeline*, or at least they'd all tacitly agreed to avoid the subject; could they have pretended to forget about that terrible night if it hadn't been the last one? Would Toby have forgiven them for whatever wrongs he thought they'd committed? Jem had felt truly hated that night for perhaps the first time in his life; he'd had plenty of sneers and casual mockery, but Toby had spoken as though Jem's crippled foot, his lowly background, his *existence* were as much an affront as his liaison with Nicky. *The bitter hate of my beloved.*

It was only a translation. He couldn't look to it for answers. Still, it was a damned unnerving thing to find left for his attention in a ruined room.

He couldn't sit here in an oversized nightshirt like an invalid, thinking of miseries and guilt. He needed to get dressed and get out, but his other clothes would still be in his room, and he couldn't face the stairs. If he walked up to the Lodge, surely a porter would go and fetch them for him? He could put on his coat and shoes over his night things to go and ask; he'd look highly eccentric, but this was Oxford.

There was no sign of his coat on the coat-rack, or of his shoes anywhere. Jem looked around, wondering where on earth Nicky had concealed them. He tried a couple of cupboards and found nothing.

This was bizarre. His coat might have suffered from the oil and required cleaning, but his shoes had not, and he needed them; Nicky knew perfectly well they had to be specially made and cost more than Jem could easily afford. He wouldn't have been careless with Jem's shoes. He looked in every cupboard, telling himself he was missing somewhere obvious, then went through to the bedroom again, and tried the wardrobe. His coat wasn't hanging up among Nicky's suits; he went through them twice to check, with a rising and stupid feeling of panic. Of course he'd been wearing a coat when he came here; of course Nicky hadn't thrown his one adequate winter garment away—

He could smell oil. Just a faint scent, but there.

Jem looked down. There was a blanket on top of a pile at the bottom of the wardrobe. He picked the blanket up and saw it covered his coat, neatly folded on top of his small, battered suitcase, next to which were his shoes.

He hauled the lot out, noting the weight of the case, and was absurdly relieved to discover his clothes and other possessions were inside, carefully packed, presumably by the porter. Well, that made sense; of course he should have brought Jem's things here. But why had Nicky hidden them away like that?

The note had said *I have sent your clothes for laundry.* It wasn't a lie, as such, but Nicky could have added *Your other clothes are in the wardrobe.* He hadn't.

In the wardrobe, hidden under a blanket. Jem dressed slowly, with automatic movements, thinking about why Nicky might have wanted to force him to stay in here.

He finished dressing and decided to shave since he hadn't bothered yesterday. He was making the best job he could of a sadly creased necktie when he heard the sound of the door being unlocked, footsteps, and the key turning again. There was a brief silence, then Nicky, in the other room, said, 'Jem?'

'Here.' Jem came through into the sitting room, dressed except for his stockinged feet, and saw Nicky's brows twitch. He cocked his head. 'Did you hide my clothes?'

'I hoped you'd have the sense to rest.'

'Why did you hide them?'

'I put them away. Put the kettle on, will you?'

It had to be filled at the bedroom sink. Jem returned to see Nicky standing by the fire, holding a small piece of paper. The pamphlet page, he realised.

'You found that,' Jem noted.

'In your jacket last night.'

'It had been left on the desk, in the middle, lined up, so I—or whoever came in—couldn't miss it.'

Nicky went very still. 'Is that so.'

'It's hard not to feel there was malicious intent there.'

'It is, isn't it.' His voice was flat.

'I'm hardly going to take the word of whoever sent me down those stairs. But it does seem like someone wanted me—or anyone looking into what had happened to me—to look at you. Why would they do that?'

'Everyone looks at me,' Nicky said. 'And since you are looking at me now, what do you conclude?'

'A devil of a lot,' Jem said. 'Can we sit down? I think I may know who killed Toby. Or, at least, I've found a damned good reason for it to be done.'

Nicky's face was tense, expressionless. 'And that is?'

'A crime. Something that could get one of us in appalling trouble. It will ruin this person if I go to the police with what I know. And if I'm wrong about Toby's death, that would be an unspeakable thing to do.'

'I did warn you,' Nicky said. His voice was flat.

The kettle was sounding shrilly, like a police whistle. Nicky took it off the fire and poured water into the teapot. Jem watched him as he made the preparations, trying to make a decision. What was right, what was fair, who to trust. Nicky worked without speaking, letting the silence stretch till the pressure on Jem's chest forced him into speech.

He took a deep breath as Nicky handed him a cup. 'Aaron was doing something, at college, that could have got him a very long prison sentence. Not something terrible—or some people would count it terrible, perhaps—'

'A crime against law but not humanity?' Nicky suggested. 'My speciality.'

'Toby found out. He threatened to go to the police if Aaron didn't end things with Ella.'

Nicky's face was very still. 'And?'

'He says they broke it off that night. That she went to Toby to tell him he'd won. And he still claims he was with her all evening after she left Toby, although he'd insisted on breaking the engagement and I gather she didn't want to. I don't believe that.'

'It doesn't sound likely. I can't I imagine Ella taking that well. Any of it.'

'No. And Aaron said he hadn't seen her since, but they were together in Seal's yesterday. I saw them having coffee in the afternoon.'

'Were they now,' Nicky said slowly. 'But that doesn't necessarily mean they have been associating in secret.'

He was always quick. 'All I know is, I wrote those letters and now they're here, in Oxford, together. And it's not just them. Hugo is here too.'

'Hugo? What the blazes is he in Oxford for? The government is teetering and there's talk of Balfour resigning at any moment. The Liberals might be asked to form a government as early as next week. I can't imagine him leaving Westminster except to sleep, and perhaps not even that.'

'Well, he's here. On his father's business, he said. He sought me out because of the letter.'

Nicky grimaced. 'What did he have to say?'

'He was awfully nice, actually. He said he wanted to be sure I was all right and that he'd stand by me if there was trouble.'

'Really.' Nicky tapped his fingertips together, slow and reflective. 'Did you come back to your room at any time between all this dissipation with old friends?'

'No. I left around six, saw Aaron and Ella in Seal's, then I met Hugo in the Lodge, and we went to the Randolph for a drink.'

'So your room was vandalised between six and whatever time it was I found you?'

'Yes. It could have been Aaron or Ella, while I was with Hugo.'

'Or it could have been Hugo while you were in Seal's with Aaron and Ella. Or it could have been me at any time. Or someone else.'

'Aaron could have faced a life sentence for what he did,' Jem said. 'Toby was blackmailing him and succeeded in breaking up their love affair. It was one of them, with the other's knowledge. I think the evidence is pretty convincing.'

'And if you take it to the police and you're wrong, Aaron could presumably still face a gaol sentence for these nameless and, I assume, victimless crimes, despite not being the killer,' Nicky said. 'Are you prepared to risk that over the death of a blackmailer?'

Jem felt the breath rush out of his lungs. 'He wasn't just a blackmailer. He was *Toby*.'

'I know who he was. Better than you, I suspect. That aspect of his personality was not unprecedented, and it was worsening. Or perhaps he just hadn't previously found himself so affronted, I don't know. Do you recall the Sherlock Holmes story of the blackmailer who is murdered? What does Holmes say? "There are certain crimes which the law cannot touch, and which justify private revenge."'

'Holmes is fictional,' Jem said. 'And if it was Aaron or Ella who went through my room and poured oil on the stairs in an effort to break my neck, they also tried to incriminate you with that page of Anglo-Saxon. So I'm not sure why you're defending them.'

'Because neither Aaron nor Ella killed Toby.'

'How can you say that?' Jem demanded. 'How can you assert they didn't kill him if you don't know who did?'

Nicky raised a brow. 'In the same way I can assert that the prime minister didn't do it. I still have some small faith in a few of my fellow men.'

'Well, I don't,' Jem said. 'I think the person who booby-trapped that stair did so to stop me looking into the murder, and I'm not going to back down in the face of that.'

'Why the hell not? You might have died!'

'Yes. I might. And, you know, it's one thing to say we should let Toby's killer go free because they were intolerably provoked, but that person could have killed me yesterday. We're talking about a potential double murderer now. Is that still forgivable?'

'Jem…' Nicky paused, and exhaled. 'Will you promise me something? Will you give me, let's say, twenty-four hours before you go to the police or make any accusations to anyone?'

'Why?'

'Because I want to think about this, and I have tutorials from twelve and going on all afternoon. There are certain other facts you should take into account before you accuse Aaron and'—he kept going over Jem's interruption—'an accusation could ruin him even if he is not accused or convicted of murder. For God's sake, Toby's been dead for ten years. Another day won't hurt.'

'What other facts? What do you know?'

'I am asking for twenty-four hours before you destroy a life, and I am telling you that there are things you don't know and need to know. Can you give me that trust, and that time, Jem? For the sake of past glories?'

Jem swallowed hard. 'Why can't you tell me now?'

'Because I have a student arriving in five minutes. Fine: just give me the day. Only that. Meet me back here at seven, and we will talk then.'

'All right,' Jem said. 'But after that, I act.'

'Understood. At seven. I hate to throw you out, but there is an illiterate on his way, fearing my undivided attention.'

Jem retrieved his belongings from the bedroom and made his way out, with a distinctly queasy feeling about the day to come.

He went to the Lodge first to speak to Moffat about the vandalism. The Head Porter was suitably apologetic, though Jem couldn't help but feel he was being regarded with a jaundiced eye. He was trouble and had brought trouble back to the college.

'Very bad business, Mr Kite,' Moffat said. 'Very nasty accident.'

'It wasn't really an—'

'We've given you a room on the ground floor of Bascomb instead, as Dr Rook requested. You'll be with us two more days, I think?'

That was right. It was Friday now, and he'd booked for a week. 'I think so. I might need to stay a little longer, but—'

'Well, do let the Lodge know, Mr Kite, and we'll see if that's possible.'

If that's possible, not *We'll see that done*. 'Right. Uh, I think the porter last night took my stained clothes?'

'They'll be brought to your room, Mr Kite. And I hope we won't see any more accidents.'

CHAPTER 20

Jem needed time alone. Nicky had used to do that; he'd suddenly announce, 'I must have solitude,' and head off for long walks up to Port Meadow or along the Cherwell. Sometimes Jem had seen him striding along while he'd been in the boats. Jem would have liked to do that himself, but there was a steady dull ache in his foot, and the full pea-souper had closed in at last, muffling sight and sound in its greasy blanket. Front Quad was wreathed in grey, and Broad Street a dim and bleak prospect outside.

He went to Blackwell's and picked up a new notebook and pencil, as well as cheap editions of books he'd wanted, *The Club of Queer Trades* and *The Four Just Men*. It was an unjustifiable indulgence and he winced as he fished out the coins, but he needed not to think for a while.

So he didn't. He lay on the bed in his ground-floor room and read *The Four Just Men* through, held by the drama and letting the mystery pass him by. He did not stop to reflect that its heroes were vigilantes, imposing justice in the teeth of inadequate law, or try to guess the solution to the locked-room mystery. He just wanted space not to think about the shadows closing around him, and, when he came to the end of *The Four Just Men*, he moved straight on to the Chesterton. Anything but his own company.

He'd read a couple of the stories when there was a knock on the door. He rolled out of bed to unlock it, and saw Hugo.

'Hello, old man. Lounging around?'

'Last night was tiring. Do sit down.'

Hugo looked around the small, bare room. There wasn't even a kettle. 'Would you care to come out for a cup of coffee?'

'My foot hurts,' Jem said. Hugo blinked, startled, and it occurred to Jem that he might never have said such a thing before. He'd been so desperate not to be limping Tiny Tim among the splendid physical presence of his friends. 'If you don't mind—'

'Of course, old man.' Hugo took the straight-backed chair, while Jem sat on the bed. 'So, what were you up to last night? You didn't look fit for adventures, I must say.'

'I wasn't. Unfortunately, while I was out, someone ragged my room and booby-trapped the stairs.' He gave Hugo a brief, unemotional account. He felt anything but unemotional, yet somehow his feelings seemed to be tidied away, hidden in a wardrobe under a blanket.

'Good *Lord*, Jem. Well. You wanted to stir things up and look what you've provoked. For heaven's sake. Will you please listen—'

'I know, you want me to stop. It's a bit late. Everyone's in Oxford now, did you know? All of us except Prue, and I can hardly blame her for not wanting to come back under the circumstances.'

Hugo's eyes widened. 'Circumstances?'

Jem felt an urge to shake him. Tall, privileged, wealthy Hugo, sailing through life without noticing the people frantically paddling to keep afloat. 'It ruined her life—this place, this group of so-called friends. Was it you who told me I'd regret digging all this up? Well, I don't. And the reason I don't is that I've spent ten years in mourning for a wonderful thing that was ripped away from me, and now I know it never existed. I thought we trusted each other, that we cared for each other, but I was wrong, wasn't I? All this time I've been weeping at a grave, and the coffin was empty.'

'Jem—'

'I'm tired, Hugo, and, honestly, I'm sickened,' Jem said over him. 'I believed in you all. And now this.'

'What do you mean by that?' Hugo demanded. 'Are you accusing me of something?'

Jem couldn't bring himself to say no. He wanted to hurt Hugo, in all his confidence and privilege and superiority, to find a weak point in the gleaming, expensive armour, to stick the knife in and twist. 'What are you doing here, when everyone expects your party to be in power by Monday?'

'I beg your pardon?'

'You rushed down to see me when you had that letter. Why aren't you in Westminster now?'

'I can attend to my own career, thank you. If you must know, I was deeply concerned by your letter, and clearly I was right to be.'

'Toby was blackmailing people,' Jem said. 'He was using things he knew to make people do things he wanted, and it seems he knew a lot. Why did you propose to Ella?'

'What? Jem, why are you being like this?'

'Because I'm fed up to the back teeth. I'm tempted to take everything I know to the police, and suggest they do their job.'

'What's stopping you?' Hugo demanded. 'A lingering regard for people for whom you once cared, perhaps?'

'For Prue, at least. I don't want to drag her into this mire; I think she's suffered enough already.'

'Then you should stop this, because she will not emerge from any examination of her behaviour with credit. For God's sake, man, listen to yourself. *Look* at yourself. You are underfed and in clear physical distress, and all this talk of murder and police and past crimes sounds frankly unhealthy. Obsessive. You need a long rest.'

Jem stared at him, incredulous. 'Are you implying I'm unbalanced?'

'It's what happened before, isn't it? You thought too much about all this—about Toby, and his murder, and that business with Nicky—and it was too much for you. Nervous collapse, wasn't that what you called it?'

'I am not having a nervous collapse.'

Hugo ignored him. 'People do odd things under stress. Ten years ago, it was hurling unwarranted recriminations and the kind of things that were said that night. Now you're telling me someone's tried to harm you, and we're all guilty and goodness knows what—'

'Someone did try!' Jem snapped.

'I'm not trying to insult you. I am trying to *help* you, before you at best make a damned fool of yourself, and at worst cause serious harm. You are developing some kind of complex about this, believing God knows what—'

'You don't know what I believe.'

'Well, I hope you believe that I am your friend,' Hugo said. 'And as such, I would be very happy to provide you with a bit of peace and quiet. We've a little place in the country, with an excellent doctor who could take a look at your foot. You could come and stay, get away from it all for a while. And if after, say, a month of rest and good feeding, you still think there is substance to your fears, you'd be in a much better position to make your case. Because, I fear, you're not giving the impression of a reliable witness at the moment. What do you say, old fellow?'

Jem had to take a minute to calm himself. He wanted to shout, and knew very well that wouldn't help, and he also had a horrible sneaking feeling that Hugo had a point. He'd been hungry for weeks, desperate for years, and the conversations and contradictions of the last days were a simmering brew in his mind. He probably looked like a man at the end of his tether, because he was.

'It's very decent of you to offer,' he said as levelly as he could. 'But there is nothing wrong with me. And I am not going to walk away from this.'

'I didn't say walk away, just take a breather. Will you at least think about it? I'm worried for you.'

'You don't need to be.'

'I think I do,' Hugo said. 'Either somebody tore up your things and poured oil on the stairs in a deliberate attempt to threaten and hurt you—and if that's the case, there's someone dangerous and ruthless out there who wants you to stop. Or—'

'Or what?'

'Or that didn't happen,' Hugo said steadily. 'And if it didn't, I am even more worried.'

Jem felt himself going scarlet. 'Of course it happened. Ask Nicky, or the porter who saw the room.'

'I don't doubt the damage was done.'

'Are you suggesting I did it myself?'

'Did you?'

'No!'

Hugo let his exclamation hang in the air for a long moment, then gave a tiny shrug. 'So someone else did, which brings me back to my first point: you are in danger. Potentially serious danger from someone who wants you to stop what you're up to. And, not to put too fine a point on it, you aren't a great hand at self-defence. It would be sensible to pull back and regroup, old chap. At least think about it?'

'You're very kind,' Jem said. 'But I don't need to think about it. I know what I have to do, and I won't be warned off or bought off. I've had enough of being quiet, Hugo. I've been quiet for ten years, and I'm not the only one. It's time for us to speak.'

Hugo stared at him, face unreadable. The silence stretched for a few moments, then he rose.

'Well,' he said. 'The offer stands if you come to your senses. I just ask that you consider it.'

When Hugo had gone, Jem went to stare in the mirror, looking at what other people saw. Prematurely lined eyes ringed with exhaustion, hollow cheeks, greying hair that needed a cut. Shaving had helped, but nothing could hide the expression of fear and desperation, from himself at least. He'd been afraid for so long. It had left its mark.

He couldn't shake off Hugo's words. He knew he wasn't being irrational, or at least that he had good reason for his suspicions, and he knew what nervous collapse felt like. But to hear someone doubt one's sanity in such a calm, kind voice was enough to make a man sick.

There *had* been oil on the stairs. His notebook *had* gone. Nicky *had* hidden his clothes. Or put them tidily away, of course, and Jem had simply, fearfully assumed they were hidden…

No. He wasn't inventing this, and he wasn't collapsing again. He was almost sure of that.

He tried to focus on *The Club of Queer Trades*, but its whimsy couldn't hold his attention. He wished more than anything he could go for a long walk. Stride out in the cold and fog, defy the weather, because he had a good greatcoat and money in his pockets to stop for a pint in some pub with a blazing fire.

He thought of that, sitting on the bed with a blanket doubled over his feet in the small, chilly room, and then started *The Four Just Men* again. Anything to let time pass; anything rather than think about what he was going to do, what he should do, what other people might do in response.

* * *

He was standing at Nicky's door when the chapel clock struck seven. Nicky looked drawn as he let Jem in, paler than usual, lips tense.

'Jeremy. Good evening. Would you care to eat first?'

'No,' Jem said. 'I want to talk. I think we have to.'

Nicky exhaled. 'Yes, we do. *Have* you eaten?'

'I don't want anything.'

'I'd like you to,' Nicky said. 'You look in need of it.'

'Has Hugo been round here, by any chance?' The upswell of rage was instant and overwhelming. How dare he sow doubt about Jem's mental state to Nicky, of all people?

'In fact, he has. God, he's got pompous, hasn't he? Give it another decade and he'll be indistinguishable from every other sleek walrus on the benches. Do you know, he suggested we had a bout with the foils for old times' sake. I was almost tempted to take him up on it as punishment for hubris. Yes, he gave me all sorts of dark warnings about you not looking well, and what did I think about your precarious mental state.'

'And what do you think?'

'That I am not your keeper,' Nicky said. 'I am, however, your host, and I want sustenance even if you don't. I'm making toasted cheese; will you have some?'

Jem just wanted the conversation over. But he said, 'Go on, if you must,' and settled on a chair, watching Nicky's preparations. He moved in silence, with concentration, but not his old limber, youthful grace. Jem's heart hurt.

Nicky handed him a plate and settled back to his own chair. Jem felt too miserable to be hungry, but it smelled wonderful. He nibbled a corner to be polite, and soon found he had finished the slice. Nicky's toasted cheese had always been comforting.

'Another?'

'No, thank you.'

Nicky put his plate down, leaving half of his own portion untouched. 'All right, then.'

'You said you wanted to talk to me,' Jem said. 'I think it's time we did speak. I've had you and Hugo and Aaron tell me to drop this, in your different ways. Aaron made his feelings clear, Hugo cast doubt on my mental state and offered me a quiet place in the country to recuperate, and you took me to bed.'

'Just a damned minute—'

'And of course someone played that little prank with the stairs that might have broken my neck. I'm tired of this. So I am going to the police tomorrow, to tell them everything I know. Prue's pregnancy, Aaron's activities, Ella's lies, Hugo proposing to Ella, you and me, and Toby threatening us all. I will tell them everything, no matter what it does to us all, and no matter what else comes out in the course of it.'

'You're going to ruin us all.'

'Yes.' Jem forced the words out. 'Yes, if that's what it takes. First thing tomorrow, I will ruin us all. Unless you give me a reason not to.'

Their eyes met for a long, silent moment, and then Nicky rose. He stood very tall above Jem, looking down, and Jem had just time to realise that his pulse was accelerating before Nicky turned. He went to the sideboard, poured two glasses of whisky, handed one to Jem, then folded his long limbs back into his chair. 'Well. Right. I suppose you know most of it anyway, don't you?'

'Tell me.'

Nicky knocked back about half his glass in a single swallow. 'Very well. Christ, what am I supposed to say? It's a fair cop. I done it.' His lips moved in a faint, humourless, stillborn smile. 'It was me.'

CHAPTER 21

Jem had once, at school, seen an experiment where a frog had been placed in a glass jar that was then emptied of oxygen. The class had watched, first laughing and then dropping silent as the frog thrashed, and stilled, and died. He'd had nightmares afterwards about being trapped in a chamber, feeling his lungs collapsing inward. He felt that now, and the sense of terrible inevitability too.

He'd known, of course. He wondered if he'd always known.

'Wh—' He had to lick his lips. 'Why?'

'I believe the done thing in detective novels is for the murderer to say it will be a relief to confess. Take my word for it, it is not.' Nicky stared into his glass. 'Where to begin? That night, that term, that year? The previous year, perhaps. That was when life stopped going Toby's way, long before the end.'

He took a meditative sip of whisky. Jem moistened his lips with his own drink and felt the burn of alcohol.

'He was jealous of the rest of us. He tried not to be, at first, but after a while he stopped trying. He wanted to be the lead in that accursed play, and he was not happy to relinquish that glory. I don't remember much about that last day, but I do recall he came round with three bottles of champagne at ten that morning.'

'He got you drunk? On purpose?'

Nicky shrugged. 'I drank it. My fault. But Hugo didn't look like such a romantic hero afterwards, did he? And Toby experienced the unique pleasure of seeing one's friends fail—Hugo, me—and he liked it.'

'God.'

'Then his damned uncle had the child. And there I was in our third year, trying my hardest to believe that the idol of my heart was not in fact a spoiled, capricious, manipulative, whining shit, and finding it harder on a daily basis. Sitting listening to Toby night after night, wondering why I wasn't in the library, or fencing, or with you. Trying to soothe him, because Ella had entirely delegated that duty to me by then, and who can blame her. You can't segment the story, you can't say Toby's murder—my murder—happened on the fifteenth of May as though it were a discrete and singular event. All through that spring and summer I was falling out of love with him; Ella was falling in love with Aaron; and Toby was indulging his temper more and more. He was savage in private.'

'He bruised your wrist.'

'He hit Ella at least once. And then he found out that she returned Aaron's affections, and everything was so much worse. For Christ's sake, drink your whisky. I need another one and I don't want to drink alone.'

Jem took a sip while Nicky poured himself a generous measure. 'And then?'

'And then that night.' Nicky's hand was trembling slightly, just enough to make the amber liquid quiver in the glass. 'You all left; Toby spouted his unpleasantness; I told him he was a cunt and went back to my room. I was sick of him, and of myself for what I'd said to you in order to curry favour with a man I was coming to loathe. Plus, I wanted to work, for which I needed a particular book, and, in the way of irritated nerves, it seemed impossible I should change to another task. So I decided I would go and borrow it and speak to Toby while I was there. I would go and tell him he was a cunt again, in significantly more detail, and we would have the damned great row I should have had with him months before, and it would be the last one because I should not speak to him again afterwards.' He smiled without humour. 'I was right about that, I suppose.'

Jem's own hand was shaking. He thought he might drop his glass. 'And then?'

'I got the book and took the cellarway to Thirty-One because the quad was full of people and I couldn't bear it. I passed nobody: everyone was at Summoner's Gift. That was a relief then, more so later. I found him in a hell of a rage. He said Ella had just been to see him, and the engagement was off, but she had told him that she hated him, would always hate him, and would do her best to ruin him if he harmed Aaron. He might have asked himself how much pain he had caused her to provoke that, but, as ever, he couldn't see past his own hurt. He was spitting. He told me he was going to destroy Aaron and she'd grovel on her knees to accept Hugo when he was done. I said Ella's affairs were surely her business. He said, "No. She's mine." I told him to stop behaving like the most tiresome character in a Jacobean revenge tragedy. And that was when he turned on me.'

Nicky paused to take another mouthful of whisky. His eyes looked very brown in the firelight.

'He told me that Aaron had been involved in carrying out abortions. That's your discovery, of course? Damned fool. I reminded him that not only would Ella never speak to him again if he reported Aaron to the police, but that none of the rest of us would, or any other decent human being. But he had a solution to that. I was going to do it for him.'

'What?'

'He informed me,' Nicky said remotely, 'that he would be obliged if I went to the police station the next day, lodged a complaint against Aaron, and carried through the business until a prosecution was mounted. I told him to go fuck himself. And he said…he said, if I didn't, he would report me to the police, for gross indecency, with you.'

Jem's stomach plunged. 'He—'

'That was the choice he gave me, Jem. Ruin Aaron or be used to ruin you. And at least Aaron's crime would be his own fault, whereas your fall would be entirely down to me. I'd felt guilty as sin about you for much of that term, but I didn't know until then—well.'

Jem couldn't speak. Nicky's knuckles were white on the glass.

'I told him to go to hell. He started talking about you, and what he'd say about you, us. And the thing is, I believed him. He wasn't talking wildly, or rather he was, but I was quite sure it wasn't just words. That he'd do it.'

'You are saying that Toby would really have—But he was my *friend*,' Jem said, and heard himself sound like a bewildered child.

'Yes,' Nicky said. 'He was, except in all the ways he wasn't. Do you not recall how, in that damned argument, he said something about *you two wouldn't want to be caught?*'

Jem clenched his hands. 'Yes.'

'It was a threat. Much as unsavoury people might say, *What a nice shop, wouldn't it be awful if it burned to the ground.* I didn't know if you'd realised it, but I heard it very clearly indeed. It's why I said what I did. I was trying to tell him, "I don't care about Jem, so you've no need to hurt him." He didn't believe me, of course, so I achieved nothing except to cause you pain.'

'Maybe that was what he wanted,' Jem said thinly.

'I don't know. I don't know how much he'd planned and how much he was reacting, feeding off his own anger. I don't know if he wanted to hurt you or me or simply anyone available. Anyway, there we were. He threatened to use me to hurt you and vice versa, and, at that moment, having known him since we were eight years old, I had had absolutely enough.

'Perhaps I should have conciliated him even then. Maybe if I'd given in, Ella and I might have talked him round in the morning. But I couldn't, or at least I didn't. Instead, I told him precisely what I thought of him, as viciously as I could. We had an exchange of words. And—'

'What?'

'And he picked up that damned paperknife,' Nicky said. 'He said, did I not understand that he could stab me here and now and get away scot-free? All he'd have to do was tell the police I'd made advances that he had to fight off, and everyone would believe him. And, you know, he was right. That's what finally did it, I think. Not that he was jabbing at me with a stiletto, but that he was right.

'And he slashed at me—sliced my shirt open, didn't graze the skin—and I went to take the knife off him, and we struggled, and I stabbed him.'

The fire crackled gently in the hearth. Jem could hear Nicky's breathing and his own.

'I'd love to say I did it because he threatened you, or to save Aaron,' Nicky went on. 'I don't think I can. I didn't plan to do it, I swear that. But he wanted me to know that, despite having a quarter of either of our brains and none of your character, none of your courage or determination or steadfastness, despite never having worked for one single scrap of what he had, he was going to use our nature to destroy us, and he would get away with it. And I hated him for it, and I had a knife in my hand, and I killed him.'

Jem's hands were so tight on the tumbler that the crystal edges felt as though they were cutting into his fingers.

'It was damned quick,' Nicky said reflectively. 'And clean, considering. He went down. I tried to catch him—I remember his sleeve slipping through my fingers, the feel of the material. His mouth moved a little, but only for a second, and he looked confused, really utterly confused, and then he was dead. I would have run for aid, if there had been any chance. I do think I would have. But he was dead, and I looked at him and…I don't know. I'd felt half-mad for such a long time, and I looked down at my best friend, the man I'd loved for years, and I didn't feel anything at all.'

He sounded calm, but the whisky shuddered in the glass. Jem watched that because he couldn't watch Nicky's face.

'I felt entirely self-possessed, in a distant sort of way, the dispassionate observer of my own actions. I made sure the windows were fastened, and then I looked for the key, but I couldn't find it. You know he always put it down in some damn fool place and we'd all be searching for ten minutes, and it would turn up in a shoe. I couldn't lock the door and I had a feeling I should, so I tricked it—which was a damn fool thing to do, in retrospect, but there we are—and I took the cellarway back to the JCR and returned to my digs. There was blood on my shirt. I took it off, and I worked on my translation for an hour or so, and then I went to bed. In the morning I went for my usual walk with the shirt in a brown paper bag and threw it in a waste bin. After which I simply carried on until I was arrested.'

'And so was Aaron. You *let* the police arrest him.'

'I didn't want to hang,' Nicky said. 'I had no excuse to give the police except the frustrated homosexual yearnings they suspected, and there would be no clemency for that. I would have swung, still will, and I'm sorry to be a coward, but I don't want to. I'd rather cut my wrists, if it comes down to it. I'm not afraid of blades. And—this will sound extraordinary, but since I'm telling all, anyway—I wanted to know that, if I were caught, it would be because the police did their job. They arrested me purely because someone told them I was a queer, and I found myself entirely reluctant to help the useless swine. So I decided I'd admit what happened if and when someone else was charged. I wasn't going to let Aaron go to the gallows for me: I hope you believe that. But they didn't charge anyone, and they let me go in plenty of time to sit Finals. Which I did with some success, and with the same feeling of not quite being there. I saw you fall by the wayside, and Prue flee Oxford, and I passed my exams and went home and locked myself in my room without food or water. My parents had the chauffeur kick down the door eventually.'

'And you came back here,' Jem said. 'You killed Toby and then you came back here to teach.'

'Where else could I go? It seemed necessary that there should be some sort of consequence. The Anglo-Saxons sent their murderers into exile. I exiled myself here, where Toby died, and spent a little while trying to persuade myself I had acted rightly, and rather longer coming to terms with the truth.'

'Not long enough,' Jem said. 'Because you didn't tell the truth, did you? You let us, all of us, wither up in fear and mutual suspicion, and look at us. Look at the damage.'

'I know.'

The firelight picked out his angular features, pooling shadows on his face. Jem swallowed. 'And now what?'

Nicky shrugged. 'That's up to you. My main concern is that you don't plunge Aaron into trouble—though I suppose you weren't going to really, were you?'

'No,' Jem said. 'I knew it was you. I think I always did.'

'Then why in God's name would you—' Nicky began.

'Because it helped me pretend, I suppose. I wanted it to be anyone else and I tried my hardest to persuade myself it was, but nobody could hate Toby that much except someone who loved him. I just wanted time with you before it had to be true.'

Nicky put his face in his hands. They sat in silence for a long moment, then he looked up again, interlaced his long fingers and flexed them outward. 'Well then. You've done what you set out to do, found the who and the why of Toby's murder. There only remains what you're going to do about it.'

'What *I'm* going to do? You're going to confess. Aren't you?'

'No, I am not. If you choose to take this to the police, feel free, but I will not give myself up. *From this time forth I never shall speak word*, as another villain so neatly puts it.'

'But you can't make this my responsibility,' Jem said blankly. 'It's not up to me. I don't want to—' He cut himself off.

'But you *are* responsible,' Nicky said. 'Everyone told you to leave it alone and you chose to persist. If you carry on this course to the end, I shan't hold it against you. I'm not going to pretend it will be a relief, but at least it will be an ending, and that's something.'

'That's what I wanted,' Jem said numbly. 'An ending.'

'Then you'll have to decide what it is. Just—' His mouth moved in an effort at a smile. 'Warn me first?'

Jem got up, movements ungainly, stumbling. He moved blindly for the door, grabbing for his hat and coat as he went, screwing up his eyes because he refused to let the tears fall. Nicky didn't speak as he hurried out.

Old Quad's single gas lamp glowed feebly against the thick wreaths of grey fog. Jem stumbled away from it, towards Summoner Quad, not sure where he was going except away.

It wasn't fair. It ought not be this way. It ought to be Ella, or Aaron, or that imaginary fucking passing lunatic, not Nicky who had kissed Jem and loved him and ruined him. Nicky, who had said that first night on the rooftop that, if he could change a single thing about back then, he would choose not to have betrayed Jem that night.

Jem sobbed aloud, one horribly loud, painful gulp that was flattened by the fog. He headed down the gardens, along the path to the far gate, not that there were any people to see him, but he needed to be as far as possible from anyone. He couldn't go back to his little bare room in Bascomb Stair, his empty life.

Nicky, Nicky…

And Toby too. Laughing Toby, their flame, always full of life. Jem would never have taken up with the others, or started rowing, or acted, he'd never have done any of it without Toby sweeping him along. He'd been so wonderful until he wasn't.

He should have lived up to himself, to everything he could have been, and then he wouldn't be dead, and Nicky wouldn't be a murderer.

Jem walked down to the garden gate, almost stamping, grinding his feet into the ground because the pain in his foot was better than the pain everywhere else.

The gate was locked, as he'd known it would be. He stared through the bars into the street, then put his hands out experimentally to grasp them. They were very cold, running wet and dirty with the fog. He held on until his hands began to hurt, then turned.

Halfway up the garden, a side path ran behind the Master's Gardens to the shadowy mass of Bascomb Wood, and he took that rather than threading through Summoner Quad and Old Quad. It was unlit of course, but he could have walked it blindfolded, and at least nobody would see him, since nobody would walk for pleasure in this. The freezing fog settled on Jem's face in a clammy, dank blanket, colder where it met the tears.

He walked up to Bascomb Wood. The white trunks of silver birch glimmered faintly in the fog like a forest of bone. He ought to keep to the path that ran by the Master's Gardens wall, but he plunged between the trees anyway, taking a perverse relish in the way his shoes sank into the mud and mulch of fallen leaves. They'd sat here in summer sometimes, taking advantage of the shade, with Nicky reciting Elizabethan love poems—

He was not going to think of that. Toby had hated them all and Nicky had killed Toby, and there was nothing else.

The leaf-mulch was sodden and pliable. Jem's footsteps made only a faint squelch, flattened like all sounds by the fog. He plodded towards Bascomb Stair and that hateful room, but then stopped. If he went back inside, he would have to decide what to do next, and he couldn't.

He stood in the dark and fog under a dripping tree, despair twining through his blood and bones with every breath, and wondered if this bleakness was how Nicky felt every day of his life.

As he stood, there was a muffled clap from Front Quad, the sound of an incautious footstep coming down on an unexpected paving stone, and someone in front of him moved.

Jem wouldn't have seen anything if he hadn't been in the dark for so long. Bascomb Stair's front door was shut against the fog, its edges limned in the gaslight from inside. A little yellow light from Front Quad leaked through the archway, tinting the murk. And between those two faint areas of light, someone was standing in the sodden air. Not under the arch or in the doorway, in the light where a friend to be met could see him, but in a pool of darkness outside Bascomb Stair.

Someone was waiting in the dark. Just as someone had spilled oil on the stair.

Jem hadn't even thought about that. Nicky's confession had obliterated every other consideration from his mind, and so he hadn't said, *Did you try to break my neck yesterday?*

Nicky had confessed to murder: would he really have concealed setting a booby-trap? Would he have carried Jem back to his room and had his clothes cleaned, if he had been responsible? Would he have confessed at all, with Jem small and helpless and locked in his room, if he intended to get him out of the way?

Jem had known in his heart that Nicky was the killer, but he could not make himself believe Nicky had set that trap. It seemed too petty. Perhaps he was a gullible fool and Nicky was a monster.

Or perhaps someone else had poured oil on the stair, and that person was over there now, waiting for Jem in the darkness.

He needed to get out of here. That meant backtracking through the Wood, and round the end of the Master's Gardens and the chapel, both dark and silent, to get back to the lights of Summoner Quad, and people, and help. It would be no distance at all for a man who could turn and sprint. Jem wasn't even sure how fast he could walk. His pulse was thudding uncomfortably in his throat, echoed by the throb in his foot.

He retreated one step, and another, keeping his eyes fixed on the dim shape. If he moved slowly and quietly, perhaps he could fade into the fog and disappear. A small grey man, vanishing into the mists where he belonged. He took another step backwards, and this time his bad foot landed on something that wasn't mulch, a stone or hard lump of earth that skittered away. It didn't sound loud to Jem, perhaps because of the blood roaring in his ears, but the waiting man, now just a dim shape in the fog, looked up, and moved.

Jem turned and ran, in the childhood hopping gait everyone had mocked but which at least carried him along, heading back towards the gardens. He thrust himself onwards, stifled a cry of pain as his foot hit the ground with too much force, and realised that noise was exactly what he needed. He let out a yell that sounded terribly small and flat in the fog, like a scream for help in a dream, and managed another half-stride, and then the other man was on him, giving him a powerful shove that sent Jem stumbling into a tree trunk. He shouted out for help into nothingness, and was grabbed and thrown down, hitting the ground painfully, earth and leaves striking his open mouth. His assailant landed over him, his weight on Jem's back knocking the breath out of him, grabbing Jem's arm and twisting it up behind his back. His other hand came over Jem's mouth, fingers digging into his cheeks.

Jem kicked his legs fruitlessly, like a child, pinned and helpless under the weight. He jerked his head, hard and sharply enough that the man's hand slipped and he had the edge of a palm pressing into his mouth.

Jem bit savagely, clamping his teeth together and chewing with all the force he could muster. The man roared with pain and snatched his hand away, and Jem screamed, as shrill and carrying as he could. A solid blow sent his head snapping forward into the mud, and his arm was wrenched again, so high and hard he could feel the sinews tearing and thought, with odd clarity, *No, don't do that, it's going to break.*

'Hoi!' It was a deep voice in the distance, sounding over the dull buzz in his ears. 'You there, stop! Hey!' The newcomer came pounding through the trees as he shouted. The assailant pushed himself up off Jem, using a hand against his skull to grind his face into the clammy earth, then the weight was gone, and the man was running, spraying leaf-mulch as he sprinted away to the gardens.

'Hey!' bellowed the newcomer. 'Come back!' Jem, sprawled stunned in the mud, felt a warm hand on his shoulder. 'Good heavens, sir, are you all—*Jem?*'

It was Aaron. Jem was lying on the cold, wet earth with a mouthful of leaves, and he couldn't seem to get his breath back, and Aaron was right there. Of course he was.

'Great Scott,' Aaron said. 'Did he attack you? Can you sit up?'

Jem managed to get to his knees with Aaron's help, since his shoulder was on fire, and took a moment to spit out the dirt and fill his lungs. As he did, so another set of footsteps approached. He wasn't even surprised to see Ella come picking her way through the trees.

'Good God,' she said, looking down at him.

'Someone attacked Jem,' Aaron said. 'I saw him running off. Who was it, Jem?'

'Don't know. Second time.'

'Second—He attacked you before?'

'Someone did.'

Aaron and Ella exchanged looks, then Aaron took his arm. 'Can you stand?'

It proved possible, leaning on Aaron's strength. Upright, if filthy and freezing, Jem looked at them both. 'How are you here?'

'We were coming to see you,' Ella said. 'You did write to us.'

'Let's get him inside before we do this,' Aaron said. 'He's soaked to the skin. How long have you been out here? For heaven's sake. Come on, take my arm.' He reached out. Jem pulled back, because he couldn't trust Aaron and Ella together, and then he remembered that yes, he could, because they hadn't killed Toby, and it was a stiletto to the heart all over again.

'Jem?'

Jem nodded, grabbing Aaron's arm. Its solidity was a tiny comfort. 'Watch out for traps,' he managed as they set off.

'I beg your pardon?'

'There was oil on the stairs before. That's why I'm on the ground floor now. Watch out for booby-traps.'

'Is he drunk?' Ella asked. 'Because that would explain a great deal.'

'He smells a bit of whisky. And I've seen him look better,' Aaron said. 'Come on, let's get you warmed up and settled down. And yes, yes, I'll look out for traps.'

He tried to lead Jem up the stairs, and Jem had to plant his feet on the floor and repeat twice that he was in a different room now. Apparently, he didn't seem very reliable.

The door was intact, and the room had not been tampered with this time. That was a relief, in an academic sort of way; Jem didn't have the capacity to care any more. Ella waited outside while Aaron helped Jem strip off his sodden garments, washed the mud off his face, towelled him down, examined his arm, and concluded it was not seriously damaged. He helped Jem into dry clothes and wrapped the blanket round his shaking shoulders.

Jem huddled on the bed while Aaron went out and exchanged a few quiet words with Ella. The shock was subsiding under the warmth of being looked after, but that only let the misery rush back in.

Aaron and Ella came back in together. They stood, not quite together, a little too far apart, looking down at Jem.

She wasn't much changed, Jem thought. Perhaps a little thinner where she had before been statuesque, hair still vibrantly red, a few lines around eyes and mouth, a harder look. Her expression was not kindly now.

'I should like to know what's happening,' she said. 'Starting with what you meant by your repeated harassment of me at my place of work, and that extraordinary and impudent letter.'

'Give him a chance,' Aaron said, sounding rather weary. 'He's had a very nasty shock. Jem, what did you mean about being attacked before, and booby-traps?'

'It happened—last night, I suppose.' It felt like months ago, the day had been so agonisingly long. 'Someone tore up my books, poured ink all over my bed, and stole my notebook. They also, uh, they poured oil on the stairs, right at the top, and extinguished the gas. So when I came up here in the dark, I slipped and fell.' His hand moved automatically to the line of bruising across his chest.

'At the top of the stairs to the second floor?' Aaron demanded. 'You were lucky not to break your neck!'

'Or someone was unlucky he didn't,' Ella said. 'I suppose this is related to your recent activities?'

'I wanted to kick the hornets' nest and succeeded beyond my wildest dreams. I need to apologise,' Jem said. 'I wrote that letter to you all to provoke a reaction because I wanted to know who killed Toby. I didn't realise that I was going to cause trouble for Aaron over the other matter.'

'You thought investigating a murder might be done without consequences?' Ella enquired sardonically. 'Don't bother to answer that. *Have* you caused trouble for Aaron? Gone to the police?'

'No. I don't—it's not—' His throat closed. 'No. And I shan't, not about Aaron. It's none of my business and I don't care. And I know that neither of you killed Toby. So I'm sorry. You…you needn't worry any more. I shan't cause any trouble.'

There was a long silence. Neither Ella nor Aaron moved. Finally, Ella said, 'And how do you come to say that with such certainty? Because if that's an expression of faith in both our characters, I can assure you it's not widely shared. Even in this room.'

Jem made himself meet her eyes. 'Because I know who did it.'

'Know?' Aaron said hoarsely. His fists were clenched, the knuckles standing stark. 'Not think, or deduce, but *know*?'

'He confessed,' Jem said in a thread of a voice.

Ella put a hand to her mouth. Aaron shut his eyes, face contorting with what looked like agony. There was no sound in the room but harsh breath.

And Jem wanted to cry out for comfort, because coming even that close to proclaiming Nicky's guilt out loud felt like a jagged tear along his soul, but Ella looked as though she'd been struck. She reached out blindly with her other hand, and Aaron began to move to her and then pulled abruptly back. He picked up the chair instead, placing it behind her, and she sank into it in a rustle of skirts and put her face in her hands.

Aaron stared down at her. His face was a rigid mask, his eyes dreadful. Jem couldn't understand the horror on his face, and then he did.

'You suspected each other,' he said before he could stop himself. 'You both thought—'

Ella shook her head, a tiny motion. 'Never. I never did. I *never* believed it.'

'I didn't *want* to believe it,' Aaron said. 'I never—'

'I *told* you,' Ella said through her teeth. 'I gave you my word. And you still couldn't trust me, could you?'

Aaron looked like a man in a nightmare. 'I tried. I thought—Ella…'

'I don't care. I don't want to hear it. Who killed Toby, Jem?'

Jem looked between them, then pushed himself off the bed. 'Come on. Both of you, come with me. You need to hear.'

CHAPTER 22

They followed him through the fog-wreathed Front Quad, through to Old Quad and Staircase Thirteen, walking in silence. There was nobody out, nobody waiting, no lurking figure, and Jem realised he wasn't afraid of one now, because Ella and Aaron were with him.

He led them to Nicky's door and knocked. There was no answer, and a sudden image came, as vivid as if it was in front of his eyes, of Nicky, who feared the gallows, alone in his loveless room with a bottle of whisky and a razor blade.

Jem yanked frantically at the doorhandle. It turned, the door opened, and he half fell through the doorway.

Nicky didn't appear to have moved since Jem had left him. He sat holding the empty glass, and didn't even look up from the fire, now mostly dully glowing coals, as Jem clattered in. Nobody moved, until Ella said, with a kind of resignation, 'Nicky?'

He looked up then, at Ella and Aaron, and he didn't need to speak.

Jem was the first to break the silence. 'Let's all sit down. Aaron and Ella need to know. It's only right.'

Aaron and Ella moved forward. Jem hung up his sodden coat and locked the door, then took his previous chair opposite Nicky, since Aaron and Ella had taken the settee, sitting together.

'Well,' Ella said. 'I suppose I ought to hear you out.'

'Not if you don't want to,' Nicky said. He was watching his hands, loosely clasped on his knee. 'I killed Toby. I'm sorry, Ella. And I am deeply sorry for the damage caused by my cowardice afterwards, to all of you.'

'Why did you do it?' Her voice was very level.

'He knew about Aaron's extracurricular activities. The abortion ring. He told me that I'd do his informing and bear witness for a prosecution, or he'd lay a complaint of gross indecency and sodomy against me and Jem.'

Aaron inhaled sharply. 'Are you serious?'

'We argued. He picked up the knife, but I killed him. That's all.'

Ella's breathing was harsh, Nicky's a thin hiss. Nobody spoke.

'And you said nothing,' Aaron said after a while. 'Not when I was arrested, not when we…' His voice failed.

'I would have spoken if they'd charged you,' Nicky said. 'I wouldn't have let anyone else take the blame.'

'You *did*!' Aaron shouted. 'You let Ella take the blame for ten years! I thought—'

'Yes, *you thought*,' Ella said. 'You thought I killed him, and you wouldn't listen to me. You can't blame Nicky for that.'

'You—' Aaron began hotly, then snapped his mouth and eyes shut at once. He was silent for a moment, then spoke carefully. 'No. You're right. I didn't believe you. You were so angry when you went to confront him that night. And then he was dead, and you gave that false alibi. I should have trusted you in the teeth of the evidence and I didn't, and I am sorry, Ella. I'm so sorry. You trusted me, and I—' He turned away.

Ella looked at him, face unreadable, then back at Nicky. 'So. I should have guessed, I suppose.'

'Probably you should.'

'Why?' she asked. 'And I know what you just said. Now tell me *why*. You owe me that.'

Nicky inhaled, a long shallow breath, and let it hiss out between his teeth. 'In the moment, because he was jabbing a knife at me with intent. In the larger moment, because he had given me the choice between destroying Aaron or destroying Jem, and I did not choose to do either of those things. In the round, because—' He stopped. Ella cocked her head, waiting. Nicky's nostrils flared. 'Because when he was good, he was very, very good, and when he was bad, he was horrid.'

'Yes, he was,' Ella said. 'He might have recovered himself, given the chance.'

'A thought on which I have reflected every day of the last ten years,' Nicky said. 'Do you think that hasn't occurred to me? That if I had just been more patient, had more sense, if I had given him *time*—'

'You're suggesting he might have grown out of it,' Aaron said. 'I think he was, if anything, growing into it. You are both letting the man he could have been blind you to what he was becoming. To me, in that last argument, it was very clear indeed.'

There was a moment's silence, then Ella exhaled, long and deliberate. 'Perhaps. I don't know if it matters, really. He knew you didn't love him any more, Nicky, and I quite believe he would have destroyed you for it, and Jem with you. Perhaps he would have been sorry afterwards, but he was too angry, too hurt, to consider that. I saw as much in our—our last conversation.' Her voice faltered on that for the first time.

'What happened?' Jem asked, almost in a whisper.

'I told him he'd won, and Aaron had broken the engagement, but that I hated him and he was no longer my brother, never would be again. I meant it with my whole heart, and he knew I did, but he wouldn't retract. He had to win, even if it meant he lost me. I told him he had, and the next day he was dead, and I have felt as guilty as though I struck the blow myself ever since. No wonder you didn't believe me, Aaron.'

'I'm sorry,' Aaron said again. 'I should have trusted your word.'

'And I'm sorry, Nicky,' she said quite levelly. 'If you came to him after that conversation, he would have been desperate for someone to take it out on. And also...ugh. I told him that if he laid information against Aaron, I should let the world know he had betrayed his friend. It's possible I made him realise he needed a catspaw.'

'Perhaps,' Nicky said. They both sounded calm, in the way a man might be calm crossing a tightrope above an abyss because, if he lost control at all, the fall would be terrible. 'But he always liked to have people dance to his tune. It's just that the tunes used to be pleasant ones.'

'Especially you,' Ella said. 'He got you drunk for *Cymbeline*, didn't he? Do you think, when he picked up the knife, he intended to hurt you? Physically?'

There was a long silence.

'I don't know,' Nicky said at last. 'I think what he really wanted was to make us both know our place. For me to admit that he could kill me and get away with it.'

'Because you belonged to him.'

Nicky's face twitched. 'Not as much as you.'

'No. Toby thought you belonged to him, but he *knew* I did. Grandfather used me as an example to teach him how to run a household. "Your sister has stained her dress with playing at scientific investigation, how should she be punished?" "Your sister wishes to attend the Royal Society lectures, should that be permitted?" When I wanted to attend a women's college, Toby and Grandfather agreed that it could only be Anselm Hall. I wanted to go to Girton, but Toby was going to St Anselm's and that was that. It never crossed his mind that he didn't have a say in my marriage; as far as he was concerned, he had the only say.

'I loathed Nicky growing up, because my importance in life was entirely related to Toby, and I couldn't afford for him to care about other people. And he liked the devotion, the competition. He had Nicky for school and me for home, and he loved us because we loved him best of all. And when we failed to do that, when we put our own lives and loves first, we betrayed him unforgivably. We betrayed him, and you two *stole* from him.' She glanced between Aaron and Jem. 'Because Nicky and I were his. And if he'd only thought about it—if he'd just *tried* to be generous or magnanimous, as he could be…'

'Because he could be wonderful,' Nicky said harshly.

'But he had to be the main character, or he'd ruin the play,' Ella finished. 'I miss my brother. I miss him every day. And I'm so relieved he's gone.'

She swiped angrily at her eyes. Nicky was huddled in his chair, both arms wrapped around himself. Aaron was stiff with tension, hovering by Ella, not touching her.

'And what does that mean?' Jem said, more roughly than he intended. 'Where does all this get us?'

'Toby's life was worth no more and no less than any of ours, no matter what he may have thought,' Aaron said. 'The question is whether Nicky's life is required to pay for Toby's.'

The words thudded into silence. Nicky swallowed. 'I—would prefer to avoid a trial. My family, you understand. If you give me until tomorrow, I will do the decent thing. I'll leave a letter, of course, to be made public.'

'*No*,' Jem said.

'The law—' Nicky began.

'Be damned to the law,' Aaron said. 'Laws are what got us all into this. The three of us most affected by Nicky's act are here—'

'Prue, too,' Jem said.

'Prue *caused* this, when she went running to spill our secrets,' Ella said, with a savage bite in her voice. 'If there is one single act of stupidity that precipitated this whole disaster—'

'It was mine,' Nicky said. 'Whatever anyone else did, I'm to blame.'

'Yes, you are,' Aaron said. 'And yet I cannot see how driving you out of the world will do the slightest bit of good. It won't bring Toby back, or restore his memory, and it certainly won't clear our names: I expect the letters will only increase in volume. So I ask again, does justice require an eye for an eye?'

'I don't want vengeance,' Jem said through a dry throat. 'I wanted to know what happened because I thought that would be the only way we could ever put anything right.'

Ella steepled her fingers in front of her face, as though she were praying. 'Putting things right. How do we do that?'

'By looking at what went wrong,' Jem said. 'Aaron suspected you, and he was wrong, and now he knows that, and you know it, and maybe you can talk about it. And, just so you know, every time I spoke to him, he stuck to your alibi like glue.'

Ella's brows shot up. Aaron's cheeks darkened slightly.

'Prue lost her husband and her child, and she is dreadfully unhappy,' Jem went on. 'But I spoke to Miss Keele and she's writing to her, and perhaps something can be done. I wanted to know why my life fell apart, and now I do. And maybe, if I don't have to distrust all the people I ever believed in and cared for—'

Nicky made a stifled noise. Jem said, 'That's what it did. I haven't settled to anything or made friends with anyone because I was too afraid. It's been a state of limbo.'

'Yes,' Ella said. 'That is exactly it. Limbo, with no resolution of the past, and no way to a future.' She looked up at Nicky, lowering her hands. 'There is nothing you can give me back that makes up for what you took. And if you hadn't killed Toby, I'd be saying exactly the same thing to him.' She stood, towering over the three seated men, chin up, eyes shining in the firelight. Her mouth was working, but she managed to say, 'Live, and deal with others better,' blurting the words out before she turned away.

It was one of the last lines of *Cymbeline*, the hero forgiving the villain Iachimo. Nicky had knelt for it on stage, curling into himself to show Iachimo's shame. He didn't move at all now.

Aaron rose and went to Ella, putting his hands gently on her shoulders. She didn't look round at him, but she didn't pull away. Jem looked back to Nicky, and saw his face convulse.

Jem made a strangled noise, shoving himself out of his chair, down on one knee so he could reach out for Nicky with both hands, and Nicky fell forward into his arms, gripping with a terrible desperation, body shuddering with silent sobs.

'There are other things,' Aaron said reluctantly. 'What happened earlier—'

'Not now,' Jem said into Nicky's hair. 'I *can't*. I'll lock the door and we can deal with that tomorrow, but I can't—any more—'

'No,' Ella said. 'I think we've all had enough for tonight. As long as you will be safe here?'

'I think they're both safer if Jem stays here,' Aaron said. 'Alive and well for breakfast, please. I don't want to lose either of you now.'

CHAPTER 23

Jem woke with a bleary suspicion that he'd been awake most of the night and only just drifted off to sleep. There was the faintest glimmer of pre-dawn light in the room, which suggested he needed to get up, and there was someone next to him. Nicky, quietly breathing.

Nicky.

Jem twisted his neck as gently as possible to check the clock, so as not to disturb his companion, and saw it was a quarter past seven. Time enough. He lay for a moment, memorising the sensation of the warm, heavy body by his, the sound of his sleep. Then, because life never let you keep anything for long, he sat up.

Nicky grunted, rolling over as Jem stood. 'Ugh.'

'Morning.' Jem looked around hastily for his clothing, and pulled on his drawers in the dim light before he lit the gas.

Nicky groaned, blinking. 'Right. Yes. Morning.' He had a vague sound to his voice. Jem supposed he was going over the events of yesterday in his mind, and wasn't entirely surprised to hear a very quiet, 'Christ.'

'Mmm.'

Nicky dropped an arm over his eyes. 'I can't imagine why you're still here.'

Jem wouldn't have left at gunpoint. For himself and the terror of the man in the dark; for Nicky, and the bottle of whisky and the razor blade. In the morning light, those things seemed sufficiently far away that he could breathe. 'We should get up. I think Aaron and Ella might be coming for breakfast.'

'I suppose it would be ungracious of me to complain about the social awkwardness attendant on confessing murder and then meeting one's confessors for breakfast.'

'*Nicky*.'

'Sorry. I...may take a little while to come to terms with this. Permit me my defences?'

It was a painful question. Jem turned to face him, bare-chested, and Nicky said, in quite a different voice, 'What the hell is that?'

'What?'

'Your face is bruised, and your shoulder. That's not from the fall. What—' He stopped. 'Wait. Did Aaron say something last night?'

'Someone attacked me,' Jem said, and recounted the incident as unemotionally as he could.

Nicky heard him out, his mouth hardening. 'Someone did that last night. And you said nothing?'

'You weren't in a state to hear it,' Jem pointed out. 'I locked the door.'

'Right.' Nicky massaged the bridge of his nose. 'Could we set my histrionics aside for the moment and concentrate on discovering who is bent on harming you? And has tried to do so twice, since we must assume this is a sequel to the oil incident, about which we have *also* done nothing yet because of me. I am going to do better by you, I swear.'

'Start by putting the kettle on,' Jem suggested.

They were drinking tea when a rapping knock sounded, so familiar that they both said, 'Aaron.' Nicky went to answer the door, and Ella and Aaron entered in a blast of fog and chilly air. Jem rose, mumbled greetings were exchanged, and then they all looked at each other.

'Well,' Ella said. 'Is there tea in the pot?'

Jem went to refill the kettle while Aaron and Ella took off coats and hats and scarves, and claimed their sofa of the previous night. Jem thought they sat a fraction closer than before.

They all took a mug of tea. Nicky looked around and said, 'Is everyone else paralysed by a sense of déjà vu?'

'I expect someone to burst in complaining about tutorials at any moment,' Ella offered, and winced, because *Toby* hung in the air unspoken.

'They probably will,' Jem tried. 'Nicky is one of *those* tutors.'

Ella smiled a little at that. 'Of course he is.'

'We'd expect nothing less,' Aaron said. 'I missed you, all of you. This is the devil's own reunion, but I'm glad you did it, Jem.'

'So am I,' Nicky said. 'For good or ill, and against all common sense.'

'He always was obstinate,' Aaron said. 'We need to talk about what happened last night, Jem. You were violently attacked, and you said that was the second time. Of course the, uh, the obvious culprit...'

'It wasn't Nicky,' Jem said. 'The chap who attacked me put his hand over my face and it didn't feel like Nicky's. Also, I bit him jolly hard.'

Nicky extended pale, unmarked palms, which allowed Jem a moment to recover from having announced his familiarity with Nicky's touch. 'Moreover, it was the second incident,' Nicky added. 'Someone poured oil on the stairs outside his second-floor room. Without prejudice, would either of you know anything about that?'

Aaron narrowed his eyes, but said only, 'It was not us.'

'You can only assert that it wasn't you,' Ella said. 'It could have been me.'

'Was it?'

'No. Is it possible the attacker was a lunatic of the letter-writing type?'

'You might think anyone lunatic enough to attack me would have had something to say about it,' Jem said. 'But he didn't speak at all. Which raises the question of whether I would have recognised his voice.'

The others exchanged glances. Ella said, 'Yes, but if it wasn't Nicky, or Aaron, and Hugo isn't even *in* Oxford—'

'Yes, he is. He came down two days ago.'

'What's he doing here with Balfour's resignation expected any day?' Ella demanded.

'That's what Nicky said. But he arrived the same day you did, after receiving my letter,' Jem said. 'And he was still here yesterday afternoon.'

'What for?' Aaron demanded. 'It can't be related. Nobody ever suspected him of Toby's murder and now we know for a fact that he didn't do it.'

'But my letter wasn't an accusation of murder,' Jem said. 'What I said was that, before his death, Toby had intended to lay accusations of a serious crime against a fellow student.'

'So you did,' Ella said. 'And that brought Hugo here?'

'He said he was on his father's business, but he sought me out twice to talk. He said that I was under sustained nervous strain and needed a long break in the country for my health.'

'He visited me to make the same observation,' Nicky said. 'He seemed extremely keen that I should not think Jem reliable. What are you leading up to?'

Jem took a deep breath. 'The person who burgled my room stole my notebook while he was at it.'

'Your notebook,' Aaron repeated. 'And in this notebook was—?'

'My early conclusions. Addresses and personal details for you all. Notes of my conversations with Prue and Aaron and Hugo before I came to Oxford. Nothing after I met Miss Keele. I had started to feel unhappy about committing anything to paper.'

'Thank God for that,' Ella said. 'What exactly are you saying?'

'Let me put this fairly. Person A burgled my room and took my notebook, and I assume what he read in it made him unhappy enough to put oil on the stairs. Then Hugo made a jolly good stab at telling me and others I was going mad, and I didn't take up his offer to go away and be quiet. Then Person B attacked me.'

Ella's brows drew together. 'And you think A equals B equals Hugo.'

Aaron cleared his throat. He had both his large hands clasped round the mug, almost hiding it. 'I couldn't say anything for certain, and I would not be prepared to swear it in court. I was coming in a hurry through Bascomb Wood in the dark and fog, responding to a scream. But I saw a man running away, and I ran with Hugo almost daily for three years. And when I saw the attacker fleeing, the thought in my mind was, *He runs like Hugo*.'

'Good God,' Nicky said. 'But why?'

'That's the question.' Jem poured more tea. 'Ella, why did Hugo propose to you?'

'I have no idea. It was unprovoked, believe me.'

'And it was hardly the most ardent proposal. You refused, and I remember him saying something to Toby like, *Well, I tried.* And when Nicky confronted Toby the, uh, the last time, he was still talking about Hugo marrying Ella.'

She frowned. 'Do you mean Toby somehow pressed Hugo into proposing? I can see why Toby would have liked a wealthy, and white, brother-in-law, but why would Hugo do it?'

'Consider Toby's new hobby,' Nicky said. 'Blackmail. Is that what you mean, Jem?'

'Yes. I think he knew something about Hugo that he used, and when Hugo got my letter, he concluded I knew it too. I think it was Hugo who burgled my room and spilled the oil. And when I wouldn't accept the padded cell on his country estate, he attacked me in person.'

'But are we to understand that Hugo was harbouring a dark secret alongside and separate to mine and Aaron's? Is that entirely likely?' Nicky said.

'I don't think it was separate,' Jem said. 'Prue told Toby about Aaron's secret, didn't she? Suppose she told him about Hugo in the same conversation?'

'Told him *what* about Hugo?' Aaron demanded. 'What in heaven's name is in this notebook?'

'About the only thing I found out,' Jem said. 'That Prue learned she was expecting not long before Toby's murder.'

The others glanced at one another. 'That's not illegal,' Aaron said at last. 'It might not even be considered particularly shameful for the man involved.'

'Did Prue tell you who the father was?' Jem asked Ella.

'No. She wouldn't talk about it, only that she was expecting and didn't want to be.'

'And you, uh, recommended Aaron?'

Ella's face tightened. 'She was talking wildly about how she couldn't bear to have the child, the shame to her parents. I was afraid of what she might do, what sort of quack she might go to. Aaron had told me stories and it was awful. I told her, in strictest confidence, that Aaron knew people who could help.'

'You didn't tell me any of this,' Aaron said.

'Of course I didn't,' Ella snapped. 'Prue had sworn me to secrecy. I respected that. I trusted her with Aaron's secret in return, and she ran straight to Toby with it. I have never understood why.'

'She did adore him,' Nicky said. 'All the adoration he could have wanted.'

Ella blinked slowly. 'Are you suggesting Toby was responsible for her predicament?'

'I'm not,' Jem said. 'I think it was Hugo. I think he got Prue with child, and she went to Toby to ask for his help.'

'What help could *he* offer?' Aaron asked.

'And why would Hugo worry about that being revealed?' Nicky said. 'It's not a crime.'

'It could have been a crime.' Ella's eyes were on Jem's, as vividly blue as Toby's had been, and much, much harder. 'Is that what you mean?'

He nodded reluctantly. 'Hugo said to me, several times, that I wasn't to listen to rumour or false allegations, and that Prue would suffer if there was any talk. It was, oh, framing the debate, much like the way he's gone about making me seem unbalanced. I think he's afraid of her accusing him.'

'She refused to tell me anything about the father,' Ella said slowly. 'I thought she was ashamed. I thought she might be jealous, even, because Aaron and I were happy. I have rather a habit of distrusting people's motives, which...which I didn't quite realise until a few years ago. Oh, the devil.'

'I think she said something to Miss Keele,' Jem said. 'She asked me if Prue had loved her son, and sounded surprised when I said yes. One wouldn't normally ask that about a child, would one?'

'No,' Ella said. 'I don't suppose one would. Oh God. Why didn't she *say*? I was full of our engagement, I suppose, and Finals, but still—'

'He's Hugo Morley-Adams. Would people have believed her?'

'I would!' Ella snapped.

'Engagement rings and wedding bells can be a little off-putting to those for whom they aren't available,' Nicky said. 'She might not have felt able to speak to you at that time. Jem was as insignificant as she, socially speaking, I am no one's first choice for a sympathetic ear, and Aaron ran with Hugo. But Toby—Toby who could do wonders when he put his mind to it, Toby who was the only one of us to be Hugo's social superior… If she was afraid of retaliation, or of the consequences of going to the police, to have Toby stand by her would make all the difference.'

'Dear heaven.' Aaron was massaging his temples. 'This is appalling. Can we be sure?'

'If anyone has another explanation, I'll listen,' Jem said. 'And perhaps I'm wrong, perhaps he and Prue had an affair of the normal kind and he's merely afraid of it becoming known that he had an illegitimate child, but I don't think so. I think Hugo committed a rape, and Toby used that to blackmail him into proposing to Ella. But Toby died and Prue vanished, and Hugo got away with it. And then he had my letter just when his ducal marriage was coming off and the Liberals are set to form a government for the first time in ten years. There's not a chance that he could be gaoled now, but this would be the worst possible time for an accusation.'

'Or for you to drag the murder up,' Nicky said. 'Suppose Prue had been accused of murder: her reasons would be all over the front pages. Suppose Toby's blackmailing activities became known to the police, and they started asking hard questions. If Hugo saw the possibility of a scandal, he might well have panicked.'

Aaron scrubbed his hand over his hair. 'We have to talk to Prue. We need her confirmation, her voice. We can't do anything without that.'

'If she wishes to talk to us,' Ella said. 'She didn't before. Which is, in itself, suggestive. Hell and the devil.'

'Undoubtedly we should talk to Prue. But there is also the attack on Jem,' Nicky said. 'I should very much like to speak to Hugo about that, and I'm disinclined to wait.'

'I want to see him too,' Ella said. 'I want to see his face.'

'Mr Morley-Adams has a lot of explaining to do,' Nicky said. 'Are we going en masse?'

They left Nicky's rooms together: Ella, Aaron, Nicky, Jem, striding through Front Quad in an uneven line, long coats flapping like scholars' gowns, as if nothing had ever changed. Moffat was in the Porters' Lodge. He looked round at them, and his slack-jawed expression brought a suppressed snort from Aaron.

'He's going to have a seizure,' Ella said as they passed. 'Shall we all book tea with the Master as well?'

The Randolph Hotel was all quiet, oaken, intimidating elegance. Ella swept up to the concierge without the slightest regard for his magnificence, and demanded Hugo.

She received a bow. 'I regret to say, Mr Morley-Adams left us this morning, madam, not half an hour ago.'

'How extremely tiresome. I wanted to speak to him.' Her tone suggested Hugo's absence was the hotel's fault, and that she expected them to deal with it.

'I do beg your pardon, madam. I believe he received and sent a number of telegrams this morning, so I am sure the matter was urgent.'

'I suppose he must have hurried back to London,' Nicky said. 'Might we still catch him at the station? What train was he taking?'

'He's travelling by motor, sir, but I don't believe he was going directly to London,' the man offered. 'He requested a motoring guide.'

'He can't possibly have gone off sightseeing,' Ella said. 'A guide to where?'

'He asked for a motoring map of Hertfordshire, madam, and if I knew of any good hostelries in Aylesbury. I recommended the King's Head off Temple Street.'

'Aylesbury?' Jem asked. 'Do you have another map, please?'

One was produced. Jem leaned over and traced the road from Oxford through Aylesbury to Aldbury, Prue's village. It was very nearly a straight line.

Ella was leaning next to him and saw where his finger rested. 'Aldbury. Do you think—'

'Aylesbury's on the way.'

'But does he know where she lives?'

'Her address is in my notebook,' Jem said. 'So either I'm wrong and he doesn't know where she lives—or I'm right, and now he does.'

'Yes,' Ella said. 'I see. Well.' She sounded calm, but her hand was tense on the wooden desk. 'Well, then. It's about an hour in a motor car from here to Aylesbury, is that correct?' she asked the concierge.

'More like two, madam. The roads are rather winding, and of course it depends on the motor car and the driver.'

'What's Mr Morley-Adams driving?'

'One of the new Wolseley line, madam. A beautiful machine, if I may say so.'

'Thank you,' Ella said. 'Just one more thing, then.'

'Certainly, madam. How may I assist?'

She smiled at him. 'A motor car, at once.'

CHAPTER 24

Jem had no experience with motoring, but he hoped it was normally more comfortable than this. He felt every jolt of the rough surface as they bowled along at what felt a terrifyingly unsafe speed. Ella had gone through the foggy Oxford streets too fast, but, once the visibility and countryside had opened out towards Headington, she really let rip, far exceeding the speed limit. Jem feared she was doing well over thirty miles an hour; he didn't want to lean forward and look because he was too busy clinging white-knuckled to the passenger handle. Even with the hood up, the wind whipped their faces violently at this speed, and stones showered up from the roads. None of them had proper motoring clothes. Ella had wrapped a scarf around her face and borrowed a pair of goggles from the obviously motor-mad concierge; the rest of them were simply huddling. Nicky pulled Jem over, wrapping an arm over his shoulders, and they leaned into each other against the buffeting wind and the biting cold.

'I'm walking home,' Nicky shouted in his ear at one point, and Jem nodded as vigorously as he could.

Headington, Wheatley, Tiddington. Thame and Haddenham, then the long busier stretch to Aylesbury. Ella came off the London Road there, with Aaron in the front reading the map.

'It's market day in Aylesbury,' she shouted over her shoulder as she whipped them along narrower lanes without any noticeable reduction in speed. 'It might slow us down.'

'That would be awful,' Nicky muttered.

The roads twisted and turned horribly. Jem concentrated on trying not to be sick. Ella gave the Saturday traffic in Tring no quarter, blasting her horn and causing many astonished leaps out of the way. Then they were passing Tring station, on the road Jem had trudged not so many days ago, and Ella dropped the motor back to a sane speed, while Aaron twisted round to ask for directions.

'Straight on up Toms Hill Road, I'll warn you when we get there,' Jem said. 'How fast—'

'Thirty-three miles in an hour and eleven minutes.' Aaron sounded stunned.

'Well, the roads are very poor,' Ella said. 'I did my—' The motor came to an abrupt halt, sending them all lurching forward.

'God's sake!' Nicky snapped. 'What was that?'

'That motor over there is a new Wolseley,' Ella said.

'It's right in front of her cottage.' Jem's lips felt numb.

The motor roared up the last few yards to the cottage. Nicky didn't wait for it to come to a complete stop but vaulted over the side, and sprinted up the path. Aaron reached him within a couple of seconds, the pair of them shoulder to shoulder. Jem had to lower himself down carefully out of the motor; his legs were shaking. He and Ella caught up with the others at the cottage door, which was still firmly shut after Nicky's third barrage of knocks.

Aaron thumped the heel of his hand against the door. 'Come on, open up!'

Jem ducked to the side, and pressed his face against the little window, not caring that his foot sank into a bare and struggling shrub. He couldn't see much through the net curtains, only shapes, but that was enough.

'She's inside and so's he. I can see them.' He slapped his hand on the window as he'd used to do at college. 'Prue! It's us!'

'I vote we break the door down,' Aaron said. 'With me?'

'Shoulders or feet?' Nicky asked.

Aaron cast an assessing look at the low doorway, weighing up the distance, and delivered a kick to the door that seemed to rattle the house.

He stepped back again, ready to repeat the kick as the door swung open. Hugo stood there foursquare in the hall. He opened his mouth and Aaron strode right into him, planting a hand on his chest and sending him stumbling back. Jem ducked under his flailing arm and darted through to the parlour.

Prue was there, seated in a hard chair, back rigid, tear-streaks glistening on her too-pale face, eyes wide. She whispered, 'Jem,' and he came to her with arms out, gripping her hands hard. 'Oh, God, Jem!'

'We're here,' he said. 'All of us. It's all right. We're here now.' *Ten years too late. We're here.*

Aaron and Nicky were walking Hugo backwards into the parlour. They were three tall men, and they took up a lot of space. Ella followed, shutting the door behind her. She came over to Prue and sank down by the chair, taking her other hand, so that she and Jem were flanking the small woman.

'Well,' Hugo said. 'This is something of a surprise. Is it a reunion? I must say, I didn't expect all you fellows. Bit of an unceremonious entry, what?' The forced bonhomie rang like cheap tinware.

'If you could try not to embarrass us all, *old man*, that would be marvellous.' Nicky's voice was lethally dry.

'I beg your pardon?'

Prue's hand felt very cold in Jem's, her fingers tight around his. He cleared his throat. 'What are you doing here, Hugo? Why did you need to rush off to visit Prue like this? Why aren't you in London?'

'I hardly think I need answer any of that.' Hugo was still smiling.

'I think you must,' Aaron said. Nicky strolled back to the door and propped his shoulders against it, folding his arms in a way that suggested he didn't intend to move.

'Why don't I start,' Jem said. 'And if Prue wants to add anything, she can.' He felt her fingers twitch. 'I'm going to start with the last few weeks. And then I'm going to go back to what happened ten years ago. And you can correct me if I'm wrong, but I don't think anyone's in the mood for bluster, so please don't bother. You must realise, we all know.'

The smile stayed on Hugo's mouth. His face settled around it, though, eyes and cheeks losing their cheerful lift, dragging his lips down.

'I set out to discover who killed Toby,' Jem said. 'Perhaps that was foolish—in fact, every one of you told me not to do it, but I did it anyway, and learned a number of things. And one of those was that Toby had had incriminating information about a fellow student, that he'd considered going to the authorities, and that he hadn't. And the reason he hadn't was that he was using his information for blackmail. Hugo, why did you propose to Ella?'

'If you're suggesting Toby forced me to do so, that is an insult to a very lovely and accomplished woman. Since you ask, I felt it was the right thing to do. She found herself—if you will excuse my frankness—in a very difficult entanglement that would have had disastrous consequences.'

'No, I didn't,' Ella said. 'It was an *engagement*, and the consequences of that were and are none of your business. Why did you feel compelled to suggest I, who had just lost my chance of a title and my inheritance and thus was absolutely no use to you, marry you? What was in it for you?'

'Perhaps I proposed *because* you had just lost your chance of a title and your inheritance.'

'An act of charity. I see. How very kind.'

Jem desperately tried to marshal his thoughts as they bickered, to remember what was assumption and what fact. Hugo was a politician, and a good one; he would have a story ready, and Jem felt a sudden panic. He was out of practice with verbal battles. Why was Nicky not taking charge?

He flung a desperate glance at Nicky, who was lounging against the door. Nicky met his gaze and winked. It was just a flicker of an eyelid, a twitch of the lips, there and gone, and Jem took a deep breath.

'As I was saying,' he said loudly. 'Toby had the goods on one of you. I wrote to you all, the same letter. It was a fishing expedition and it got bites. Because the other night, Hugo, I met you coming out of St Anselm's, and when I returned to my room, I found it burgled, the stairs booby-trapped, and my notebook stolen. I suppose that was intended to put me off. But when you came to see me the next day, I told you I intended to take everything I knew to the police. You weren't happy about that, were you?'

'I was not happy at your obvious state of exhaustion and dishevelment,' Hugo said. 'You looked and sounded unbalanced, if I must say so, babbling of crimes and conspiracies. In fact, you do so now, and I fear the police will give you short shrift if and when you reveal whatever fantastical tale—'

'No speeches,' Nicky said. 'You're not in the House now.'

'Quiet!' Hugo snapped. 'If Jem insists on insulting me, I have the right to speak in my defence.'

'I don't think I've insulted you yet,' Jem said. 'I'm merely recounting what happened. And the next thing was a heavily muffled man, waiting in the fog outside Bascomb Stair, coming after me, and attacking me. Aaron came up then, thank goodness, and you know, Hugo, he saw your face clearly.'

'No, he didn't,' Hugo snapped.

Nicky laughed aloud. 'Well played, Jeremy.'

'I meant, he couldn't have seen my face because it wasn't me.'

'I didn't see a face,' Aaron said. 'What I saw was a man running away. I ran with you for three years, Hugo, and I was not always out in front. You still have that kick to your gait, don't you?'

'This is some sort of plot between you all,' Hugo said savagely. 'I don't know what envy or spite is motivating this attack, but it is a malicious confection. I have no idea what this is about.'

'Liar.' Prue's voice was thin but clear.

Jem gave it a second in case she wanted to add anything. She didn't, so he went on. 'Let's help you, then. How did you find Prue's address?'

'I—what do you mean?'

'It's a simple question. How did you find the address of a woman going by a married name you didn't know, to whom you hadn't spoken in a decade?'

'I had my secretary find it.'

'You gave him too long to think there,' Nicky observed. 'When did you have your secretary do this, precisely?'

'This morning—no, yesterday.'

'Yes, it *is* Saturday,' Nicky said with mock approval. 'Well remembered.'

'We can establish the truth easily enough. Aaron, Nicky?' Jem said. 'Could you see if he's got my notebook?'

The two larger men moved. Hugo moved too, attempting to elbow Aaron, and suddenly it was a scuffle. Aaron put his weight into it, shoving Hugo back against the wall as Nicky came in to grab his hand. The china on the dresser rattled. Prue sucked in a breath.

'Are you all right?' Jem asked her, voice low.

'What are you doing?'

'Trying to put things right.' He squeezed her hand. 'Was he threatening you?'

Prue nodded, a tiny movement, just as Nicky gave a triumphant hiss Jem knew from the fencing court, and held a small card-bound notebook aloft. 'Look here.'

Hugo shouldered violently forward. Nicky threw the notebook to Jem, who fumbled the catch and managed to slap it against his chest. Aaron shoved Hugo against the wall with both hands. 'Don't be a fool.'

'There are two of us, and you've had too many late nights with cigars,' Nicky added. 'Is that it, Jem?'

'My notebook. Including Prue's address. Do you want to explain how you had it, Hugo?'

'He—' Hugo began, and stopped.

'Please don't say Nicky put it there because we all know he didn't,' Aaron said. 'He's right. It's embarrassing.'

'Quite,' Nicky said. 'I also observe a very nasty bruise on your hand, Hugo, not unlike a bite mark. Tell me, did you intend Jem to break his neck when you poured oil on a second-floor staircase, or did you merely not care?'

'You came down to Oxford because you had my letter and were afraid of what I'd found out,' Jem said. 'You burgled my room and stole my notebook and attacked me because you were afraid of what I'd found out. And then when Aaron got in your way and you couldn't scare me into silence, you decided to come here and bully Prue instead. And do you know, Hugo, she hasn't said one word to me or anyone. I worked it out myself. All you've done is prove your own guilt.'

'What guilt?' Hugo demanded. 'For heaven's sake, let me go.' He straightened. Nicky and Aaron stepped back, not by much.

'Very well, Jem, suppose I did try to prevent your reckless, selfish attempt to upend everyone's lives. Have you considered why? I was attempting to protect the good name of another individual, who might have made a foolish decision and one that would meet with the world's disapproval, but who does not deserve to be humiliated for it. I attempted to protect that individual's name by, yes, acceding to Toby's extraordinary demands, and I will protect it now.'

'Shut up,' Prue said very quietly. 'Shut up. Shut up, shut up, *shut up*!' She pushed herself to her feet, pale and shaky, still gripping Jem's hand. 'You filthy liar. I can see what you're doing and I will not have it. I didn't make a *foolish decision.* I said no and you would not stop, so don't dare say you wanted to help me. I told you no!'

Her hand felt clammy. The silence in the room was absolute. Hugo looked around, at Jem, Ella and Prue together, at Nicky and Aaron flanking him. 'That is not—I'm sorry to deny a lady, but that is not how it happened. Not at all. I understand the urge to disclaim responsibility, considering the outcome, and of course I must regret that we both behaved improperly, but I must defend my own reputation. You may have regretted it afterwards; so did I. But you were willing, Prue. I remember it well.'

'I wasn't,' Prue said. 'I was *not*.'

'This is nonsense. You came to my digs of your own accord. There were people nearby. If what you say is true, you would have fought.'

Prue gave a harsh little gasp. Ella said, 'Ah. Well, that does change things.' She walked into the centre of the room, pacing to the window and turning back. Jem watched her as though she were a judge in the High Court. She slid her finger absently along the edge of a heavy pewter candlestick, as though considering. Then she picked it up, turned, and was already swinging it as she took two strides towards Hugo.

'Jesus!' Nicky yelped, diving to the floor under the weapon's arc. Hugo threw his arms over his head, ducking but not far enough, and screamed as the heavy metal slammed his elbow with a meaty thud. Ella raised the candlestick again, Nemesis in a walking dress, and brought it down with skull-splitting force. Aaron grabbed her just in time, dragging her back so the candlestick missed Hugo's head by an inch, and Hugo rose, swinging a furious fist.

Jem didn't know if he meant it, or if he'd have pulled the blow before it hit her. It never landed. Aaron yanked Ella away with a roar of fury, and went in with a brutal right hook. Ella staggered backwards into Jem, who grabbed her wrist as she raised the candlestick again.

'They'll wreck my house!' Prue shouted. 'Stop it!'

'Nicky!' Jem shouted. 'Get them outside! Ella, don't, you'll kill him!'

Aaron and Hugo were struggling together, two gentlemen in good suits wrestling like street fighters. Hugo's face was patchy red, teeth bared in a snarl; Aaron's neck muscles were corded with effort. Nicky skirted them cautiously.

'Nicky!' Jem roared. He couldn't hold Ella back much longer.

'Borrow your fire irons?' Nicky reached over to the fireplace as he spoke, grabbing the poker, skirted around the struggling men, and thrust the poker into the melee with a high upward fencer's lunge.

Prue gave a shrill squeak. Aaron recoiled, looking startled. And Hugo was suddenly very still, standing on his tiptoes with the poker's point jabbed disturbingly deep into the underside of his chin.

'That,' Nicky said into the deafening silence, 'will do. It will do from you, Aaron, so calm down; it will do from you, Ella, so hand Jem the bludgeon before we have a second murder on our hands; and it will do for the rest of your natural life, Morley-

Adams, you contemptible specimen. I take Prue's word over yours a hundredfold, and if you open your mouth I will put this poker right through your soft palate, so help me God.'

Ella turned to Prue. 'Are you all right?'

Prue nodded slightly. Ella put her arms around her, a little awkwardly. Prue was stiff against her for a second, then she started to shake.

Aaron cleared his throat, jerking his disarranged clothing back into place. 'I beg your pardon, ladies. Is anyone hurt?'

Hugo made a noise in his throat. Aaron said, 'Not you,' with a calm simplicity more devastating than Nicky's most baroque contempt. 'Anyone who matters? Good. Well. What are we going to do with him?'

That was the question. He didn't have to say, *Nobody else will believe Prue*; that was entirely obvious. Hugo would say she hadn't fought, and that was that.

'Prue,' Nicky said very gently, considering the tension of his posture. 'I will stand by you—we all will—if you should wish to prosecute. I trust you know that.'

'My word against his, in a courtroom?' Prue said. 'I never wanted to go through a trial, as if there would be justice. I never told anyone it was him, except Toby. And even so, he came in here and threatened me, he said he would ruin my reputation if I spoke about what had happened. He said, if I *told lies*. I've never lied. How could I when I've never spoken? He said he'd make sure I lost my job and nobody else would employ me and I'd lose this cottage. I have *nothing*, and he wanted to take it away anyway.' Her voice was trembling, with rage or fear or both. 'I was never going to speak, and he came to my home and threatened me to keep silent!'

'That's my fault,' Jem said. 'I'm sorry, Prue. I didn't mean to drag you into this.'

'If you want to consider prosecuting—' Ella began.

'I want him out of here,' Prue said. 'Get him out!'

'Just a moment,' Jem said. 'I've something more to say. Nicky, hold Hugo there, won't you? I'm sorry, Prue, but I need to go over what I think happened. Hugo had done this dreadful thing, and you went to Toby. You thought he could help, that he *would* help, and you ended up telling him about the engagement too, among other things. Is that right?'

He could feel everyone's eyes intent on him. If Prue mentioned Aaron's activities, they'd have a problem; he prayed he'd judged this right.

'Yes.' Prue swallowed hard. 'I told him everything, I told him… all sorts of things I shouldn't have, but I was—it was—I thought he'd help me. I thought he'd tell me what to do, and—and all he cared about was Aaron and Ella. He didn't care about me in the slightest. He told me to have a hot bath and chalk it up to experience.'

'My God,' Ella said. 'I'm sorry. I'm so sorry.'

'Toby used what you'd said to blackmail Hugo into proposing to Ella.' Jem moved around Nicky, so he could see Hugo's face. 'But she wouldn't have it. So what happened next, Hugo? When Toby held a charge of rape over your head, and you'd failed to meet his conditions, what did you do?'

Aaron and Ella made simultaneous noises. Nicky inhaled, a sharp hiss.

'What did you do to silence him?' Jem repeated. 'We all know what you're capable of. Did you go to his room when you dropped in on Summoner's Gift? Did you decide he needed to be got out of your way, just as you tried to get me out of your way?'

Nicky's arm had slackened along with his jaw. Hugo wrenched himself free of the poker. 'I did nothing! This is an absolute—I didn't kill Toby!'

'In the last ten minutes you've claimed you didn't attack me, you didn't steal my notebook, and you didn't force Prue,' Jem said. 'Forgive me if I don't find this latest denial any more convincing. You might as well admit it. We couldn't think worse of you.'

'I didn't do it!' Hugo yelped. 'I swear it! For God's sake, man, I might have made mistakes—'

'*Mistakes?*' Jem and Prue shouted together.

'I have done…things I'm ashamed of,' Hugo said, forcing the admission through his teeth. 'Evidently I have fallen short of the, ah, the standards of decency to which I should—' Nicky raised the poker again, meaningfully. Hugo swallowed. 'I didn't kill Toby. I'm not a murderer.'

'Just an attempted one?' Jem asked.

Hugo made a brushing gesture, raising his chin. 'I intended nothing of the sort. Any serious harm would have been an accident.'

'You have no idea how badly I should like to hurt you,' Nicky said. 'Jem, you make a convincing case, but may I ask your intention?'

'That's the question,' Jem said. 'I don't know if, at this distance of time, we could persuade a jury of the murder, let alone his crime against Prue. But we could try. We could tell the court and the papers and the world what he did, and make the case that he committed a murder to hide a rape. I don't know if a court would convict, but oh, the court of public opinion would. The St Anselm murder solved at last. His political career, his grand marriage, his society friends—we could take them all. It wouldn't make up for what you did, but by God it would be a start.'

Hugo had gone an unpleasant sallow-grey colour. Ella smiled without kindness. 'Yes, indeed. Oh, yes. Do you think Lady Lucy will stand by you, Hugo? Perhaps exhibit herself in the dock as a character witness?'

Prue was shaking her head, a tiny motion. Jem said more levelly, 'The problem is, it would be dreadful for all of us too. I know nobody wants to be thrust back into the public eye, and it would be by far the worst for Prue. I'm not going to ask anyone here to put yourselves through that. Not unless we all agree that we want to, and we're quite sure Hugo killed Toby.'

'I didn't!' Hugo almost screamed.

'And if we don't agree?' Ella enquired.

'Then I suppose we don't take it to the police,' Jem said. 'But there still have to be conditions, and there have to be reparations. His actions had consequences. He should face some himself.'

'Yes. I see,' Ella said. 'Prue, I think you and I should talk about that in private. We'll tell you what she decides.'

The two women went upstairs. Jem sat down on one of the uncomfortable chairs. Aaron stood by the door, arms folded; Nicky idly slapped the poker into the palm of his hand, pacing the tiny parlour, up and down. Hugo attempted to speak once, and was invited to stop by all three of them at once. Upstairs, Jem could hear the sound of weeping.

Eventually, Ella came back in alone.

'We've discussed it,' she said. 'Prue would rather not go through the misery of a trial and the insult of whatever repulsive lies this repulsive liar will tell. So we're not going to take this to the police unless Mr Morley-Adams makes it necessary by any sort of aggressive manoeuvre. That is her decision, and we will all respect it.'

Hugo sagged slightly. 'It is the correct decision because I did not kill Toby, and let me say—'

'No,' Ella said. 'There are conditions. You may never come near Prue again, not in person or by letter or by proxy. If you do, all bets are off, and we will ruin you. You know we can; I don't think you know how much some of us would like to.'

'You don't approach Jem either,' Nicky said. 'Ever. If you try, you will regret it more than I regret I ever introduced you to decent society.'

'Well put,' Ella said. 'That's the first demand. The second is… well, I hope you have your chequebook with you, because you're going to need it.'

'*How* much?'

'Five thousand pounds,' Ella said. 'In itself an admission. He's guilty as sin and he knows it.'

They sat in Prue's sitting room, the women in the two chairs, the men pretending to be as comfortable on the floor as they would have been ten years back. Aaron had got the fire blazing. Ella had driven to the village shop and returned with substantial quantities of bread, ham, cheese, milk and tea, and a bag of coals, as well as some borrowed mugs. Nicky was now sprawled in front of the fire making toasted cheese, because it seemed entirely appropriate that they should return to old habits.

Hugo had gone. Jem had no sympathy for him, casually taking what he wanted because he always had and always could, but, when Hugo had stood by his expensive motor and looked back at the five of them in alliance, his face had slackened with something like grief, and Jem had seen, just for a second, the man he'd liked. The runner, the fencer, the friend.

'But,' Prue said helplessly. 'But, five *thousand*? Really?' It was a staggering sum, ten years of wages at Jem's last post.

'It had to be enough to hurt,' Ella said. 'And as much as he could scrape together without setting off investigations. I had him make the cheque out to me: I don't want him accusing anyone else of blackmail later on. I thought a thousand to Jem and the rest for you. Since you two suffered the most material harm from all this.'

'But what about Toby?' Prue said. 'If he murdered him, surely you must want to see him prosecuted? I'm sorry, I didn't think—'

'He didn't kill Toby,' Ella said composedly. 'Jem was lying. It scared him pretty effectively, didn't it?'

Prue gaped. 'How do you know?'

'Because Jem found out who did it,' Ella said. 'Toby was up to a great deal of shameful things in that last term. He was blackmailing more people than just Hugo, and betraying more people than just you.'

Prue put her hands to her temples. Ella patted her knee, an uncharacteristically affectionate gesture that looked a little odd. 'He went badly wrong, and did a lot of harm, and he paid for it. We all did.'

'So who *did* kill him?'

'Someone whose name I shan't disclose, even to you. The whole business is well beyond the reach of the law now. It's over.' Ella spoke with finality, voice resonant as the chapel bell. *Send not to know for whom the bell tolls: it tolls for thee.* Jem glanced at Nicky, and saw him raise his chin, accepting.

Prue frowned. 'Can it be over?'

Ella gave the little scowl that said she was thinking. 'When Toby died, and nobody knew why or who did it, it felt unfinished. I recall people saying that my brother wouldn't rest in peace till his killer was found. But really laying Toby to rest involves undoing the harm he did to us and to himself, and the harm we all did to one another around him. I am deeply grateful to Jem for putting that in motion. And I'm sorry I was a poor friend to you when you needed me, Prue. I can't tell you how sorry. I wasn't good at having friends who weren't Toby, and I was every bit as self-centred as he was. I wish to heaven I had been better.'

'You came now,' Prue said. 'I was so frightened. Hugo… the way he walked in…I didn't know what he was going to do.' Her free hand was clenched into a tight fist. 'I couldn't speak. I couldn't breathe. And then you started banging on the door and Jem shouted, and I thought I was hearing things. I wanted it to be someone coming to help, you can't know how much, and I knew it wouldn't be, but it *was*. It actually was.'

Ella reached for her hand. Prue gripped it.

'And I'm so sorry about Toby,' she went on. 'I thought I could trust him. I desperately needed someone to tell, and it all came spilling out. I told him things I shouldn't, and I'm so sorry for what I caused.'

'You didn't cause it,' Ella said. 'He was looking to hurt people and you were the weapon he found to hand, but if it hadn't been you, there would have been something else. You should have been able to trust him, and you have nothing to apologise for.'

'No, I do.' Prue swallowed. 'I wrote the letters. The one you came here about, Jem, the one that made you lose your job. I wrote them to all of you. I had been putting away Joe's things—my son, who died—and I was so angry and I wanted to hurt someone. I wanted everyone to feel as I did, as if the past wouldn't ever let go. I'm so sorry.'

'I'm not,' Nicky said. 'If you spurred Jem into action, I think all of us owe you as well as him a debt of gratitude. I have been mired in the past for a decade. I should like to experiment with a future, if I am to be permitted one.'

'So should I,' Jem said. 'I mean, a future for me. I need to pick myself up. Find better work. Settle to something instead of settling for nothing.'

'I should be very pleased to help with any aspect of that,' Nicky said. 'If you wished, of course.' He handed Jem a plate of toasted cheese as he spoke, and their eyes met.

'I—Yes. I mean, yes, I'd appreciate that. If you'd like.' Jem clamped his mouth shut and concentrated furiously on his plate.

'I had a letter from Miss Keele,' Prue said, to his relief. 'She thinks I should come and speak to her.'

'Will you?'

'I think I might. What about you, Ella? And Aaron?'

The two exchanged glances. Aaron coughed. 'I don't know.'

'We'll see,' Ella said. 'I suppose we'll all see.'

Jem looked between them, once seven, now five. Ten years older, endlessly wearier, but with that same quiver between them he remembered from the golden days. It was the sensation of potential, possibility, things going to happen. Toby had always been bursting with it. Jem had believed it had died with him.

He raised his plate high in the air. Nicky gave him a quizzical look. 'What are you doing?'

'Isn't it obvious? A toast.'

Aaron gave a deep bark of laughter. Nicky said, 'My *God*, Jeremy.'

Prue raised her own slice, molten cheese slipping dangerously sideways. 'A toast. To what?'

'Absent friends. Forgiveness. What happens next.'

Nicky, Aaron, and Ella raised their mugs. 'What happens next,' Ella said. 'Yes. I'll drink to that.'

A LETTER FROM THE AUTHOR

Dear reader,

Thank you for reading *Death in the Spires*. I hope you enjoyed the story. If you want to join other readers in hearing about my new releases and bonus content, sign up here:

www.stormpublishing.co/kj-charles

If you enjoyed this book and could spare a few moments to leave a review that would be hugely appreciated. Even a short review can make all the difference in encouraging a reader to discover new books. Thank you!

Cymbeline is my husband's favourite play, and he directed it as a college performance at Cambridge, his stories of which indirectly served as a kernel of inspiration for *Death in the Spires*. (No students were murdered in the making of his production.) He supported me unstintingly in my decision to become a full-time writer, I suspect in large part because he wanted to read this book, which is of course dedicated to him. Thank you, Charlie: I quite literally couldn't have done it without you.

Thanks again for reading!
KJ Charles

www.kjcharleswriter.com

Bluesky: @kjcharleswriter.com

KJ Charles Chat